Murder Begins In Pieces

Also By Murray Moffatt

*Murder Best Unsolved**

*Murder Maybe Relative**

*Murder Maybe By Evil**

*Murder Sometimes Cold**

*Murder Not Quite Buried**

*A Murder Solved Twice**

*Never Murder At Home**

*Go West For Murder**

*Murder Begins In Pieces**

Play

Murder And No Play

*A Tale of Play and Murder*****

**A Shane Daniels Mystery*

***Play and Murder And No Play- combined edition*

Murder Begins In Pieces
A Shane Daniels Mystery

A Novel by
Murray Moffatt

ISBN: 978-1-0688512-6-1

Cover Design: Murray Moffatt, Sarah Autio

Author's Note:

In this, my ninth Shane Daniels novel, I've gone substantially deeper into what motives both Shane and his partner, Emma Carstairs.

People change and sometimes they re-evaluate their lives, depending on the circumstances they find themselves in. Those of you who have been with me from the beginning know that the direction of Shane's life changed when he was eighteen years old. He solved his first murder and also found out that his father was not the man he thought he was. Those two events put him on the path to being a cop, but his life changed again when he was shot in the knee and disabled.

In the novels since the first in the series, 'Murder Best Unsolved, Shane has been completely focused on solving murders, which he believes is the most important part of his job as a law firm investigator. But while Shane hasn't changed, Emma has, from a free-spirited career-oriented woman to the protective mother of a precocious foster daughter who has suffered a lot of tragedy in her young life.

In 'Murder Begins In Pieces', Shane and Emma's differing visions of what their lives should be about clash for the first time. And there is a very deadly reason why.

As always, I want to extend a sincere thank you to everyone who has taken the time to read my novels and for all of the support and encouragement of my retirement hobby.

This is a work of fiction. The cities and towns are real, but many locations within them are not. Names, characters and incidents are all products of my imagination. Any mistakes are mine alone.

Murray Moffatt
November 2025

For my wife, Jill, my daughters Sarah and Laura, and my grandchildren, Winnie, Archie, Wyatt and Hailey. You all bring great joy to my life.

"Tis one thing to be tempted, another thing to fall"
William Shakespeare

"I generally avoid temptation unless I can't resist it"
Mae West

Vengeance is mine; I will repay

The Bible (Romans 12:19)

Chapter One

I apologize for keeping you in my freezer.

I know it's not a dignified thing to do to a body, and you would probably prefer to be in the ground like most bodies, letting nature do its thing.

I promise you won't be in the freezer forever, and although your final resting place will not involve me digging a hole, I will incinerate your body and scatter your ashes in a nice secluded spot, maybe with some nice trees around. Or maybe I can put your ashes in a lake. That would be nice, wouldn't it? But I am sorry to tell you that not all of you will be going to the woods or the lake. I need a few parts of your body to send to some people who need to know, in a rather graphic way, what they've taken from me.

What? You don't see the logic in what I'm planning to do? What you think doesn't matter. What matters is how I feel, and I don't feel anything. I'm dead inside and have been since they took away the person I loved the most in this world.

I go about my life trying to be a normal person, but it's a facade. I might as well be in the freezer with you. I think the only way to save myself is to show those responsible the parts of me they killed. And after I've done that, I'll hurt the ones they love so they know how it feels.

Why now, you ask? Because I had to bide my time until I could be close by and watch events unfold firsthand.

You know, you should be happy that your miserable life at least ended with a purpose. You were likely going to die under a bridge somewhere, all alone except for an empty bottle of cheap rotgut wine. You may have had a past life, maybe even a successful one until the booze took over, but you had no future.

But I do have some good news for you. You're not going to be stuck in my freezer all by yourself. I need one more donor to the cause. It may take me some time to find someone like you, who, and I'm sorry to say this, but it's true, won't be missed. So you'll just have to be patient.

Oh, and I should let you know that I will have to remove you from your new home for a few hours. I will need to let your body thaw for a few hours so I can harvest what I need.

Sorry about that. But you really don't care, do you?

Chapter Two

"Okay, everyone, I have an opening statement to make in a couple of hours, so let's get started," Jason Burke said as he entered the conference room at Burke and Associates and sat down in the plush leather chair at the head of the long, wide oak table.

Jason was considered one of the best criminal defence lawyers in the province, if not the country, and was a formidable presence no matter what room he was in. He was a big man, six feet tall and heavily built, which made him an imposing and often intimidating figure in the courtroom. He had a dark complexion, sharp facial features and silver hair combed straight back from his forehead.

In addition to his reputation as an excellent lawyer, Jason was also well known for his impeccable sartorial taste, and today was no exception. He was wearing a tailored, dark, three-piece suit with a silk handkerchief in the breast pocket of the jacket, which matched his pale blue dress shirt. His tie, also silk, was a deep red.

It was Jason's tradition that after the jury was selected for a trial, and before the opening statements from the Crown Prosecutor and himself, he called a meeting of his defence team for one final discussion about their strategy. Jason would do an overview of the case against their client and point out the key evidence expected to be presented by the Prosecutor. The people sitting around the table were already more than well-versed on the details of the case because they'd been working on it for over a year, but they realized this was Jason's way of taking a deep, calming mental breath before the courtroom battle began. He would verbally strip the case back to just the basic facts, a way of clearing his head of everything that might be a distraction. Plus, it might reveal something that was missed.

Sitting to Jason's right was Shane Daniels, the firm's investigator, and to his left, Susan Cartright, who would be acting as 'second chair' during the trial. Susan was young, in her mid-twenties, and as a junior member of the firm, was eager to do a good job for Jason, who she considered her mentor. Susan was a petite woman with shoulder-length red hair, blue eyes and a freckled face. She looked significantly younger than her age and took a lot of good-natured ribbing about it. Also at the meeting were the firm's researcher, Chioma Abiola, Law Clerk Jamie Wheeler and Legal Assistant Elizabeth Pratt.

Jason pushed a button on a small remote he had in his right hand and the photo of a young man, from the waist up, appeared on a large monitor on the wall behind him. He then said, "As you know, our client, Noah Tremblay, who is twenty six years old, is on trial for second-degree murder in the death of his wife, twenty five year old Olivia Tremblay."

Jason clicked the remote again and the screen split in two so the photographs of the couple were side-by-side.

Noah Tremblay's picture was taken after he was arrested and the young man looked sleep deprived. There were dark circles under his bloodshot eyes and his naturally curly hair was a tangled mess. He had no expression on his unshaven face, his thin lips in a straight line.

Olivia Tremblay, on the other hand, had a smile on her face in what was a portrait studio photograph taken several years ago during what must have been happier times for the couple. She had a plain, pale face with some acne scars visible on her cheeks, no makeup other than a touch of lipstick, and shoulder length, straight dark hair. It was thin, and the part down the middle of her head seemed wider than normal.

"Just over a year ago, during the evening of last August second, the Saturday of the civic holiday weekend, Noah and Olivia got into a physical altercation in their townhouse on Morton Avenue," Jason said. "Olivia was stabbed with a long-bladed kitchen knife. The blade entered her body just below her breast bone, in an upward trajectory, and pierced her heart. She collapsed. Noah, in a panic, not sure what to do, left the knife in Olivia's body and called 911."

Jason changed the image on the screen to a photograph of the crime scene. Olivia was on her back on the carpeted floor of a living room, a large blood stain on the front of the sundress she was wearing. There was a breathing mask on her face, an IV line still attached to the top of one wrist and a medical equipment bag was visible on the floor beside the body; all evidence of a desperate attempt by paramedics to save Olivia, even though they already knew it was too late.

"Right from the beginning, Noah has claimed that he didn't mean to kill Olivia and that he jabbed her with the knife purely out of self-defence," Jason said. "Olivia was bipolar and would often refuse to take her prescribed medication. The file from her psychiatrist says he believed that Olivia may have had anosognosia, a condition that caused her to go through periods during which she refused to accept the fact that she was bipolar. Experts believe anosognosia results from damage to the area of the brain involved in self-reflection."

"There are some people who are bipolar, and Olivia was one of them, who experience periods of anger and rage," Jason continued, "Noah says that's what happened that night. He says the evening started out fine, they had a drink, and Olivia seemed to be in a good mood. But then they got into an argument over the fact Olivia allowed herself to get pregnant and he thought it was a mistake given her disorder. Olivia flew into a rage, went into the kitchen, got a carving knife from a set on the counter, returned to the living room, and tried to stab Noah."

"Noah says he tried to calm Olivia down, but she wanted no part of it and continued to try to slash and stab him. Once she got close enough, Noah says he managed to wrestle the knife away from

Olivia and then jabbed her in the chest. He says he didn't mean for the knife to go into Olivia as deeply as it did."

Jason changed the image on the screen to a close-up of a knife. A police evidence tag was attached to the handle and blood stains were still visible on the blade.

"Susan, you want to take over from here?" Jason asked.

Susan Cartright leaned forward in her chair and consulted the notes she had on the screen of the laptop sitting on the table in front of her.

"The knife is a typical one that's found in most wooden butcher block sets," she said. "Stainless steel blade and hard plastic handle. The fact that it came from the kitchen is not in question. There was an empty slot in the block and the knife matched the others of various sizes."

Susan was very soft spoken and Jason had been working with her to change that, at least in terms of her trial work. The acoustics in many Ontario courtrooms were notoriously bad, and Jason had told Susan how critical it was that the Judge and the jury, if there was one, could clearly hear what she was saying. And just as importantly, hear confidence and sincerity in her voice.

"Both Noah and Olivia's fingerprints were found on the handle of the knife, not surprising since they both likely used it in the kitchen at some time prior to their altercation," Susan said and then nodded at Jason, who put up a new image on the screen. It showed Noah from the waist up, wearing a prison-issued t-shirt, arms at his side, turned so the palms of his hands were visible. Jason put up a second image of Noah, this time with his back to the camera.

"I have no doubt that the Prosecutor will present these photographs to the jury to show that Noah suffered no defensive wounds when Olivia attacked him with the knife," Susan said. "It will be part of proving their theory that there was no altercation and that Noah got the knife and stabbed Olivia. The autopsy showed that Olivia had no other wounds on her body other than where she was stabbed. Sadly, the autopsy revealed that Olivia was two months pregnant."

"The Crown's theory is that Noah was angry because Olivia stopped taking her birth control pills and got pregnant without discussing it with him," Jason said as he took over from Susan. "He didn't think she was fit to be a mother because of her extreme mood swings and the fact that she wouldn't take the bipolar medication. When Olivia rejected Noah's demand that she have an abortion, he flew into a rage and murdered her. The Crown has a witness, Noah's best friend, Jamie Wilcott, who will testify that Noah had expressed anger to him about Olivia's pregnancy. Wilcott claims Noah told him that he was demanding Olivia have an abortion and she was refusing."

Jason changed the image on the screen to another photograph of Noah, but this one was a police mug shot.

"I tried to get the Crown to agree to a lesser charge of manslaughter, which Noah is willing to accept, but the Prosecutor, Evan Gregory, refused," Jason continued. "Gregory wants to have a trial because he believes he can win, and the photograph on the screen behind me is one of the main reasons why."

Jason turned slightly in his chair and looked at the image.

"This photo was taken two years ago when Noah was arrested for assaulting Olivia," Jason said. "Police were called to the Tremblay's townhouse by a next door neighbour who complained about hearing a screaming match and things getting smashed. The officers who responded found Noah and Olivia in the kitchen, which was in shambles. There were smashed plates and mugs on the counter and the floor, and two of the wooden chairs were broken. Olivia was sitting on the floor, covering her face with her hands and crying. She reluctantly admitted that Noah had hit her, but blamed herself and didn't want Noah arrested. But there was clear evidence that Olivia had been hit in the face, so the officers arrested Noah and he was charged. He received a suspended sentence with probation for two years, and was still on probation when Olivia was killed."

Jason paused long enough to have a drink of coffee from the mug on the table in front of him and then continued. "So, there's the assault charge, police reports on previous domestic disturbance calls, and Noah already had a criminal record for assault related to a fight in a bar. Taken all together, it allows the prosecution to show that Noah has a propensity for violence."

"And it's all admissible?" Chioma Abiola asked.

"Yes, the judge ruled in favour of the prosecution during the pretrial hearings," Jason answered and then said, "I know you are all well versed in the case, so I appreciate you allowing me to do a final overview before I head over to the courthouse to give my opening statement."

"Does anyone have any comments? In going back over the general details of the case, did anything come to mind that we might have missed? Shane, do you have anything?" Jason asked.

Shane Daniels didn't say anything for a moment as he gathered his thoughts. As the firm's investigator, Shane had been responsible for researching and interviewing many of the people expected to testify at Noah's trial. Shane was a tall man, well over six feet, and kept himself in excellent shape thanks to almost daily workouts. A star basketball player in high school and university, Shane chose not to enter the NBA draft in order to pursue his dream of becoming a cop. But that career was cut short when Shane was still a rookie with the Brantford Police Service and his left knee was heavily damaged when he was shot during a domestic disturbance call that he and his training officer had responded to.

Despite a series of operations on the joint, including insertion of an artificial kneecap, Shane suffered chronic pain but he had learned to live with it without relying too heavily on painkillers, which he had gotten addicted to during his initial recovery.

Wherever he went, Shane had an old-fashioned, curved handled wooden cane with him, which was currently leaning against the chair beside him. But the cane was actually no longer necessary thanks to a specially-designed knee brace which allowed him to walk with little sign of a limp and, just as importantly, substantially less pain. While keeping it with him was a sign of some mistrust in the brace, Shane was also quite proficient in using the cane for self-defence. And it had saved his life once when a murder suspect tried to shoot him, but the bullet lodged in the top of the cane.

Shane's partner, Emma Carstairs, often remarked that Shane was one of the very few handsome men she knew who didn't seem to realize the fact that he was good-looking. Shane had blue eyes and short dark hair with a touch of gray showing at his temples. He had a heavy beard, which meant he often had to shave twice a day to maintain a clean face.

After his slight hesitation, Shane responded to Jason's question. "I'm sorry to say that I've been unable to change one of the more serious problems you might have to face with the prosecution's case," he said. "One, or both, of Olivia's parents, Jim and Charlotte Crombie, will likely be called to testify."

"Yesterday, I attempted to meet with them again, but they refused," Shane continued. "I fully understand their grief and their desire to get justice for their daughter, whatever it takes to achieve that. So, at this point, I believe there's more than a good chance that they will perjure themselves while testifying."

"I assume you got that impression back when they did agree to meet with you," Jason said.

"They openly expressed their dislike of Noah and how they tried to convince Olivia not to marry him," Shane said. "They claim Olivia faithfully took her medications, and if she stopped, it was because Noah forced her to do it. As illogical as it may sound, Charlotte is convinced that Noah wanted Olivia off her meds hoping she would eventually have a manic episode and he would have an excuse to harm her ."

"Did they know Olivia was pregnant before they received the results of the autopsy?" Susan asked.

"They said 'no', but I got the impression Olivia and her mother were close, so I am a bit surprised Olivia didn't tell her," Shane replied. "However, she may not have told her parents because of how they felt about Noah. Now that they know that they lost both a daughter and a grandchild, it has galvanized their hate for Noah, and I believe Charlotte will say just about anything on the stand if it means a conviction."

"Thanks, Shane," Jason said. "I know that when I cross-examine Olivia's psychiatrist, he will confirm that he had a difficult time convincing Olivia to remain on her meds. If her mother claims something different during her testimony, I'll have to walk a fine line between questioning her credibility and making it look to the jury like I'm trying to intimidate a grieving mother."

"Possibly a no-win situation," Shane commented.

Jason then said, "Before we wrap up and I head to the courthouse, I think we should discuss some of the issues I will face during the trial. The best outcome, obviously, is a not guilty verdict, but that's highly unlikely given the fact that Noah admits he stabbed his wife. The best case scenario is that I'm able to convince the jury that Noah didn't intend to kill Olivia, that he acted in self-defence, and the knife going deep enough into Olivia's body that it pierced her heart was a terrible accident. If I'm successful, the jury will find Noah not guilty of second-degree murder but guilty of the lesser charge of manslaughter. It would mean the difference between a life sentence or something substantially less with a much earlier parole eligibility."

"But in order to do that, we have to clearly draw the jury's attention to Olivia and her mental issues, specifically her actions as a result of not taking her meds," Susan said. "We have to shift some or all of the blame for what happened the night she was killed from Noah to Olivia."

"Exactly," Jason responded. "And we have to be very careful how we do that. The chances it could backfire are very high."

"There must be another way to defend Noah's actions other than demonizing a woman with a very serious mental condition," Legal Assistant Elizabeth Pratt said with emotion in her voice. Elizabeth had been with the firm for five years and was both competent and compassionate about her work. She was in her early thirties and the mother of two young children.

"I'm sorry, but Olivia is the victim," she continued. "Aside from the issue of why she refused to take her meds, she was not in control of herself that night. Noah said he had been through outbursts of rage from her before. He should have reacted differently; not jab at her with a knife."

"Never apologize for speaking up with your opinion when we have these meetings," Jason said to Elizabeth. "I welcome the input. And you're right, Olivia is the victim and I can't lose sight of that during whatever strategy I use to defend Noah's actions. But I do have to prove that based on Olivia's behaviour during her previous manic episodes, Noah had every reason to fear for his life when she attacked him with the knife. The jury has to believe that there was absolutely no intent on Noah's part to kill his wife and therefore he's not guilty of second-degree murder."

"Have you thought any more about whether you'll let Noah testify?" Susan asked.

"As you know, it's very rare for a defendant to testify at their own trial," Jason said. "But I'm not ruling it out. I'm going to wait and see how the prosecution's case is laid out and how much success I have with cross-examining their witnesses. It's been over a year now, and Noah is still struggling every day with guilt and grief. He comes across as sincere and I think he would make a compelling witness in his own defence. The jury may need to hear directly from the man who was forced to stab his own wife."

"We would have to spend a substantial amount of time preparing him for cross-examination by Evan Gregory. Gregory is very good," Susan commented.

"That's why defence lawyers seldom take the risk of putting their client on the stand," Jason said. "But I think if properly prepared, Noah could handle the tough questions about his relationship with Olivia and what happened the night she was killed."

"Jason, it hasn't been brought up, but can I ask how you plan to handle the fact that Olivia, knowing that she was pregnant, was drinking the night she was killed?" Law Clerk Jamie Wheeler asked, speaking for the first time. Jamie had been with the firm less than two years, but everyone agreed he was going to be an excellent lawyer.

"It's one of two significant issues that we're facing that will have a serious impact on how the jury views Noah," Jason said in answer to Jamie's question. "Noah admits he made a terrible mistake telling Olivia it would be okay for her to have one drink that night, even though she was pregnant, and he insists he only put a small splash of rum in her glass, not even an ounce. But the pathologist's toxicology report will show that Olivia had a lot more than just a tiny amount of alcohol in her system. I'm going to have to find a way to deal with that discrepancy. The other thing is testimony around Noah's insistence that Olivia consider having an abortion. Just the mention of that word will, no question, have an impact on the jury and divide their opinions."

Jason used the remote to turn off the monitor on the wall behind him, closed the laptop in front of him, and then said, "There's a tough road ahead if we have any chance of convincing the jury that Noah is not guilty of second-degree murder."

Jason then smiled and said, "Thanks everyone. If there's nothing else, I'll take the time left before I head over to the courthouse to review my notes again."

Everyone stood up and were collecting their laptops and notebooks, when Office Manager and Receptionist Jill Langley appeared at the door and said, "I'm sorry to interrupt, but Judge Wendal's Clerk just called. Judge Wendal is ill and opening statements have been delayed until tomorrow."

Langley was a thin, gray-haired woman, long past retirement age, but continued to work because she said she hated the thought of sitting at home trying to knit, which she hated anyway, or watching daytime television. She had been with the firm since the day Jason opened his practice and knew everyone's business, whether they wanted her to or not.

"Thanks, Jill. I was afraid something like this was going to happen," Jason said.

Superior Court Justice Oliver Wendal was rumoured to be in ill health and many had expected him to retire. But he had presided over the preliminary hearing for Noah's case and had insisted he would be able to handle the trial.

"Okay, I guess I get another day to prep," Jason said and headed for his office.

Chapter Three

Shane and Chioma walked back to their offices together, both deep in thought about the Tremblay trial since they had both spent countless hours over the past year preparing background documents on the various expected participants.

Chioma Abiola was a statuesque black woman with short, tight curly dark hair and always had a smile on her pretty face. She and her husband had immigrated to Canada from Nigeria when their two sons were very young, but they're both grown men now and are attending McMaster University in Hamilton. Chioma is an outstanding researcher and Shane had come to rely heavily on her to get information that very few people have access to. They had a deal; Shane was never to ask Chioma what databases she accessed using the internet so that in the event she was ever caught searching someplace where it was illegal for her to be, Shane would have plausible deniability.

Chioma's dream when she came to Canada was to become a lawyer and even though she had a law degree from the University of Lagos, she was required to undertake further studies and examinations to get the required accreditation to meet Canadian legal standards. She had recently achieved that with flying colours after years of online classes and studying during evenings and weekends, and was now preparing to take the bar exam. In Ontario, that involved two multiple-choice open-book exams: the Barrister Exam and the Solicitor Exam. Shane was behind Chioma one hundred percent, but if she was successful in becoming a lawyer, he'd really miss her excellent research skills.

When they reached the door to Chioma's office, Shane said, "I hear that Jason has offered you paid leave to prepare for the bar exam."

"He has. It's very generous of him because I couldn't afford to be off work without pay," Chioma said.

"I suspect he's thinking ahead to when you become a lawyer, then he can keep you around, but in a different role," Shane said.

"I suppose, we'll see," Chioma responded noncommittally and then changed the subject by asking, "Have you met the new Law Clerk?"

"I didn't know we needed one," Shane responded.

"Sherrie Morrison has gone on long-term disability," Chioma said. "She's been really ill, in and out of the hospital, and they can't figure out what's wrong."

"I'm sorry to hear that. Hopefully, she'll be back soon," Shane said sincerely. "Who's the new Clerk?"

"Come on, I'll introduce you," Chioma said and led Shane to one of several office cubicles located in the central area of the firm's office space. The one she stopped at was occupied by a young Asian man who stood up and smiled when they approached.

"Tin, this is the firm's investigator, Shane Daniels. Shane, this is Tin Tran," Chioma said.

The two men shook hands and then Shane said, "Welcome to Burke and Associates."

"Pleased to meet you, Mr. Daniels. You're quite famous around here as some kind of super sleuth," Tin said.

"I don't know about that," Shane said sheepishly and then added, "No Mr. Daniels is necessary, Shane is fine."

"Okay," Tin said with a smile.

Tin Tan was short, maybe five foot four, Shane guessed, and had a slight build. He had a wide oval face with a bit of a golden undertone to his skin, straight, thick dark hair and brown eyes.

"Are you from Brantford?" Shane asked.

"No, I'm currently living with my Mom in Hamilton, but I'm looking for a place here," Tin answered.

Shane noted that Tin spoke without a hint of an accent, so he asked, "My nine year old adopted daughter, Lan, is from Vietnam and has been working hard to maintain her language skills. Is there any chance you speak Vietnamese?"

"I do, actually," Tin answered. "Growing up, my parents and my grandparents, who lived with us when they were alive, very seldom spoke English."

"My partner, Emma, and I make an effort to take Lan to every available Vietnamese-Canadian event here in the city to keep her connected to her heritage. Perhaps I can bring her to the office one day so you can meet her and spend some time speaking Vietnamese with her," Shane said.

"I'd be more than happy to do that," Tin replied.

Shane shook Tin's hand again, and then he and Chioma went to their respective offices. Shane's space was small; just enough room for a desk, a chair for himself and a visitor, and a filing cabinet. But Shane didn't care. Although he did have to spend a lot of time in his office working on his laptop, he preferred being away from the firm doing fieldwork.

Shane spent the rest of the morning completing a detailed background on Doctor Monique LeBlanc, the Toronto psychiatrist Jason had retained to testify for the defence during the Tremblay trial. LeBlanc was a lecturer at the University of Toronto and a preeminent authority on mood disorders, including bipolar and neurodevelopmental disorders such as ADHD. She had been given access, through the trial's discovery process, to all of Olivia Tremblay's medical records and had met with Noah on several occasions. She was expected to provide her analysis of the severity of Olivia's mood disorder and the high probability of her resorting to violence during one of her manic periods if she was not taking her medication. She was also expected to testify about Noah's state of mind. Did he have violent tendencies? Did he truly care about his wife? Was he capable of hurting her?

Shane's job was to fully vet Doctor LeBlanc to avoid any attempt by the prosecution to discredit her testimony if it was in disagreement with the Crown's expert, who was expected to testify that Olivia would not have tried to stab her husband even in a rage caused by her bipolar disorder. Shane was making sure LeBlanc didn't have any 'skeletons in her closet', such as complaints to her professional standards group and if she had ever been disciplined. He also wanted to know how many times she'd been hired recently to testify in a trial because Jason didn't want LeBlanc's credibility undermined if the prosecutor called her a 'hired gun', which he was expected to do.

At four pm, Shane decided to call it a day. His partner, Emma Carstairs, a surgical nurse at the Brantford General Hospital, had worked an early morning shift, so she would already be home, and Lan would be home from school.

Shane went out the back door of the firm to the small parking area located behind the building and started up his 1969 black Dodge Charger. The muscle car was a gift from his father when Shane turned sixteen, two years before his father murdered a young woman in his hometown of Paisley, a rural village in southwestern Ontario, north of Brantford. Shane's father died in prison while serving a life sentence for murder with no chance of parole for twenty five years. Despite the irreparable relationship he had with his father after he was arrested, Shane kept the Charger as a reminder of when he was a teenager and still loved and admired the man.

The Charger looked like it had just come out of the showroom because Shane was meticulous with its care. Everything in the interior was original, although Shane had added a Hurst gear shifter and a dash-mounted tachometer. He was about to put the transmission in first gear when he hesitated and listened to the Charger's 383 V8 four-barrel engine. He thought he could hear a knocking sound while the engine was idling, so he revved it a few times. I think it might have a couple of sticky valves, Shane thought. It was not the Charger's original engine, which had started to leak oil after Shane had turned the odometer over twice and had eventually blown a piston. He managed to find a used replacement in decent shape in a local wrecking yard and completely rebuilt it, but now, after putting another eighty thousand miles on it, it sounded like he was going to have to do it again.

Emma hated the Charger and refused to ride in it unless absolutely necessary. She thought it was a high speed death trap from another era when there were no basic safety features like shoulder harnesses and airbags. She begged Shane to take it off the road and even offered to give up using the garage attached to their house for her vehicle so he could store the Charger full time.

"It would be close by and you could go and sit in it or run your hands over it any time you wanted," Emma had told Shane. She thought that idea was amusing, but Shane did not.

Shane drove home and parked in the driveway of his house, located on a quiet, tree-lined street in East Brantford. The bungalow had belonged to Emma's parents, both now deceased, and after Shane moved in, he and Emma took out a small mortgage, which they used to basically gut the interior and rebuild it to their liking.

When Shane walked in the front door, he could hear Emma and Lan's voices coming from the kitchen. He also noted a small sealed cardboard box sitting on the bench to his left in the entryway. He took a quick glance at the shipping label and saw his name and address, and assumed Emma must have ordered something online. He left the box on the bench and walked into the kitchen.

"Hi Dad!" Lan exclaimed when she saw Shane.

He liked it, but Shane was still trying to get used to Lan calling him Dad instead of his first name. It was Lan's idea. She had decided that her parents would always be her father and mother, but now that Shane and Emma had adopted her, they could be called her Mom and Dad. Lan's parents were killed when their van was forced off Highway 403 by two members of a Vietnamese-Canadian criminal gang. Duc and Hai Pham got into Canada through what turned out to be a bogus immigrant resettlement company and were forced to live in a house with a cannabis oil extraction lab in the basement. The Phams were run off the highway as they were trying to escape to another part of Ontario with a suitcase full of cash they had taken from the house.

Emma first met Lan in the Children's Surgical Ward at the Brantford General Hospital, where the then eight year old girl was recovering from surgery to amputate her right hand, which had been crushed beyond repair in the accident that killed her parents. In addition to her nursing job, Emma worked with psychiatrist Charlene Anderson, counselling recent amputees on how to mentally and physically deal with their disability. Emma knew what she was talking about; her left leg from the knee down was blown off by a landmine when she was with the Canadian Armed Forces. She was part of a United Nations explosives disposal team searching for the thousands of landmines left behind at the end of the Bosnian War.

Emma fell in love with Lan at first sight and managed to convince Children's Services and the RCMP to let the young girl live with her and Shane. The Mounties wanted to put Lan in a safe house elsewhere in Ontario because of what she might have witnessed in her house, but Emma refused, saying the young girl had been traumatized enough. Emma had faced some heavy criticism for keeping Lan with her after there were two separate attempts by members of the gang to kidnap the young girl. One attempt was thwarted by Ben Chen, but Shane's friend was badly beaten while trying to save Lan.

Eventually, the leader of the gang, Hong Phuong, was deported to Vietnam to face murder charges, and the other top members of his organization were arrested. It then took over a year before Shane and Emma were allowed to adopt Lan, primarily because officials in both Canada and Vietnam had to search to see if Lan had any relatives willing to take her, but it turned out there was no one.

When Shane entered the kitchen, Lan was sitting at the table and drawing on a sketch pad. She was holding a charcoal pencil with her high-tech prosthetic hand, an amazing device which operated almost like the real thing. Emma and Shane happily re-mortgaged the house to pay for the prosthetic. Lan had actually taught herself to use her left hand to print and draw, but had switched back to her right once she got used to how the prosthetic operated.

Lan was a precocious nine year old, very smart for her age and an incredibly talented artist. Shane couldn't believe the quality of Lan's sketches of people, including charcoal portraits of her late parents, Emma, himself and even Shane's best friend Ben Chan. Even though there was a public school within walking distance of the house, Lan took a bus to attend a school for gifted children.

Emma, who was at the stove cooking some hamburger in a frying pan for tacos, turned her head toward Shane and said, "You're just in time for taco night."

No matter how long they had been together, every time Shane looked at Emma, he couldn't believe how lucky he was to have such a beautiful woman as his partner. Emma had a flawless light complexion, blue eyes and blonde hair, which she always kept cut very short. She was a reflection of her Nordic heritage. Her trim figure was the result of a dedication to daily exercise, including running with the use of a blade-type prosthetic, the same type used by Paralympians. Emma was wearing an oversized T-shirt and shorts. She was never embarrassed to be out in public with her prosthetic leg visible and was used to people staring because she said it was just human nature. More than once, she'd managed to hold her temper when an ignorant man or even sometimes a woman said to her, 'What a shame your missing leg has ruined your beautiful looks.'

"Is it weird that I'm Vietnamese, but I love tacos and hate the stuff from my country?" Lan suddenly asked, not looking up from her sketch pad.

"Yeah, I think that makes you super weird," Shane replied with a straight face as he went to the fridge to get a can of diet Sprite.

"Don't tell her that!" Emma admonished. "Lan, even though my family is originally from Norway, I don't like most seafood, which is a Norwegian staple. Everyone has different tastes, no matter where they're from."

"But you could still be a bit weird," Shane said.

Lan put her hand over her mouth and giggled.

"You got a package delivered today. It's on the bench at the front door. Did you order something online?" Emma said.

"I saw the box, but no, I didn't order anything. I thought it was you," Shane said.

"Can I open it!?" Lan said excitedly while she ran to the front of the house and returned with the box, which she placed on the kitchen table.

"I'll have to cut through the label for you first," Shane said as he examined the cardboard container, which was square, probably eight by eight inches. There was a standard shipping label on the top with a bar code and Shane's name and address. It said it was from 'Big Ben's Entertainment Inc'.

"Is it something from Uncle Ben?" Lan said when she read the label.

"Probably," Shane answered. "That will be the name of one of Ben's companies, maybe the one he uses for his designs." In addition to owning a Chinese buffet restaurant in the Lake Huron tourist town of Port Elgin, Shane's friend, Ben Chen, was a highly successful designer of online games.

Shane took a small, two-bladed folding knife out of his pocket, one he had carried with him since he was a teenager, and used the larger blade to slice through the label on the box top. Lan pulled the flaps open to reveal a thin sheet of Styrofoam with six small vent holes in two rows of three. Shane got concerned, but before he could say anything, Lan stuck her fingers into two of the holes and pulled the Styrofoam cover off.

"What's that?" Lan asked as she looked at a bag of white material inside the Styrofoam lined box.

"Don't touch that!" Shane said quickly. "It's likely dry ice used for shipping perishable goods."

"Ben sent you food?" Emma asked as she walked over from the stove to have a look.

"I have no idea," Shane said as he went over to the cupboard under the sink and returned with the rubber gloves Emma used for washing dishes. He put the gloves on, lifted the bag out and set it on the table beside the box.

"Eww, what is that!" Lan exclaimed as she looked into the bottom of the box.

"What the hell, Shane!?" Emma said loudly and then grabbed Lan and pulled her back from the table.

Shane was stunned as he looked at what appeared to be a human heart. On top was a thin ribbon of paper with words printed in black ink: **'YOU BROKE MY HEART AND NOW I'M GOING TO BREAK YOURS'**.

Chapter Four

Inspector Mark Stabler of the Brantford Police Service pulled his gray Kia Sorento into the driveway of his brick and siding, two-storey home on a quiet street in the city's north-end, but didn't immediately exit the vehicle.

He removed the clip-on shades from his glasses, put them in the drop down holder just above the windshield, and then just sat for a minute with his hands on the steering wheel and his eyes closed.

It was just after six pm and the sun was making its descent in the western sky, casting deep shadows off the trees that lined the street. It was beginning to cool off after the latest in a long stretch of hot days, but with the windows up and his vehicle's air-conditioning not running, it was starting to get stuffy in the Sorento. Stabler didn't care; he just wanted a moment to clear his head before he went into the house.

Stabler was exhausted after a long and stressful day, but that was nothing new for him. Since his promotion to Inspector in charge of the Criminal Investigation Division, simply known as CID, every day was long and stressful. It was something which was not unexpected. The officer he replaced had retired and before he left, he warned Stabler that the burnout rate in the position was very high.

Stabler was fifty years old and a twenty five year veteran of the Brantford Police Service. He joined later than many recruits, but signed up successfully at the age of twenty five after serving five years as a military police officer with the Canadian Armed Forces. During the years he was a uniform patrol officer, Stabler kept himself in good physical shape, but that changed once he began being promoted through the ranks and spent the vast majority of his shifts behind a desk. He was now a heavy set man with a gut that hung over the belt of his pants, a jowly face with a pale complexion, green eyes behind dark-rimmed trifocal glasses and short, very curly brown hair, which had been going gray in recent years.

Stabler took off his glasses, rubbed his face with his hands, put the glasses back on, and decided he had spent enough time sitting in the car pushing some of the events of his workday to the back of his mind so he could at least try to put up a pleasant front for Mary. He got out of the car and headed for the front door of the house, but noticed immediately that the front lawn was in serious need of mowing.

Shit, I'd better get that cut before the neighbours start complaining, Stabler thought, but he knew it was just one of many home maintenance jobs that had been ignored in recent weeks because of work. He had several major cases he was currently supervising, plus any spare time he had, he was spending it with Mary. I'm going to have to hire someone to come and do the yard work, he decided.

Stabler entered the front door of the house carrying a framed commendation he had grabbed off the passenger seat when he exited the SUV. Earlier in the day, he had been presented with it by Brantford Police Chief Charlie Oak during a small ceremony in the community room at the Police Service's headquarters on Elgin Street. The commendation was for Stabler's investigation that resulted in the arrest of Adam Talino for the murders of at least five women, several of whom were killed in homeless encampments in Hamilton and Toronto. One of the victims was a young Aboriginal woman whose body was found buried in the basement of a house Talino owned in Brantford.

Talino's arrest came as a shock to a lot of people in Brantford, a city in southwestern Ontario with a population of over one hundred thousand, and considered one of the fastest growing cities in Ontario. It was known as 'The Telephone City' because it was where Alexander Graham Bell said he invented the telephone. Talino, who was a multimillionaire at age twenty eight, was well known for his philanthropy. With his good looks and attention-getting appearances at high profile fundraising events where he was always generous, Talino was popular enough that a significant number of people had suggested through social media that he would make a good Mayor.

But Talino's public persona was a facade he had intentionally created to hide the fact that he was a serial killer who wore various disguises while he wandered around homeless encampments, primarily in

Toronto, looking for victims; often enticing young, vulnerable women with the offer of free drugs.

Talino was currently in jail awaiting trial for first-degree murder in the deaths of three of the women. Investigators are not sure exactly how many women Talino killed; they knew of five for sure, but if there were more, Talino was not saying. A joint task force of detectives from several Ontario police services was still combing through missing persons files and suspicious drug overdose deaths, looking for possible connections to Talino.

After entering his house, Stabler went into a small room off the main hallway that he used as his home office. It was the place he often escaped to when he had a lot on his mind and needed a distraction, something that had nothing to do with police work. The room contained a scarred wooden desk and chair, a gunmetal gray filing cabinet, and an old La-Z-Boy chair in the corner. Stabler had a high-end desktop computer, which he used for a hobby he was quite passionate about: Genealogy. Over the past several years, he had researched and built an extensive family tree for both his family and his wife's.

There was a closet in the room and on the shelf inside, there was a small safe. After Stabler entered the combination and opened the door, he put in the paddle holster he wore on his belt, which held his service weapon, a Glock 19, and the leather pouch containing his handcuffs. He also put in the commendation. He had several that he had been awarded during his career hanging on the walls of his office, but he had no intention of doing the same with this one.

Stabler wanted no part of the commendation when told about it by Police Chief Charlie Oak who, Stabler knew, was well aware that Talino never would have been arrested without the work done by Shane Daniels. But Oak insisted Stabler accept the award, saying he deserved it, plus it was good public relations for the Service.

Shane Daniels had been convinced Talino was responsible for killing Missy Williams and burying her body in the basement of his rental property. Daniels became obsessed with the idea that Talino was responsible for other murders. At the time, it was not that Stabler had rejected Daniels' theories about Talino, but he had continually cautioned the private investigator about making accusations against a high-profile Brantford resident without solid proof.

At one point, Daniels followed Talino to a homeless encampment in Toronto and, with the help of two Metro Toronto cops, arrested Talino when they caught him inside a tent preparing an injection of drugs for a young female addict. Talino's DNA was collected when he was charged with drug possession, and both Daniels and Stabler had hoped it would connect him to the Williams murder.

However, both the methods he used and the legality of Daniels' surveillance of Talino were called into question, and the Crown Prosecutor decided Talino's DNA would likely be ruled inadmissible at a trial.

Undeterred by the setback, Daniels convinced Talino's terminally ill mother to give police permission to search a storage shed where, unknown to her son, she kept the furniture from the bedroom he used when he lived at home. Hidden on the back of a dresser drawer, forensics officers found a necklace Talino had pulled off the neck of a teenage girl he had sexually assaulted after entering her bedroom through a window. Talino, also a teenager at the time, took the necklace as a trophy, but for a reason only known to him, he left the necklace hidden in his room after he moved out and never came back to retrieve it. Daniels' theory was that Talino left the necklace behind because, in his psychopathic mind, it was a way of giving the finger to his mother, with whom Talino had a complicated and often fractious relationship. Talino's DNA was found on the necklace, and this time, it was used successfully to connect him to the Williams' murder as well as four others.

As he had in the past when he was instrumental in solving a murder case, Daniels insisted Stabler take the lead and keep his involvement out of the public eye as much as possible. Stabler was well aware that being the officer attached to several high-profile cases that Daniels had solved in the background was one of the reasons he had quickly risen through the ranks of the Police Service. So when he was asked to say a few words after being presented with the commendation today, Stabler made it very clear to the gathering of fellow officers and members of the media that the murders would never have been solved, and Adam Talino would never have been arrested, without the work of investigator Shane Daniels from the law firm Burke and Associates.

Stabler knew the media representatives in the room would be delighted with that news. Despite his insistence on being kept out of the limelight, the media always managed to find out about Daniels' involvement and relished in writing stories about Brantford's tall, handsome super-sleuth. Stabler was cynical enough to think Daniels purposely said he wanted to stay in the background, knowing full well Stabler would give him credit and Daniels would look like a hero.

After closing the safe, Stabler left his office and walked into the nearby kitchen, where he found Jalissa Dale, Mary's personal care assistant, putting some glasses away in a cupboard. Jalissa was a petite black woman who always had a pleasant disposition, and Stabler considered himself lucky to have found someone who was very good at her job. She took excellent care of Mary, and the two women had actually grown quite close. Stabler knew that Jalissa had met her husband, who was from Brantford, when he stayed at the hotel she was working at in Kingston, Jamaica. She came to Canada after they married and was now the mother of two young boys.

"You're home," Jalissa said to Stabler as she closed the cupboard door.

"I'm sorry I'm late, but I guess that's nothing new," Stabler said with a thin smile on his face.

"It's never a problem," Jalissa said and then added, "I made some dinner, hoping Mary would try and eat something, which she couldn't do, but I made you up a plate. It's in the fridge, you just have to heat it up."

"Thanks, Jalissa. Mary had a rough day?" Stabler asked.

"This round of chemo has been the hardest on her," Jalissa answered. "She can't keep anything down and is very weak physically. She's upstairs resting."

"Okay. I'll go up and see how she's doing. You can head home," Stabler said.

"Have a good evening," Jalissa said with a smile as she collected her purse from the kitchen table. But before she left the kitchen, she pointed at a small cardboard box that was sitting on the counter near the coffeemaker.

"I almost forgot. That package was left at the front door for you," she said.

"I wasn't expecting anything. I'll look at it later," Stabler responded.

After Jalissa went out the front door, Stabler took off his suit jacket and tie and laid them on the back of a kitchen chair. He went into the downstairs bathroom where he washed his hands thoroughly with disinfectant soap and splashed water on his face to erase some of the exhaustion he felt. He then walked upstairs and along a carpeted hallway to the master bedroom.

The window blinds were closed, but a lamp on the nightstand was on. Mary was sitting on the bed, propped up by two pillows, her eyes closed. The complexion on her fine featured face was pale, and her thin lips were chapped. She was wearing a colourful kerchief to cover the hair loss she had suffered as a result of the chemo. To Stabler, she was still the beautiful woman he had met when they were both attending McMaster University and married twenty eight years ago.

After cancerous lumps were discovered in both of Mary's breasts, she made the decision, in consultation with her Oncologist, to undergo a double mastectomy. Following a series of tests, and based on Mary's family's medical history, the Oncologist recommended adjuvant chemotherapy to destroy any undetected cancer cells and reduce the risk of the cancer returning.

Stabler sat on the side of the bed and put his right hand lightly on the side of Mary's face. She opened her eyes and said in a soft voice, "You're home."

"How're you feeling?" Stabler asked.

"When I was a kid and my Dad was sick, he would say he felt like 'a bag of dirt'. I never really knew what that meant, but I do now," Mary said. She tried to smile, but her lips didn't move too far.

"Jalissa says you haven't been able to keep anything down," Stabler said.

"I've tried, but the nausea is a lot worse than the last round," Mary replied and then said, "But I am thirsty, so maybe I'll see if I can keep some water down."

Stabler handed Mary a glass of ice water that Jalissa had left on the nightstand, and after taking a few sips, she asked, "So how was your day? Did you encourage good work from your detectives with your sunny demeanour?"

Stabler knew Mary must be feeling a bit better if her sarcasm was back.

"I chewed out a few asses, but that's my job," Stabler said flatly.

"I know grumpy is your standard mood, but now that you're an Inspector and a boss, you may want to think about cutting your subordinates a little bit of slack," Mary said. "You want respect, not dislike."

"The Chief gave me a commendation today," Stabler said, changing the subject.

"A commendation? For which case?" Mary asked. "Did they have a ceremony? Why didn't you tell me? I would have at least tried to be there."

"I didn't want it in the first place. I told the Chief that, but he went ahead anyway," Stabler said and then explained the circumstances.

When he was finished, Mary said, "You may be a lot of things, Mark Stabler, but you've never been selfish, so I understand your feelings about the commendation. But you're also a great cop and deserve some recognition."

"Yeah, whatever," Stabler responded and then said, "Listen, Mary, the Chief keeps offering me some paid leave so I could be at home with you. And besides that, I've got twenty five years in, so I could take my pension. I could find something to do part-time, and that way we could spend more time together."

"You're kidding, right?" Mary said. "You're going to hang around the house with me all day? Doing what? Yard work, which you hate? Cooking, which you're really bad at? Watch television, which I can barely get you to sit still long enough to get through one show? Mark, I appreciate you offering to be here with me, and I love you for it, but let's face it, you'd be miserable within a week, and you would drive me to distraction. You're a cop, that's who you are, and you know in your heart you're not ready to give it up."

Stabler put his hand over Mary's and said in a soft voice, "But I want to be here for you."

"I'm not going anywhere just yet," Mary said. "This was my last round of chemo, and I'm confident all of the tests will show that I'm cancer free. Once I've got my strength back, I will talk to the doctor about breast reconstruction surgery. I got this beat, Mark, you'll see, and we'll get our lives back to normal."

"It's great that you're confident," Stabler said with one of his rare smiles.

"Besides, I have a feeling that Wyatt is going to propose to Rachel any day now, and I want to be around for the wedding and any grandchildren that follow," Mary said. Wyatt was their son and he and Rachel lived together in Toronto.

"Sounds like a plan," Stabler said and then asked, "Can I get you anything?"

"No, I'm just going to sip away at this ice water and see if I can keep it down," Mary answered. "Jalissa said she was going to put something to eat for you in the fridge. Why don't you go and have that, get changed out of your suit, and then we can watch some TV together."

Although they had a widescreen television in the downstairs family room, Stabler had bought a forty inch TV for the bedroom for the times that Mary needed to rest in bed.

Stabler went downstairs and into the kitchen, where he took the dinner plate Jalissa had left him out of the fridge and put it in the microwave to heat up. He then remembered the box sitting on the counter, which Jalissa said was left at the front door. Stabler carried it over to the kitchen table and looked at the label. It had his name and address, and it said it was sent by Shane Daniels. What the hell's he sending me? Stabler asked himself. Christ, I hope Daniels hasn't found some other case he's obsessing over and he's sending me files to look at, he thought.

Stabler went into the utensil drawer and got a paring knife, which he used to slice open the top of the box. When he pulled the flaps up, he saw a Styrofoam lid with a series of holes in it and then alarm bells went off in his head. Stabler had attended dozens of bloody crime scenes during his career and he was, unfortunately, very familiar with some of the smells. His nose had picked up something coming out of the box. What the hell? Stabler thought and took his phone out of his pocket. He scrolled through his contact list until he found Shane Daniels' number and sent him a text:

'Did you send me a package?'

Daniels' reply pinged on Stabler's phone almost immediately:

'Not from me. Don't open! Call in forensics!'

Chapter Five

I told you that you would not be left alone in my freezer and I have kept my promise.

In fact, you can see that I got you some female companionship.

I'm sure you'll get along famously since you've both spent so much time on the streets and your life expectancies were poor at best.

I thought you were in rough shape physically, but it was nothing compared to your new friend, whose name was Annabelle Swanson, according to an old expired driver's license she was carrying in a tattered handbag. I noted some yellowing in her eyes, a sure sign of a serious liver problem, probably advanced cirrhosis. But it doesn't matter. I don't need that part of her anyway.

So, I need one more donation from one of you; I haven't decided who yet. For now, just enjoy each other's company.

And in case you're interested, I can tell you that my plan to hurt those who hurt me is well underway.

I will be the embodiment of revenge.

Chapter Six

The morning after the packages arrived at Shane and Stabler's homes, Jason Burke was sitting at the defence table in courtroom two at the Brantford courthouse on Queen Street.

After a one day delay because Judge Oliver Wendal was ill, the Superior Court of Justice trial of Noah Tremblay for second-degree murder was about to begin.

Jason found it very hot and stuffy in the courtroom. New air conditioning units had apparently been installed on the roof of the old building, but if they were working, they weren't very effective. Jason could feel sweat on his forehead and he was starting to worry about how that would look to the jury. It might make him appear nervous and indecisive, reducing the effectiveness of his opening statement.

Jason's traditional Superior Court attire didn't help; he was wearing gray, pinstripe pants, a long-sleeve white shirt with a winged collar, a black waistcoat, white tabs and a long black robe. It was a vestige of British legal tradition, although Canadian lawyers didn't wear the white wigs.

Also sitting at the table was Jason's second chair, Susan Cartright, no doubt also uncomfortable in her formal court clothing.

Jason turned in his chair and looked around the spectator area of the courtroom behind him. There was very little room left on the benches, which was no surprise because the start of the trial had garnered a lot of public attention. One of Jason's Clerks told him that the opinions on social media sites appeared to favour the prosecution's theory that Noah Tremblay deliberately stabbed his wife. Jason was well aware that such public chatter could have tainted the jury pool and that some of the men and women selected to hear the case may have already made up their minds that Noah was guilty of murder.

Jason noticed that Shane wasn't in the courtroom and he wondered why. He didn't attend every day, but Shane always made a point of being in the courtroom for the opening day if he was involved in the case. Something important must have come up, Jason concluded. He then glanced over at the Crown Prosecutor's table and noticed that Evan Gregory was fanning himself with a couple of sheets of paper while he studied his notes. I guess I won't be the only one looking sweaty in front of the jury, Jason mused.

Evan Gregory was a short, rotund man, dark-complexioned, with thinning salt and pepper hair, a noticeably flat face and a nose that looked like it had been broken a few times. He was a tough prosecutor and Jason had been up against him in trials on several occasions over the past decade. They used to have a very cordial relationship until three years ago, in the aftermath of the Gavin Benson murder trial. Benson was a Brantford businessman accused of murdering Paige Madison, a young woman who worked at

Benson's company and with whom he was having an affair. Jason did everything he could to defend Benson, who insisted he was innocent, but the jury found him guilty of second-degree murder and he was sentenced to life in prison with no chance of parole for twenty five years. Gregory was the prosecutor in the case. Although Jason insisted to Benson that there were solid grounds for an appeal, a despondent Benson committed suicide.

In a bizarre twist following Benson's death, his son, Josh, a soldier with the Canadian Forces, kidnapped and tortured Shane Daniels and threatened to kill him if he didn't find Madison's real killer. Josh, who had a brain tumour impairing his judgement, expected Shane to solve the murder, while in captivity, using only Josh's father's trial transcript. Shane managed to escape, but he believed Josh was right about his father and eventually proved it was Gavin Benson's partner, Ethan Holdaway, who murdered Paige Madison. Josh died shortly after learning his father was innocent.

The Crown Prosecutor's office and specifically, Evan Gregory, were pilloried by both mainstream and social media for prosecuting an innocent man. Gregory found himself reduced to handling minor cases and Jason knew that Gregory resented him for the public statements he made about the prosecutor's handling of the Benson case. The Tremblay trial was Gregory's first capital case since Benson and Jason could see the intensity on the prosecutor's face as they waited for the session to begin. Gregory will consider this trial his redemption, Jason thought, and that means he'll be going all out to try and get a conviction. It will make him a tough adversary, Jason concluded, but Gregory's over-zealousness could cause him to make a mistake. I'll have to watch for that, Jason decided.

There was a stir among the spectators after a side door opened and a police officer escorted a handcuffed Noah Tremblay into the room. The officer removed the cuffs and Noah sat in the chair between Jason and Susan. Jason had arranged a suit for Noah to wear so he didn't have to appear at his trial in prison clothing. It unfortunately appeared ill-fitting and Jason realized that Noah had lost a lot of weight during his year in pretrial custody, so his normal clothing sizes were no longer correct. Noah looked pale and tired, and his eyes were noticeably bloodshot.

"How're you doing, Noah? You okay? Are you ready for this?" Jason asked with concern in his voice.

"I'm nervous. I didn't get a lot of sleep last night, worried about how this was going to go. Not that you ever get much sleep in lockup," Noah answered.

The courtroom was called to order by the Clerk and everyone stood as Justice Oliver Wendal entered from a side door and took his place on the bench, a table on a raised platform at the front of the room. After everyone returned to their seats, Wendal said, "We are here in the matter of the Crown V. Tremblay," and then turned to the court officer and said, "You may bring in the jury."

Jason watched closely as the seven men and five women entered the courtroom in single file from a door next to the jury box, which was located to his right, at the front of the room. He studied each face closely, looking for signs in their expressions that suggested things like, 'I really don't want to be here', 'I hope this doesn't take long', 'I'm so nervous', 'this is really exciting', and most importantly, 'This is a waste of time, the guy's guilty'. After years of criminal trial work, Jason had developed a talent for reading faces, a key skill during jury selection and then, as the trial proceeded, for understanding how he stood with each member of the jury. Sometimes what he saw meant he had to change his defence strategy mid-trial if he sensed the jury was heavily favouring what they were hearing from the prosecution's witnesses.

Jason also used this unique skill on trial witnesses. He studied their physical responses to his questions and knew when they were not being totally forthcoming with the facts, not being completely honest, or were outright lying. He was proud of the fact that he had taught his technique to his investigator, Shane Daniels, who turned out to have a natural gift for it.

After the jury was seated, Judge Wendal said to them, "First of all, I want to thank each of you for doing your civic duty. I recognize that being here is an interruption of your lives, but I can assure you it is of great importance."

Wendal then turned to face the courtroom and said, "I want to apologize for the current conditions in this room. It's unacceptable, but I've been assured that the maintenance staff will have it rectified within the next fifteen minutes. If not, then I may call a recess until it is fixed or, at minimum, fans have been brought in to provide at least some air circulation."

There was a loud murmuring of voices around the courtroom as everyone expressed happiness with the news. Jason was also glad, given his own discomfort, but he was much more concerned about Judge Wendal. Wendal was well into his sixties and there had been rampant rumours in the local legal community about the state of his health, both physically and mentally. There was no question he was in ill health; the delay in the start of the trial confirmed that, but he also had a reputation as a very private person who zealously guarded his personal affairs. A colleague had recently mentioned to Jason that Wendal would occasionally drift off to sleep while presiding over hearings, but no one said anything.

There was no question it was uncomfortably warm in the courtroom, but Jason was worried about Wendal, who was sweating profusely and mopping his face with a cloth, which had been handed up to him by the Clerk sitting at a desk directly below the raised judge's bench. Justice Wendal was a thin man with a chalky complexion, a hawk-like nose and a pronounced Adam's Apple. He was mostly bald, except for a thin line of gray hair circling his head just above his ears.

Some complex issues would come up during the course of the trial, and if he were ill, Jason was concerned about Wendal's ability to make legally sound rulings. Jason's defence strategy hinged on the Judge allowing testimony regarding the violent side of Olivia Tremblay's mood disorder.

When it looked like Wendal was prepared to proceed with opening statements, Jason decided he was going to strongly suggest the trial be recessed until the air conditioning issue was dealt with. He was about to stand when he felt cold air on the top of his head and shoulders. Judge Wendal obviously felt something as well because he said, "It appears the air conditioning issue has been resolved, so I will ask the Prosecutor for his opening statement."

But Jason's concerns were not alleviated. Wendal was still mopping his sweaty face with the cloth and the hand he was using was shaking slightly. His eyes were rheumy and there was a grimace on his face. If he were really ill, would Wendal be stubborn enough not to delay the trial and recuse himself? Jason asked himself. He knew it was likely a mistake, but Jason couldn't in good conscience not say anything, and he hoped perhaps he would get some support from Gregory.

"Your Honour, I apologize for interrupting my learned colleague before he begins," Jason said as he stood. "But out of concern, I'm wondering if your Honour is feeling well enough to continue this morning. It would be completely understandable if you're ill because of the conditions in the courtroom we started with."

"My health, which is perfectly fine, is none of your concern, Mr. Burke," Wendal snapped. Jason was taken aback by the sharpness of the Judge's reaction. "I'm sure dragging out these procedures would be your preference, but it's not going to happen,"Wendal continued. "Please sit down and allow Mr. Gregory to begin."

Despite his protest, Jason was convinced that the Judge was under some type of physical duress and it was going to be an issue at some point in the trial. Judges in Ontario have tenure until they reach the mandatory retirement age of seventy five, and if Jason wanted to do something about Wendal, he would have to speak to the Regional Senior Judge or begin a formal complaint process. Neither option was appealing at this point.

Evan Gregory got up from behind his table and walked to the area in front of the jury. Facing the twelve men and women, he said, with a smile spreading across his face, "Good morning, I hope you're a lot more comfortable than you were a few minutes ago."

Many of the jurors either smiled back at Gregory or nodded their heads in agreement.

"My opening remarks this morning are going to be brief," Gregory said. "Often, the prosecutor must spend a significant amount of time at the beginning of a murder trial doing a detailed outline of the case to be presented against the defendant because it might involve complex forensic science, or perhaps the motive of the defendant has to be scrutinized from various angles. Or perhaps some of the evidence is going to be called circumstantial by the defence and I have to explain to you why it isn't. This would all be in a prosecutor's lengthy opening statement so that you would know, right from the beginning of the trial, that the defendant is going to be proven guilty beyond a reasonable doubt, which is the measuring stick you must use when deciding on a guilty or not guilty verdict."

"But this case is as basic and straightforward as it comes," Gregory continued, "On August second of last year, the defendant, Noah Tremblay," Gregory then turned and pointed at Noah sitting at the defence table, "fatally stabbed his wife, Olivia, who was pregnant with their first child."

Gregory then hesitated and scanned across the faces of the jurors. Jason knew the Prosecutor was doing this on purpose because he knew the jury would be hearing, for the first time, that an unborn child was also a victim. He wanted maximum impact from the news.

"This cold-blooded murder of a young woman and her unborn child was committed by a man with a history of domestic violence," Gregory said, but before he could continue, Jason stood up and said, "Your Honour, I object! The Prosecutor's use of the term 'history of domestic violence' is not correct, has not yet been proven, and is both inflammatory and prejudicial. My learned colleague knows this and should be admonished."

"I decide who gets admonished in my courtroom, Mr. Burke," Judge Wendal said sharply, his voice coarse and strained. "Mr. Gregory is simply outlining the prosecution's case against the defendant, which is his right, and if he states the defendant has a history of domestic violence, members of the jury are smart enough to realize that he intends to prove it. Your objection is overruled. You may continue, Mr. Gregory."

Jason knew the Judge was wrong. Noah had one criminal conviction, but allowing Gregory to say 'history' leaves the jury with the belief that Noah has had multiple run-ins with the law.

Wendal, who was still wiping sweat off his face, but had switched from the soaked cloth to a handful of tissues, never should have allowed Gregory's statement to stand. The way Wendal looked at him when he overruled his objection confirmed to Jason that it was a mistake to question the Judge's health. The situation was going to be a problem.

Gregory, who had turned to face Wendal while the Judge made his ruling, then glanced at Jason with a smirk on his face, his way of telling Jason, 'Way to go pissing off Wendal'.

The Prosecutor then turned back to the jury and said, "The defendant has admitted that he stabbed his wife but says it was in self-defence. He claims she attacked him with a knife after she flew into a rage because she was not taking the medication for her mood disorder. Don't be fooled by this theory when it's presented by the defence. The defendant had no defensive wounds on his body. If he was defending himself and managed to get the knife from his wife, why didn't he just subdue her? He was much bigger and stronger. He claims he jabbed at Olivia with the knife only in self-defence, an attempt to get her to stop. But the knife accidentally plunged deep into her chest, penetrating her heart. Does that make any sense to you? There's no evidence from the scene that suggests there was even a struggle."

"A friend of the accused will testify that Noah Tremblay was angry that his wife got pregnant. He didn't want children and was upset that she tricked him by stopping her birth control. He didn't believe she would be a fit mother given her mood disorder. During an evening of heavy drinking, Mr. Tremblay's violent nature boiled to the surface, and he murdered his wife."

Ladies and gentlemen, as I said at the beginning of my remarks, this is a straightforward case for you. There's no mystery, no gray areas. Noah Tremblay fatally stabbed his wife and is guilty of second-degree murder."

Gregory turned, nodded at Judge Wendal, and returned to his table, where his assistant, a young woman, leaned over and said something to him. A congratulations for the jury's benefit, Jason assumed.

Wendal, who had finally stopped wiping sweat off his face, but still appeared to Jason to be in discomfort, said, "Mr. Burke, do you choose to do an opening statement?"

"I do, your Honour," Jason said as he stood and went to the area facing the jury.

"Good morning," he said. "With all due respect to my colleague, only one thing that Mr. Gregory said to you during his opening is not in dispute. My client, Noah Tremblay, did stab his wife, Olivia. However, he did it in self-defence. He had no intention of killing the woman he loved; he didn't want to hurt her in the first place. I can tell you that he's still emotionally devastated, even after a year."

"Yes, there was an argument that night about Olivia being pregnant. And, yes, they were both drinking that night, and as you will learn during this trial, it was the last thing Olivia should have been doing. Noah deeply regrets allowing that to happen, but when that night started, Olivia was in good spirits, happy for the first time in a week, and he wrongly thought it would be okay to have a few drinks."

"Olivia suffered periods of mania from being bipolar one, the worst form of the disorder. You will be hearing from a top expert on mood disorders because Olivia's condition is key to what happened the night she died. During manic episodes, individuals with severe bipolar disorder experience heightened agitation, impulsivity and irritability, which can lead to aggression and violence. The risk of violence is further elevated with substance abuse, or in this case, alcohol. Proper treatment and medication management are crucial in managing bipolar disorder, but Olivia had anosognosia, which you will learn more about. It's often called 'lack of insight'. It's believed that anosognosia is due to damage in the part of the brain involved in self-reflection. As a result of this condition, Olivia went through long periods where she didn't believe there was anything wrong with her and she refused to take her prescribed medications."

"The night she died, Olivia became increasingly agitated and verbally aggressive during the argument over her pregnancy and Noah telling her how serious it could be if she continued to refuse to take her meds. Olivia had also been refusing to have the MRI and CT scans recommended by her doctor, which likely would have revealed the changes in her front lobe causing the anosognosia."

"Olivia flew into an uncontrollable rage, punching and kicking Noah, and he tried his best to subdue her without hurting her. But she escaped his grip, went into the kitchen, got a knife, and started swinging it wildly in an attempt to slash or stab Noah. Luckily, she kept missing, and that's why Noah had no defensive wounds. On one of the swings, Noah managed to grab the hand Olivia had the knife in, there was a fierce struggle, and Noah jabbed the knife at Olivia's chest, only in self-defence, but her momentum pushed the knife deep into her body."

Jason paused for a moment to let the jurors process what he had just told them, and then said, "This trial is far from clear cut and straightforward as suggested by the Prosecutor. You will have a lot of things to consider once you begin your deliberations. But I can tell you that Noah Tremblay did not mean to kill his wife. There was no intent, it was self-defence, so he's not guilty of second-degree murder."

Chapter Seven

While Jason was giving his opening remarks at the Tremblay trial, Shane was standing in the reception area of the Brantford General Hospital waiting for Inspector Stabler to arrive.

Shane had a large take-out coffee in his hand, hoping the caffeine would help him overcome the exhaustion he felt after only a few hours of sleep and a night that could only be described as tense and deeply disturbing.

Last evening, after the discovery of the human heart in the box delivered to his house, Emma had hustled Lan away to her bedroom and Shane called 911. While he waited for officers to arrive, he went to Lan's bedroom to check on her and Emma, and he found them sitting on the edge of the bed. Emma, who had an arm around Lan, holding her close, was visibly upset. Lan, on the other hand, appeared calm, and Shane even detected a look of curiosity on her face.

"Christ, Shane, who would do such a disgusting thing!?" Emma asked emotionally. "What does it mean!?"

"I don't know, but I'm most certainly going to find out," Shane said. "I'm so sorry this has happened," he added and then asked, "Are you okay?"

"Well, it's not something I haven't seen hundreds of times in the operating room, but it's upsetting when it shows up in a box at your house," Emma answered. "And it's not something that our daughter needs to see."

Emma, as she gently stroked Lan's hair, asked her, "Are you okay, sweetheart? That was a scary thing that just happened."

Lan appeared to Shane to be okay; she actually had a bit of a smile on her face when she asked, "Is that a real human heart?"

"Yes, I'm sorry, but it appears to be," Shane answered.

"Can I see it again?" Lan asked with excitement in her voice.

"No, you may not!" Emma exclaimed. "You can stay in your room and play on your tablet until I come and get you to brush your teeth and get into bed."

Shane couldn't help smiling to himself. Even though she had been through a lot in her young life, including the death of both of her parents and the amputation of her right hand, Lan was surprisingly well-adjusted. She was highly intelligent for her age and always very curious.

Shane had returned to the front of the house, anticipating police officers at the door at any time, when he got the text from Stabler asking him if he had sent the Inspector a package. Shane texted back, telling Stabler not to open the box and to call in Forensics.

After a Brantford Police Service Sergeant and a Constable arrived at his house and both had grimaced as they looked inside the box, Shane then spent the next several hours watching Forensics Officers carefully put the box in a cooler before taking it away and answering a lot of questions from two plainclothes Detectives who showed up. Any idea of who would do something like this? They had asked. No, Shane answered. Have you received other threats recently? Not recently, Shane told them. What's that mean, 'not recently', they wanted to know. Well, I've been threatened a few times in my career, Shane answered.

Can we get a list? Sure, Shane told them and explained that making some enemies came with the job of being an investigator for a criminal defence lawyer.

Just as the Detective's questions for Shane, and then Emma, started to wind down, Mark Stabler called and told Shane he had heard what had happened and that the box he received also contained a human heart and a piece of paper with the same typed message in black capital letters: **'YOU BROKE MY HEART AND NOW I'M GOING TO BREAK YOURS'**

"So, whoever has done this has a grudge against us for something we were both involved in," Shane told Stabler.

"That would be a good guess, Sherlock," Stabler responded in his usual gruff manner.

"Any ideas?" Shane asked.

"I haven't had time to think about it," Stabler replied and then said, "I'm going to put an officer in a cruiser in front of your house until we find out who's behind this. If someone has murdered two people and removed their hearts to send us a message, we have to take the threat very seriously."

"And what about your family?" Shane asked.

He realized that even though he was about as close as anyone got to being a friend of Mark Stabler, and they had worked closely on several cases, he knew very little about Stabler's personal life. Shane knew he was married, but the often cantankerous Inspector never engaged in small talk about anything, including family.

"Don't worry about my family, Daniels, just look after your own," Stabler replied to Shane's question. "Get some sleep. We'll meet in the morning. I'll text you when and where."

After ending the call with Stabler, Shane went to the kitchen fridge, grabbed a can of Diet Sprite, and sat at the table, trying to get his head around the fact that there was a sick individual out there who had sent him part of a human body. A few minutes later, Emma entered the kitchen, got a beer out of the fridge, and sat across the table from Shane.

"I need you and Lan to go out of town for a few days," Shane said. "I know you've got work and Lan's in summer art camp, but until I find out who did this, I need you somewhere safe. There's no way whoever is behind this knows about the cottage in Port Elgin, so you can go there."

Shane and Emma had a time-share cottage just outside of Port Elgin, the Lake Huron tourist town where his childhood friend, Ben Chen, had his popular buffet restaurant.

"If whoever did this knows our home address, what makes you think they don't know about the cottage?" Emma asked, and Shane could hear the combination of concern and irritation in her voice.

"The only way they would know about it is if they somehow got into our files here in the house because the time-share agreement is only on paper," Shane said. "We would know if someone got past the security system."

"What about our Facebook and Instagram accounts?" Emma asked. "There are photos of us at the cottage and on the beach."

"Yes, they may say Port Elgin, but there's no specific address. It's a huge area," Shane answered.

"Okay, we'll go, but Shane, all of this has to stop," Emma said, and Shane saw that tears were forming in her eyes.

"Don't worry, Emma, I'll find out who's behind this," Shane said and reached his hand across the table for Emma to take. But she didn't.

"I don't mean just this, Shane! I mean all of it!" Emma whispered angrily, keeping her voice down so she wouldn't wake Lan.

"Just in the past few years," she said, "You've been shot at and only survived because the bullet hit your cane, you were in a deadly shootout with a Russian, you were kidnapped and tortured, and just recently, you were obsessed with catching a psychotic serial killer who hired someone to assault me. Don't you realize how dangerous the work you do has become? And now, it threatens not just me, but our daughter."

"Emma..." Shane said as he started to respond, but Emma didn't let him.

"Shane, the problem is, you can't just stick with what other legal firm investigators do with their time; background reports, witness interviews, surveilling cheating husbands and wives, vetting expert witnesses. You have to solve crimes. You have to do things that are supposed to be done by the police, not you."

"Emma, part of my job is to help Jason clear a client's name if we believe he or she are innocent. That's what I do and I'm good at it," Shane said, starting to get irritated with the way the conversation was going.

"Yes, Shane, you are good at it," Emma responded, "But you're a former cop who has never gotten over the fact you lost that career because you were shot and disabled. Now you're a wannabe cop who doesn't know when to step back when you've reached a certain point in an investigation and let the real police take over. How many times has Mark Stabler already told you this?"

"Emma, you're being unfair and, to be honest, hurtful," Shane said as he looked down at his hands.

"You know I'm right," Emma, who was clearly upset, said. "I love you, Shane, and I've been okay with your adventures, very proud in fact, but we have a daughter now and we can't be putting her in danger."

"And what about you, Emma?" Shane said in an accusatory voice as he looked up and into his partner's eyes. "How many times have you gotten yourself involved in one of your client's affairs and put yourself in harm's way? You're the same as me, Emma. If you think something's not right or an injustice has occurred, you can't let it go; you have to do something."

"Not for much longer," Emma responded. "I'm giving up my post-amputation clients at Doctor Anderson's practice because, yes, you are correct, I tend to get too deeply involved. And unless you can find a way to stop doing what is essentially police work, I think you should start considering a career change."

"I don't think I can do that, Emma," Shane said. "What I do is who I am."

"I think you've been very lucky so far, but what if that luck runs out?" Emma pleaded. "If something happened to you while you're chasing evil people like Adam Talino or whatever sick person just sent you a human heart, I know I would be heartbroken beyond repair. And do you want Lan to lose a father for a second time?"

"I didn't know you felt this way, Emma," Shane said softly. "You've never mentioned anything before."

"I really started to reevaluate things after Adam Talino had me assaulted. You caused that, Shane, because you were obsessed with Talino and he struck back to warn you off. You finally got him, and good for you, but at what cost? You weren't sleeping, you barely ate, and when you were home, it seemed like you weren't really here. And what if Talino decided to send his warning to you by harming Lan?"

"I know I need to do more to keep you and Lan safe when I'm working on murder cases," Shane admitted.

"That's not the point, Shane," Emma stated as she reached out and put her hands over his.

You shouldn't be getting so deeply involved in murder cases in the first place," she said. "You keep going beyond what I'm sure Jason expects of you. You don't stop when it's clearly time to call Mark Stabler, and that's when you put Lan and me in harm's way," Emma said.

Shane didn't know what to say, so he remained quiet out of fear that if he tried to defend himself further, he would just make matters worse.

"I'm going to bed," Emma stated. "I will go to Port Elgin with Lan tomorrow. I need to get up early to make arrangements for time off work and to let them know at the art camp that Lan won't be there."

Emma stood up to leave, but first said, "While you're hunting down the sick fuck that sent us a heart, you have some decisions to make that will affect the future of our relationship."

Emma didn't swear a lot, but when she did, it was to emphasize the seriousness of what she was saying.

Shane got her message loud and clear.

Chapter Eight

Now, the next day, as Shane stood in reception at the BGH, the coffee he was drinking had turned to acid in his stomach, and his mind was racing as he thought about his discussion with Emma last night.

Emma had made it clear that he was going to lose her and Lan if things didn't change regarding how he did his job at Burke and Associates. He knew he couldn't claim that she was aware of what she was getting into back when they started seeing each other, and he eventually moved into her house. They had met at a support group and at that time, Shane was dealing with some dependency issues and had yet to start working for Jason Burke.

What am I going to do? Shane asked himself as a lump formed in his throat as he thought about the warning Emma had given him last night. I love her and Lan so much, but I'm not sure I can do what she's demanding, he thought.

All Shane ever wanted was to be a cop. It became his dream career when he was eighteen years old and had solved the murders of his mother and a young Russian immigrant, Alina Ivanov, who was married to Shane's Uncle Max. Shane was led to believe that his mother had abandoned him and his father when Shane was a young boy. But Shane figured out that Max murdered his mother on behalf of his father because she was cheating on him. In exchange, Shane's father killed Alina because Max knew she hated him and that she was planning to escape their marriage. Shane found both bodies buried in separate areas of a wooded area outside of his hometown of Paisley. Both Max and Shane's father died in prison while serving life sentences.

Solving those murders had a profound effect on Shane. It shattered his love and respect for his father, something he still had to deal with on occasion. But it also awakened a realization that he had both the desire and talent for solving mysteries, particularly those that remained unsolved or in which the police had the wrong suspect.

Shane was a star basketball player at Niagara University in New York State and was expected to go into the NBA draft. However, after completing his criminology degree, he returned to Ontario and began applying to both the Ontario Provincial Police and various municipal police services. He got a job in Brantford, but that ended in his rookie year when his knee was destroyed during a violent domestic disturbance call. Charlie Oak, who was his training officer at the time, and is now the Chief of Police, got him the job at Burke and Associates.

Jason Burke recognized Shane's talents and had basically given him free rein in investigating cases connected to the firm, no matter how tenuous, and Shane delivered. In his first major case, Shane proved that a wealthy man didn't die accidentally when he fell down the stairs in his home and hit his head, as concluded by the police. He was murdered.

Other cases followed, and on several occasions, Shane reached a point in his investigation where he could've handed everything he had discovered over to the police and let them take over, eventually making an arrest. But he didn't. He wanted, no, he needed, the personal satisfaction of seeing it through to the end.

He needed to confront the former Soviet intelligence officer who had murdered his wife and young daughter. She had agreed to come to Canada and marry him to escape a life of poverty in Moscow.

He needed to follow killer Alec MacDonald and stop him on the doorstep of the house where his potential third murder victim lived. MacDonald, a cunning but mentally disturbed man who lived in squalid conditions in a farmhouse outside of Paisley, had tried to frame Shane's best friend Ben Chen for the murder of Ben's elderly neighbour. MacDonald had killed two women because he thought they looked like his mother, who he blamed for dying and leaving him to look after himself.

And there were plenty of times when Shane found himself all alone with his theories on a case. The police would insist the investigation was already closed; sometimes because Shane wasn't a cop and they didn't give his ideas any credibility, and sometimes, unfortunately, because the cops didn't want to lose public credibility by admitting they got it wrong. There had been times when that occurred even when Shane said he could get proof. So, he went ahead and solved it himself.

Shane admitted to himself that some of his actions were the result of his ego, his conviction that if he hadn't been shot and disabled, he would've gone on to be a great police detective. However, he never purposely took the credit for solving a crime. Whenever possible, he tried to keep his involvement hidden from public knowledge and let good cops, like Mark Stabler, take the credit. Didn't always work; the media would find out and describe Shane as a hero or a super sleuth. If he was being honest with himself, he really didn't mind when that happened.

But in the aftermath of someone delivering a human heart to his house last night, Emma had let her true feelings be known. Maybe, once she and Lan were safely in Port Elgin for a few days, and he found out who was behind the bizarre warning, Emma would have a change of heart about the future of their relationship. You know that's unlikely, Shane admonished himself, and you're a fool for even thinking that way.

"You look like shit, Daniels," Shane heard a familiar voice say. He looked up from staring at his coffee to see Mark Stabler walking towards him with another man beside him.

"You don't look too hot yourself, Inspector," Shane said.

"Too much paperwork, getting an investigation organized, and no sleep will do that," Stabler responded.

Stabler then nodded toward the man beside him and said, "I don't know if you've met before, but this is Sergeant Greg Franks from my Division. He's going to the lead the investigation because I'm obviously directly involved."

Shane and Franks shook hands. Franks was a tall man, well over six feet, and he was big; wide shoulders, thick arms, muscular legs and wide hips. It appeared to Shane that the officer was all muscle from regular weight training, not an ounce of fat. The suit jacket he was wearing was tight, and the gun holster on his hip bulged out the right side of the coat. Franks had short cut salt and pepper hair, a thick dark moustache and heavy eyebrows over intense green eyes. Shane was willing to bet good money that back when Franks was in uniform, he was one of the first officers called in to break up a fight in one of Brantford's seedier bars.

"Just remember, Daniels, you're only here as a courtesy and you will never be directly involved in the investigation," Stabler said as the three men started walking toward the elevators.

"Is there any chance the day will come when you'll start calling me Shane?"

"Probably not," Stabler deadpanned.

Once they were on the elevator and Stabler pushed the button to take them to the basement level, Franks said, "We've started pulling files for cases both you and the Inspector were directly involved with to compile a list of possible suspects who might seek revenge for something that happened to them or members of their family. I want you to do the same thing and provide us with a copy."

Shane was surprised that Franks had such a high-pitched voice for a big man. It reminded him of the first time he had heard former heavyweight boxing champ Mike Tyson speak; an almost female-like voice coming out of such a large male body.

"I will cooperate, but some lawyer-client privilege issues will have to be dealt with first," Shane said. "The files will undoubtedly involve clients of lawyers in my firm. My guess is you'll have to get a court order, or anything I give you will be heavily redacted."

After a 'ding' sound, the elevator doors opened and the three men walked into the hallway of the hospital's Pathology Department. Its painted concrete walls and tiled floor were spotless and brightly lit by overhead fluorescent lights. Waiting for them was the Coroner, Doctor Morley Johnson, who said, "Good morning, gentlemen, you have a bizarre one on your hands."

To Shane, Johnson always looked like someone other than what you expected a physician to look like. He was a short, overweight man in a rumpled, ill-fitting suit under a wrinkled, faded-white lab coat. His round, double-chinned head was topped by thin white hair combed straight back from his forehead. His pale face had a bulbous nose, purple coloured and veined, like you associate with a heavy drinker, which Doctor Johnson was rumoured to be.

In Brantford, like many cities in Ontario, the Coroner is not a full-time, salaried job. It's an on-call, part-time, fee-for-service position, which means they're paid for each death investigation they conduct. They normally have a full-time practice, but Shane knew that Johnson was semi-retired after closing his practice several years ago.

"You probably already know that Doctor Jeffrey Patterson, the Pathologist normally assigned to our area has retired," Johnson said. "Although I understand he's scheduled to testify in the Tremblay trial because he handled the autopsy on the victim."

In Ontario, coroners do not conduct the autopsies in sudden and unexpected deaths. They're done by forensic pathologists assigned by the Ontario Forensic Pathology Service.

"I'll introduce you guys to the new pathologist," Johnson said as he turned and started walking down the hallway.

Shane, Stabler and Franks followed Johnson until he reached a wide, double door of stainless steel. He took the ID badge attached to the lanyard around his neck, held it against the security plate on the wall, and the doors swung open. The four men entered the pathology suite, a large, square, brightly lit room with four areas set up for autopsies. Each area had a stainless steel rectangular table for bodies and two rolling trays covered in instruments. The wall to the right of the autopsy tables had two rows of doors for access to the freezer where bodies were kept. The opposite wall had a series of stainless steel sinks and glass-faced cabinets, some refrigerated, for holding specimens.

Johnson led the other men to the second autopsy table to the right, where a young woman in hospital blues was standing with two lidded plastic containers on the table in front of her. As they approached, Shane suddenly hesitated as he looked at the woman glancing his way because she wasn't what he was expecting. He had assumed, obviously wrongly, that the new pathologist would be a nondescript, middle-aged or older man or woman. He admonished himself for his bias. The woman standing at the autopsy table was in her late twenties, early thirties, and was absolutely beautiful; an oval face with flawless complexion, dark brown eyes, naturally long eyelashes, a petite nose, full red lips and long auburn hair pulled back into a ponytail and held with a pink scrunchie. She's got the looks of a fashion model, Shane decided. And he couldn't help noticing that her blue hospital scrubs didn't hide the fact that she had a very nice figure.

"Gentlemen, this is Doctor Amelia Martin," Johnson said. "Doctor Martin, this is Inspector Mark Stabler and Sergeant Doug Franks of the Brantford Police Service and Shane Daniels, an investigator with the local law firm Burke and Associates."

Martin reached across the table and shook the two officers' hands, and when she got to Shane, she smiled and asked, "Are you alright, Mr. Daniels?"

Shane realized she had caught him staring at her and he felt his face flush.

"Sorry, yes, I'm fine," Shane managed to get out as he felt Martin's firm grip lingering on his hand. I'm embarrassing myself, Shane thought, but quickly recovered by saying, "Please call me Shane."

"And Amelia is fine for me," she said as she finally released Shane's hand.

"Welcome to Brantford, or are you already from this area?" Shane asked.

"No, it's my first time in your city. As a matter of fact, up until recently, I had never been to Ontario before," Amelia answered. "I'm originally from Nova Scotia."

"Why'd you decide to come here?" Shane asked.

"It's a bit of a fresh start and an opportunity," Amelia responded. "During my residency, I did a rotation in pathology. I enjoyed it and found that I had a real aptitude for it. I was working part-time in the Pathology Department at the Halifax Regional Hospital when I saw an online posting for a full-time position with the Ontario Forensic Pathology Service, and I was lucky enough to get it."

"And what about you, Shane? Are you like one of those tall, dark, handsome private detectives in old TV shows who drive around in a souped-up Mustang solving crimes and hooking up with beautiful women?" Amelia teased with a smile.

"He probably likes to think so, and he drives a Dodge Charger," an irritated sounding Stabler interjected. "Now, if you two are finished fraternizing or whatever it is you're doing, can we get down to it?"

"Certainly, Inspector," Amelia answered pleasantly, not seemingly bothered by Stabler's tone.

Shane, Stabler and Franks moved up closer to their side of the autopsy table and Amelia took the lids off the two plastic tubs. The three men were hit with the strong odour of formalin, a solution of formaldehyde and water used as a tissue preservative.

"Both hearts are from adults, and as you can see, one heart is noticeably larger than the other, which means one is from a male and the other is from a female," Amelia began. "Female hearts are typically about one-fourth smaller than male hearts, even when you consider body size. Not only is the female heart smaller, but the proportions of the four chambers, the left and right atria and the left and right ventricles also differ."

"Can you tell how old they were?" Stabler asked.

"Not very accurately, I'm afraid," Amelia answered. "If we had the body, we would be able do a much better age estimation through a combination of methods, including examining the skeletal structure, teeth and other tissues. We typically don't use the heart to determine the age of a victim because the heart's aging process is influenced by factors such as genetics, lifestyle and health."

"But following dissection, I can now most certainly draw some conclusions from the age-related changes and conditions of these hearts," Amelia continued. "I believe both victims were well over the age of fifty. Neither of these victims' hearts was in very good shape when they died. I saw signs of either coronary artery disease or myocarditis. The blood test results for the female came back with elevated levels of both alcohol and oxycodone, and for the male, alcohol and cocaine."

"So, there's no chance that these hearts were supposed to be for transplants and were somehow stolen?" Franks asked.

"No. If they were sudden or accidental deaths, they would've been deemed poor candidates for donation," Amelia answered. "If I were guessing, and it would be pure speculation based only on seeing their hearts, these two people were alcoholics and addicts who had no access to decent health care."

"Street people?" Shane asked.

"Possibly, but again, just speculation based on the conditions of their hearts," Amelia responded and then said, "And sorry for being dramatic, but I've saved the most bizarre news for last. Both of these hearts were frozen at some point. I examined tissue samples microscopically. The freezing and thawing leads to the formation of ice crystals within cells and tissues, and you can see the damage it causes when the ice melts."

"Christ, that really complicates things!" Stabler groused. "So, the hearts could have been removed from the victims and then kept in a freezer or the bodies were hidden in a freezer and then thawed so the hearts could be taken. Is there any chance you can determine when these people died?"

"Even if I had the bodies, it would be extremely difficult to pinpoint the exact time of death, especially if they'd been frozen for a long period of time. Freezing significantly slows down the decomposition process, making it difficult to use traditional methods like rigor mortis and decomposition rates," Amelia answered and then added, "Because some of what I've seen is beyond my area of expertise, I've made arrangements to have the hearts transported to the Centre for Forensic Science in Toronto. I expect the experienced pathologists there might have some better answers."

"Can I ask if you can tell if whoever did this knew what they were doing when they removed the hearts?" Shane queried.

"They're both fully intact and I saw no signs of damage caused by how they were handled," Amelia answered. "The blood vessels, both the arteries and veins, were cut neatly, so the person who did this may have had some knowledge or experience, but I can't say for sure."

"DNA?" Franks asked.

"I've sent samples for DNA extraction that can then be run through the National DNA Databank, but any results will take some time to get back," Amelia said.

"Okay, thanks, Doctor Martin," Stabler said, "If you come up with anything else, let Sergeant Franks know."

"If you manage to find the bodies, then I'll be able to give you some definitive information," Amelia said.

The three men were heading for the door when Amelia said, "Shane, hang on for a minute."

Stabler and Franks went ahead and left the suite, and Shane started walking back toward the autopsy table, but Amelia met him halfway. She took a card out of a side pocket of her scrubs and used a pen from the other to write something on the back.

"It was nice meeting you today, Shane," Amelia said with a smile. "Here's my card in case you have any further questions. I put my personal phone number on the back."

"Thanks. It was nice meeting you as well," Shane responded with a smile of his own. "Have you found a place to live somewhere in the area where you'll be travelling around?"

"I did, right here in Brantford!" Amelia said with some excitement in her voice. I just bought a condo in a new building just south of the downtown area. Maybe we can get together for a coffee sometime."

"That's a possibility," Shane said without hesitation.

After saying goodbye to Amelia, Shane walked out of the Pathology Department door where Stabler was waiting for him.

"What're you doing, Daniels?" Stabler asked. "You've never seen a pretty woman before?"

"What are you talking about?" Shane responded with irritation in his voice.

"You know what I'm talking about. You've already got a beautiful woman at home. That's not enough for you?" Stabler said with some irritation of his own.

"Since when are you interested in my personal life?" Shane asked.

"I'm not," Stabler said flatly and after seeing Franks returning with a coffee he bought from a vending machine in the hallway, changed the subject.

"You need to start compiling a list of people you think might be responsible for delivering the hearts, along with all the information you have on them, and get it to Sergeant Franks," Stabler said. "And I know I'm probably wasting my breath, but that's all I want you to do. We will check them out, not you. You just worry about keeping Emma, your daughter, and yourself safe. Anyone willing to kill two people and remove their hearts to send you a message will have every intention of taking the next step. You hear me, Daniels?"

"Emma and Lan are already out of town, somewhere safe," Shane said. "The same thing goes for you, Inspector; you have to watch your back."

"I'll be in touch this afternoon," Franks said to Shane as he and Stabler turned to head toward the elevators.

Shane followed and said, "You know, the bodies those hearts came from could be from anywhere, not necessarily Brantford. In a city this size, reports of a missing man and woman around the same time should be easy to find."

"Trust me, I have officers looking into that as we speak," Franks said as the three men entered the elevator and he pushed the button for the main floor. "They'll also be in contact with nearby police services and the OPP." OPP was the Ontario Provincial Police.

"I was also thinking they could be connected to a funeral home," Shane said. "Bodies that were scheduled for cremation."

"That's a possibility. I'll check that out," Franks said.

After the elevator arrived at the hospital's main level, Stabler and Franks headed for the front entrance without saying anything else to Shane, who had stopped to think about Doctor Amelia Martin.

He hadn't been attracted to another woman like that since he met Emma and it was causing him all kinds of confusion. He tried to put it down to the fact that very few men wouldn't be attracted to a woman as beautiful as Amelia, but he knew it was more than that. And being the intuitive guy he supposedly was, Shane knew as soon as he looked in Amelia's eyes and observed her facial expression that she felt the same way about him.

Over the years they had been together, Emma had often teased Shane about being oblivious to the fact that he was a good-looking man who drew stares, and occasionally some open flirting, from other women.

"Why would I look at other women when I already have someone as beautiful as you?" Shane would tell Emma.

"Smart answer," Emma would reply with a smile and then say she wasn't the jealous type anyway.

Shane had a steady girlfriend through high school, but when he attended Niagara University, other than a few casual hook-ups, he concentrated on his studies and playing basketball. Once he got a position with the Brantford Police Service, he didn't make time for anything else but being a cop. And after he met Emma, he didn't have eyes for anyone else. Until now, apparently.

He had just stood beside an autopsy table with two plastic tubs containing human hearts sitting on it, only half listening to what was being said because he was thinking about what Amelia Martin's lips would taste like and about the body she had under her scrubs.

Why? Why now?

Why am I acting like a teenager with a crush? Shane asked himself in frustration.

Is it because of what's going on with Emma?

Am I suddenly looking around because my relationship with Emma may be broken over her demand that I give up getting so deeply involved in my cases?

Man, this is all very confusing, Shane thought to himself as he started walking toward the hospital's exit doors.

I should be feeling guilty, but for some reason, I'm not.

Chapter Nine

At the Tremblay trial, Jason was reviewing his notes as the prosecutor, Evan Gregory, completed questioning Doctor Jeffrey Patterson, the pathologist who did the autopsy on Olivia Tremblay.

Jason knew that Patterson had recently retired after over forty years with the Forensic Pathology Service and was highly respected for his expertise. Patterson had been the pathologist on several Brantford and Brant County murder cases, including some that went to trial, and Jason was the defence attorney. So Jason already knew that Patterson was a polished and well-rehearsed witness for the Crown. He was also a distinguished looking man, which certainly helped his credibility in the eyes of the jury, with his erect posture in a tailored dark suit, thin face, tanned complexion, blue eyes, wire-rimmed glasses, and a full head of silver hair.

Gregory had led Patterson through a detailed report regarding his post-mortem examination of Olivia Tremblay, including time and cause of death, her health at the time she died and the fact that she was in the early stages of pregnancy. In an obvious attempt to add shock value for the jury, Gregory used a large portable monitor to show various photographs of Olivia's body at the crime scene, as well as a generic body outline drawing used by pathologists to show locations of injuries. He also presented the jury with a photo of Olivia's bare midriff, taken during the autopsy, to show the entrance wound just below her sternum where the knife entered her body. Jason could tell by the expressions on the faces of the jurors that the photos had the desired shock value that Gregory was after.

"Doctor Patterson, the knife the defendant used to stab his wife had an eight inch blade and was an inch and a half wide at the top of the handle. Is that correct?" Gregory asked.

"That's correct. It was a German-made Henckels stainless steel knife, a very common brand found in many kitchens." Patterson answered. The pathologist had a baritone voice, which added to the credibility and seriousness of his testimony.

"At eight inches, the blade of the knife would have gone deep after it was plunged into Olivia Tremblay's body, correct?" Gregory asked.

This caught Jason's attention, and he stood and said, "Your Honour, I must object to the Prosecutor's use of the word 'plunged'. Doctor Patterson has not used that term during his testimony, and it doesn't appear anywhere in his reports submitted as evidence. Mr. Gregory is using it to try to add an action by the defendant that has not been proven."

"Objection sustained," Judge Wendal said in what was one of the first times he actually ruled in Jason's favour. Perhaps Wendal had finally forgiven Jason for his comments about the Judge's health, although he doubted it.

"Mr. Gregory, please ask your questions in a way that the adjectives are used by the witness and not you," Wendal said.

"Yes, your Honour," Gregory replied and after turning back to face Patterson, asked, "In your opinion, would there have had to be force applied in order for the knife to go into the victim's body right up to its handle?"

"Some pressure would've been required, yes," Patterson responded. "The knife entered the victim's body in an upward trajectory, and that's why it penetrated the heart, which proved to be the fatal injury."

"I have completed my questioning of this witness, your Honour," Gregory said, and Jason noted the look of satisfaction on the Prosecutor's face as he sat back behind his table.

Gregory believes he got from the Pathologist what he wanted the jury to hear, Jason thought. That when Noah stabbed his wife, it was not a reactionary self-defence move but a deliberate plunging of the knife into Olivia's body to kill her.

"Your witness, Mr. Burke," Judge Wendal said.

Jason got up from behind his table and walked to the area directly in front of the witness box.

"Doctor Patterson," Jason began," You've been both firm and confident in many of your findings regarding your post mortem on Olivia Tremblay, such as the cause of death, the fact that she was pregnant, and the toxicology results, which showed she had a blood alcohol level of point zero three. That would be below the legal limit but is still considered high enough to cause impaired judgment. Correct?"

"Typically, for a woman of Olivia Tremblay's size and weight to reach a blood alcohol level of point zero three, she would've consumed   two to three drinks within a short period of time," Patterson replied. "When we tested her stomach contents, we found a mixture of rum and Coke. Of course, being pregnant, Olivia shouldn't have been drinking at all."

Jason ignored Patterson's comment, because he knew the Doctor had made it deliberately for the benefit of the jurors who would be wondering the same thing; why was Olivia drinking when she knew she was pregnant? And why would Noah let her do it?

Jason didn't want to draw any more attention to the issue. He knew he had to deal with it, but now was not the time, so instead he said, "While you've presented some very definitive, scientifically sound information, Doctor Patterson, I want to ask you about some things you talked about during questioning by the Prosecutor which clearly fall into the area of speculation."

"Your Honour, at no point did I ask Doctor Patterson to speculate on anything and I object to Mr. Burke being allowed to use that term," Gregory said as he stood up behind his table.

"I agree, objection sustained," Judge Wendal ruled. "Mr. Burke, I also never heard the Doctor being asked to speculate."

Jason didn't respond to the ruling. He knew Gregory was simply getting him back for his objection to the Prosecutor using the word 'plunged'. Instead, he picked up a small remote from his table and used it to put the body outline diagram on the monitor.

"Doctor Patterson, on your diagram, you drew an arrow pointing to a small black circle you put on the right wrist and noted it simply as discolouration," Jason said.

Jason then changed the image on the monitor to a colour photo of Olivia Tremblay's lower right arm and hand, facing up, that was taken during the postmortem. The skin was very pale, almost white, and on the wrist, there was a noticeably darker area.

"I'm curious why the Prosecutor didn't ask you about this dark spot, Doctor Patterson," Jason said and then asked, "Why is that? What does this discolouration represent?"

"I put in my notes that small areas of bluish-purple discolouration like this, left behind during lividity, are not uncommon," Patterson said, then turned to the jury to offer an explanation. "When a person dies and their heart stops pumping blood, gravity pulls the blood downwards, causing it to pool in the capillaries and small vessels in the lower part of the body. The vast majority of the discolouration caused by lividity is seen in the buttocks and lower back, but small splotches on the lower arms are not uncommon."

"It's a bluish-purple colour, so did you not consider the possibility that this mark was a bruise?" Jason asked.

"Bruises caused by a blow or by a strong grip tend to be uniform in shape; this was not," Patterson answered.

"But can you definitively rule out the possibility that this is a bruise caused by Noah Tremblay's thumb as he gripped his wife's wrist to stop her from stabbing him?" Justin asked.

"If that was the case, I would have seen corresponding bruises on the top of the victim's wrist left by fingers during a very tight grip," Patterson said, in what was clearly becoming a defensive tone.

"But what if it wasn't a very tight grip?" Jason responded. "What if it was someone trying to prevent themselves from being stabbed, but was desperately trying not to hurt the person attacking them?"

"Your Honour!" Gregory exclaimed while he jumped to his feet. "Doctor Patterson has already given his professional opinion on the cause of the discolouration on the wrist. But now, Mr. Burke is not only badgering the witness, he's using the opportunity as a platform for his own theories."

"I agree," Judge Wendal said firmly. "Move on, Mr. Burke."

Jason glanced at the Judge, said, "Yes, your Honour," and then went to the Clerk's desk, where he picked up a clear plastic evidence bag containing a long-bladed knife. He took the bag to the witness box and handed it to the Pathologist.

"Doctor Patterson, can you identify what I handed you, marked as a Crown Exhibit?"

"Yes, this is the knife recovered at the scene of Olivia Tremblay's murder," Patterson answered and then added, "After it was checked for fingerprints and blood by the Forensics Lab, it was transferred to me for examination and comparison with the stab wound on the victim."

"So everyone who examined this knife, including yourself, believes this is the weapon used to kill Olivia?" Jason asked.

"Yes," Patterson replied firmly. "I received it through the proper chain of custody to compare it against the wound on the victim's body. It was a match in terms of the length of the incision and depth of the wound."

"Did you take note of how thin and very sharp the blade is?" Jason asked.

"Henckels knives are a thin type. This one appears to be brand new, so it would be sharp," Patterson replied.

"A thin, razor-sharp knife like this would deeply penetrate a human body very easily, correct?" Jason asked.

"Yes it would, if there was nothing to impede its path, like a bone, for example," Patterson responded.

"However, in this case, the knife entered Olivia's body just below her sternum, on an upward angle and into her heart, correct?" Jason stated.

"Correct," Patterson answered with a questioning tone, obviously wondering where Jason was going with his questions.

"So, Doctor Patterson, going back to what you told the Prosecutor, it's not necessarily true when you said that some pressure would be required for the knife to go as deep as it did," Jason said. "During a struggle between two people close to each other, a thin, very sharp knife would very easily go into a body up to the handle, correct?"

"Well...," Patterson started hesitantly, "That would be speculation on my part."

"Just like the speculation you used with the Prosecutor?" Jason asked facetiously.

"Your Honour!" Gregory started as he jumped to his feet.

But before Gregory could say anything else, Jason said, "I'm finished with this witness, your Honour," and walked back to his desk.

Gregory glared at Jason, and Judge Wendal was doing the the same thing before he turned and said to the pathologist, "You're excused, Doctor Patterson. Thank you for your testimony."

After the Judge called a recess and before Jason left the courtroom to use the washroom and freshen up, he spent a few minutes talking quietly with Noah about how the trial was going so far and, more importantly, he asked Noah how he was feeling. Jason's client had been sitting stoically since the trial resumed this morning and had put his head down anytime crime scene photos or autopsy diagrams were shown on the large monitor.

Jason had become increasingly worried about Noah's state of mind in the weeks leading up to the trial. Over the past year, while in custody, Noah had suffered periods of deep depression over killing his wife and unborn child. Getting proper mental health care can be a painfully slow process in Canada's corrections system, and many prisoners who legitimately need help don't get it promptly because of under-funding and a shortage of qualified staff. Noah eventually began to receive a daily dosage of antidepressants, but Jason had quietly requested a suicide watch while Noah was in the holding cells for the trial.

When the allotted time for the recess was over, everyone was back in their places in the courtroom except for the Judge. Another ten minutes passed, and the room was noisy with the restless chatter among the spectators over the delay. Eventually, a side door opened, the Clerk entered the courtroom, and announced that Judge Wendal apologized for the delay and would return shortly.

Another ten minutes passed before Wendal returned. He was very slow and deliberate as he made his way to his seat on the bench, and when Jason saw him, the old phrase, 'He looks like death warmed over', immediately came to mind. Wendal looked even paler than he did at the start of the morning session, if that was even possible considering how bad the Judge looked at that time.

"Okay, I apologize for the delay," Wendal said in a shaky voice. "Mr. Gregory, you may call your next witness."

Jason was unsure what to do considering how Wendal had reacted earlier, but he was convinced something bad was going to happen if he didn't say anything. He was also sure that Gregory wouldn't be blind to what was going on and would support him.

"Your Honour, before we begin, could my colleague, Mr. Gregory and I approach?" Jason said as he stood up.

Wendal made a 'come over' motion with his hand, and Jason and Gregory walked to the front of the bench.

"Your Honour, with all due respect, while I admire your fortitude, it's obvious to me, and I believe to Mr. Gregory as well, that you continue to suffer some type of medical duress," Jason said in a low voice so no one else in the courtroom could hear him. "Out of concern, could we recess for at least the rest of the day?"

Wendal looked at Gregory, who didn't say anything, then back at Jason.

"Mr. Burke, you've already voiced your opinion about my health once today," Wendal said, clearly irritated. "And my answer has not changed; it's none of your concern. So, gentlemen, please step back, and Mr. Gregory, call your next witness."

Stubborn old fool, Jason thought, as the two men returned to their respective tables, but he did whisper to Gregory, "Thanks for your support," which elicited a smug look from the Prosecutor.

The next witness was Brantford Police Service Sergeant Duncan Campbell, the detective who was in charge of the investigation into Olivia Tremblay's death. Jason knew Campbell was an eighteen year veteran of the Service and worked under Inspector Mark Stabler.

Campbell was a tall, thin man with fiery red hair, short at the top and shaved on the sides, and a trimmed but bushy moustache. He had a light complexion and a very freckled face. He was wearing a blue suit with a Brantford Police Service pin on the lapel, a white shirt and a red silk tie.

Gregory led Campbell through a very detailed explanation of his investigation into Olivia Tremblay's death, starting from when he first arrived at Tremblay's house, through to when he arrested Noah and eventually charged him with second-degree murder.

In order to get the best possible impact on the jury, Jason had assumed, correctly as it turned out, that Gregory would wait until the end of Campbell's testimony to ask the Detective if Noah said anything when they first arrived at the crime scene. Jason had tried unsuccessfully during voir dire to have anything Campbell heard Noah say before he was advised of his rights ruled as hearsay and therefore inadmissible.

A voir dire is a separate hearing, a trial within a trial, held without the jury present, where the judge rules on the admissibility of evidence or testimony. Gregory argued that Noah's statements fell under the 'excited utterance' exception to the hearsay rule because they were made spontaneously while Noah was under the stress of a startling event. The idea is that statements made in such a state are likely to be truthful because the person hasn't had time to fabricate or carefully choose their words.

"Sergeant Campbell, after you first arrived at the Tremblay house and the defendant let you in and showed you his wife's body, did he say anything?" Gregory asked.

"Yes, he said, 'I killed my wife. I did it'," Campbell replied.

"And you accepted that as the defendant saying he murdered his wife," Gregory stated.

"Yes, I did," Campbell responded.

"Objection, your Honour," Jason said as he stood up. "According to what Sergeant Campbell just testified, my client didn't use the word 'murder' or 'murdered'. He shouldn't be allowed to add words that my client never used or to give a personal interpretation of what Noah was thinking when he said, 'I did it' in the heat of the moment."

"Your Honour, I think an experienced police detective should be allowed to infer the meaning of what a suspect said if that suspect is standing over a murder victim," Gregory responded.

"And what? That includes putting words in the suspect's mouth? Is that what an experienced officer should do!?" Jason exclaimed.

"Okay, that's enough!" Judge Wendal tried to say firmly, but his voice came out hoarse and weak. "The officer is allowed to say what he inferred from what the defendant said. Objection overruled."

The Judge then turned to face Campbell in the witness box and said, "But officer, refrain from quoting words the defendant didn't say."

"Yes, your Honour," Campbell said.

Gregory then said, "Sergeant Campbell, just to reiterate for the jury's benefit, the defendant said, 'I killed my wife. I did it'."

"That's correct," Campbell responded in a firm voice.

"Your Honour, I have no further questions for this witness," Gregory said.

"Mr. Burke, you may cross-examine the witness, if you wish," Judge Wendal said.

Jason got up from his table, approached the witness box and said, "Sergeant Campbell, you testified that you and your team found no signs that there had been a struggle in the room where Olivia Tremblay was killed. What kind of signs were you looking for?"

"Overturned furniture, scuff marks on the floor, damage or perhaps blood splatter on the walls, things like that," Campbell answered.

"You also testified that you, your partner, Detective Constable Hailey Mosher, and the Forensic Unit specialist, all concluded that because there were no physical signs of a struggle, Noah Tremblay must have just walked up to his wife and stabbed her. Is that correct?" Jason asked.

"Yes, that's what we believed happened," Campbell responded.

Jason returned to his table, where he picked up a remote and used it to bring up a photo on the large monitor. It showed the area of the living room where Olivia was killed. A dark bloodstain was visible on the carpet.

"Sergeant Campbell, I assume you noted that the Tremblays didn't have a lot of furniture in their living room," Jason said. "A couple struggling with mortgage payments on their first house don't have the discretionary funds to spend on things like a dining table and chairs, end tables or maybe a love seat. In this photo, we can see that the living room in the house was large. You measured it, right?"

"I did, and if you give me a minute, I'll refresh my memory," Campbell said, and then went into the inside pocket of his jacket and removed a small, black, ringed notebook, the type commonly used by police officers and reporters.

"The entire room is sixteen by twenty feet," Campbell then said.

"A much larger than average living room and all the Tremblays had in it so far was a sofa, coffee table, and an entertainment centre at one end. Would you agree with that description?" Jason said.

"Yes, that's true," Campbell agreed.

"Your Honour, do we know where Mr. Burke is going with this house tour?" Gregory asked sarcastically.

"I'd like to know as well, Mr. Burke," Judge Wendal said.

"It will be clear following my next question, your Honour," Jason answered.

"Okay, go ahead," Wendal said.

"We have this large room with a lot of space," Jason began, "Olivia Tremblay's body was lying in the middle of a six by eight foot section of the room. There was no furniture nearby to get damaged, there's carpet on the floor, so no scuff marks would show, and Olivia was stabbed once, not slashed, so, of course, there would be no blood splatter on the walls. Sergeant Campbell, given these facts, how could you possibly conclude there was no struggle? There's enough open space, with nothing nearby, that two big men could have had a fight and there would've been no evidence it ever happened."

Campbell hesitated before he answered and Jason saw the officer shift uncomfortably in his chair.

"We felt there would have been some physical indication in that section of the room if there was a struggle as Mr. Tremblay claimed," Campbell finally answered.

"What indication, Sergeant? This was two people up close to each other in a struggle over a knife, in an open, carpeted area," Jason said testily.

"This was a conclusion I accepted from the expert forensic officer who examined the scene," Campbell responded with irritation in his voice.

"Wouldn't you agree, Sergeant Campbell, that if it's the forensic officer's opinion, then he or she can testify to that opinion and you have no business trying to make it a fact on the stand today?" Jason said, purposely speaking louder and with a measured amount of disgust in his voice to ensure what he said was memorable to the jury.

"Your Honour!" Gregory started, but Jason cut him off by saying, "I'm finished with this line of questioning."

Judge Wendal didn't respond and instead just made a weak gesture with one hand at Jason, who accepted it as a signal to carry on.

"Sergeant Campbell, are you aware that there's a major discrepancy between what you heard my client say the night his wife was killed and what your partner, Constable Mosher, heard?" Jason said.

"There's no discrepancy," Campbell responded flatly.

"I'm afraid there is," Jason stated firmly. "During pretrial discovery, I received copies of both yours and Constable Mosher's notebooks." Jason got the remote from his table and used it to put up an image on the monitor of a page of handwritten notes.

"This is Constable Mosher's notebook, and about halfway down, you can see where she wrote in quotation marks, 'I killed my wife. I didn't mean it', Jason said. "But as we can also see, Constable Mosher scribbled over the words, 'didn't mean' and wrote 'did it' underneath."

Jason then changed the slide to show a printed document on Brantford Police Service letterhead.

"This is Constable Mosher's official statement, which she prepared, signed and submitted later," Jason said. "In it, she quotes my client as saying, 'I killed my wife. I did it'. Sergeant Campbell, did you and Constable Mosher have a discussion about what you each heard at the scene that night?"

"Constable Mosher realized that she had misheard what Tremblay said," Campbell answered.

"She misheard? Maybe you misheard," Jason said in a questioning tone. "Because I'm sure you realize there's an important distinction between 'I didn't mean it' and 'I did it'. My client's intentions are a critical question for the jury to decide."

"She misheard. I was much closer to Mr. Tremblay when he said it," Campbell said.

"So, tell me, how did that work? Did you, as her superior officer, tell Constable Mosher what she was supposed to hear and then instruct her to change her notes?" Jason asked, with some irritation in his voice, which he did on purpose.

"That's not what happened. She changed the notes on her own because after she had time to think about it, she realized she had misheard what Tremblay said," Campbell responded defensively. "It's not uncommon for young, inexperienced officers to make mistakes about what they see and hear when first arriving at a horrific crime scene because there's some shock involved. Later, when they've had a chance to calmly think things over, they realize they made a mistake. It happens."

"I don't believe that for a second, Sergeant Campbell, and I'm sure the jury doesn't either," Jason retorted. "You and I both know that an officer's first impression when arriving at a crime scene is the right one the vast majority of the time."

"I'm not sure why you're asking me about Constable Mosher's notes and not her," Campbell said as he shrugged his shoulders.

Then Gregory stood up and said angrily, "Your Honour, I think we would all like to know why my colleague is not asking Constable Mosher."

Before the Judge could respond, Jason said, "I'm asking Sergeant Campbell because he's Constable Mosher's superior officer and was in charge of everything that occurred at the crime scene that night. It's a safe bet that Constable Mosher will not be testifying for the prosecution at this trial," Jason stated sarcastically and then, staring intensely at Campbell, said, "But when I subpoena her as a defence witness, are you sure she's willing to lie for you, under oath, about what she really heard that night?"

"Your Honour!" Gregory exclaimed, "This is an outrageous attempt by Mr. Burke to discredit a police officer who has a sterling record!"

"You're the one who pushed to have what my client said to the police officers allowed to be heard by the jury!" Jason retorted. "So I should be allowed to question the credibility of exactly what they heard!"

"Gentlemen!" Judge Wendal called out weakly and then collapsed face-first on the bench in front of him. By the time anyone reached him, Wendal was already dead.

Chapter Ten

After he left the Brantford General Hospital, Shane drove to the Burke and Associates offices on King Street.

He tried, mostly unsuccessfully, to put meeting Amelia Martin out of his head because it was causing him a lot of confusion he didn't need right now. There was someone who was a serious threat to him, Emma and Lan, and he had to find them before something else happened.

After he entered the front door of the office, Shane stopped to pass pleasantries with Office Manager Jill Langley, who was sitting at the reception desk.

"Have you heard from Jason about how the trial is going?" Shane asked.

"He called during a recess to see if he had any important messages, but really didn't say much about the trial," Jill answered. "He did ask if I knew what you were up to. Don't you usually attend the opening few days of a trial?"

"I do, but I had a few things come up regarding defence witnesses I'm still vetting," Shane lied. The only person he had told so far about what was going on was Chioma Abiola, whom he had called early this morning because he knew he was going to need her help.

"If you talk to Jason again, you can mention that I have completed the background on psychiatrist Monique LeBlanc and she's all set to testify for us," Shane said.

"Will do," Jill responded.

Shane went to his office and checked his laptop to see if he had any important emails or inter-office messages that had to be dealt with right away. Not seeing anything, he took his phone out of the inside pocket of the sports jacket he was wearing and checked his personal email. There was one from Emma he had already seen, which had a photo attached; a selfie of her and Lan on the beach in Port Elgin, both smiling. Shane hoped the fact that Emma was smiling was a good sign.

There was an email from his friend Ben Chen with a video attachment, which Shane didn't open. Ben, who had a very weird view of the world, was always sending videos, most of them from TikTok, that Ben thought were funny, but Shane didn't and, in fact, most of the time he didn't even understand.

Shane and Ben grew up together in Paisley and became friends in elementary school after Shane successfully took on three other boys who were bullying Ben, primarily because he was one of the very few Chinese-Canadians who lived in the village. Ben's family lived in Paisley, but his parents owned a Chinese buffet restaurant in Port Elgin, which Ben inherited after they passed away.

Ben had a manager to run the restaurant while he concentrated on his highly successful career as a designer of online games. Even though he was a very wealthy man, Ben didn't live a lavish lifestyle and still lived in his parent's modest home in Paisley.

While Shane and Ben were very close and would do anything for each other, they couldn't possibly be more different. Shane was tall and in good physical shape. Ben was short and had battled a weight issue his entire life. Shane had a perpetual five o'clock shadow, but Ben said he couldn't grow facial hair even if his life depended on it. Ben had an oval face with fine Asian features, dark spiky hair and sometimes wore round wire-framed glasses, not for style, but because he decided it made him look like how they depicted Chinese men in the old Western films Shane liked to watch. Ben's sense of humour was always hard to figure out.

Even though he had a temper, which showed its ugly self from time to time, Shane tended to be quiet and thoughtful. Ben, on the other hand, was loud, brash, easy-going, and almost always politically incorrect with his opinions. Ben was also completely unable to finish a sentence without at least one 'fuck' in it or some other foul word.

Ben's girlfriend, Michele, also had an opposite personality to Ben, but with one glaring exception; she was also unable to talk without saying 'fuck' a lot.

While Shane was reviewing his email, his phone rang and the caller ID said it was from the Brantford Police Service.

"Shane Daniels," he answered.

"This is Sergeant Franks. Do you have that list of names and files for me?" Franks said without any introductory pleasantries.

"Working on it," Shane replied and then asked, "You have anything for me?"

"Forensics has been all over the two cardboard boxes the hearts came in, and the notes, but there's nothing so far," Franks said. "Whoever is responsible was very careful, likely wearing gloves. The notes were on standard computer paper, and the letters were made by a very common type of inkjet printer."

"Has Inspector Stabler suggested the names of people he feels we might be both connected to?" Shane asked.

"A couple," Franks answered. Shane realized Franks wasn't prepared to share very much information with him. He obviously didn't trust Shane.

"Where's Adam Talino?" Shane asked.

"Talino is still in the Maplehurst Correctional Complex in Milton awaiting trial on murder charges," Franks said. "Despite the efforts of his expensive legal team, he's been denied bail twice, even with an offer that he would wear a monitoring device."

"Talino is at the top of my list," Shane said. "He's a psychopathic killer of young women who Stabler and I caught. He hates me and would want revenge. He likely has money stashed in offshore accounts and still has, for some reason, influential supporters in the city. He would also likely know how to get in contact with other sick individuals like himself who would be more than happy to cut up some bodies for the right price."

"I know all about Talino and we're already taking a close look at who he hangs around with at Maplehurst, who's been to visit him, and who he has talked to on the phone," Franks said.

"He's the top candidate for this, but I'll think about some other names," Shane said.

"And right away," Franks said and then hung up.

The abrupt end to the call didn't bother Shane because he knew Franks would be under a lot of pressure. Brantford Police Chief Charlie Oak was also shot during the same domestic disturbance call where Shane's knee was irreparably damaged. Oak was saved when the shotgun blast hit his protective vest. Shane and Charlie remained friends as Oak rose through the ranks to Chief, and it was Oak who elevated Mark Stabler from Sergeant to Inspector in charge of the Criminal Investigation Division. The Chief was probably personally supervising the case and Franks would be aware of that.

Shane decided the rest of his emails could wait and was about to head to Chioma's office when his phone buzzed with an incoming message. It was a text from Amelia Martin:

Just wanted to say again how much I enjoyed meeting you today. Don't forget that if you have any questions, call my personal cell phone number on the back of the card I gave you. And also don't forget about getting together for a coffee! Regards, A.

A shot of unexpected excitement went through Shane's body. Christ, what have I started! Shane thought, as the excitement was quickly replaced with a sense of panic. What kind of signals did I give off to Amelia that I didn't mean to? Or did I do it on purpose because I was attracted to her? Shane admitted to himself.

Even Inspector, 'I don't care', Stabler picked up on the fact that he and Amelia were flirting with each other. I've got to stop doing that when I see her before it goes any further, Shane decided. I don't need this distraction, not with everything that's going on. I need to fix things with Emma. But even as Shane was thinking this, the image of Amelia's beautiful face, enticing eyes and full lips entered his mind, as well as speculation about the body under her hospital scrubs.

Shane closed the email program on his phone, desperately pushed Amelia to the back of his mind, and walked down the hall and into Chioma's office. She was sitting at her desk, her chair turned to her left, where she was working on a keyboard in front of two large monitors. Shane closed the office door behind him and sat in the chair facing the desk.

Chioma stopped typing, looked at Shane and asked, "How are you, Shane? It's terrible what's happened. I don't know what to say. How could anyone do something so cruel?"

"I'm doing okay, especially now that Emma and Lan are safely out of town," Shane said.

"And what does Jason have to say?" Chioma asked.

"I haven't told him yet," Shane said flatly.

"What!? Why not? He needs to know what's going on with his firm's investigator, who is also his friend!" Chioma exclaimed as her face took on a questioning look.

"Jason is in the opening phase of a murder trial and the last thing he needs under that kind of pressure is this kind of distraction," Shane said defensively. "I will tell him when the time is right."

"Well, I can guarantee he's going to be some kind of peeved at you for not telling him right away," Chioma responded.

"I know. I'll deal with it," Shane said and then asked, "What have you got for me so far?"

"Given your obsession with the guy and how much he despises you, Adam Talino has to be a key suspect, even though he's currently in jail," Chioma said. "I'm sure you already consider him number one."

"I've talked to Sergeant Franks about Talino," Shane said.

"I'm also gathering information on what Ava Evans is currently up to," Chioma said.

Shane was responsible for Brantford businesswoman Ava Evans being arrested for conspiracy to commit murder after she paid her personal driver to travel to the small town of Innisfail, Alberta and murder her brother Will. Ava was angry that when their father died, he left half of his successful business and his personal fortune to Will, who was estranged from the family at the time. Shane, at the behest of Ava, had gone to Innisfail to find her brother, who had been recently paroled from the nearby Bowden jail, and to tell him about his inheritance. Shane was unaware he was being used by Ava to locate her brother so she could have him killed.

"Ava is currently on bail under strict conditions and is being allowed to live in the family home until all of the complex legalities around her father's estate are straightened out," Chioma continued. "The thing is, with the estate currently tied up, Ava is basically broke, so I'm assuming she doesn't have the financial means to find and pay someone to murder two people, remove their hearts, and send them to you and Inspector Stabler. Unless, of course, she did it herself."

"I can tell you that the day I sat beside Ava in Jason's office and told her I knew she had her brother killed, and the police were coming to arrest her, there was a malevolence in her eyes that gave me chills," Shane said. "She's cold-hearted enough to kill someone herself, and I can see her wanting revenge. If he hasn't done it already, I'm going to tell Sergeant Franks to put Ava under surveillance. If he doesn't do it, I'll do it myself or have one of our contract employees do it."

"But if it's Ava Evans who sent the hearts, then why not one to Jason?" Chioma asked. "She hired the firm to handle her financial affairs after she received her inheritance and she asked Jason, who then asked you, to find her brother. After you found out what she did, Jason immediately dropped her as a client and refused to be her defence attorney. So she would have good reason to seek revenge on Jason rather than Inspector Stabler."

"That makes sense, but who knows what she's thinking." Shane replied.

"There are other people who might have a motive to hurt your family to get revenge, but they're all currently in prison," Chioma said and then added, "You've managed to make a lot of enemies."

"I suppose. It comes with the job," Shane said offhandedly.

"Really, Shane? Not this many names," Chioma retorted. "You're an investigator for a law firm who doesn't stay in his lane. You see a mystery or an injustice, and you have to get involved until it's solved. That's why you have so many enemies."

"Yeah, well, Emma and I've been arguing over the same subject recently," Shane said.

"You've been on a dangerous path for a long time now, Shane, and now it's caught up with you. A sick individual seeking revenge in this way is a consequence."

"Are you done with the lecture, Chioma?" Shane asked with rising irritation.

"For now," Chioma said with a bit of a smile on her face.

Shane heard a ding coming from Chioma's computer, meaning she had received a priority message.

"If this is what I hope it is, I'll have a number one suspect for you," Chioma said as she turned toward her monitors and worked the keyboard. She looked at the screens for a moment and then said, "How about Troy Finn?"

"Troy Finn. It's been a while since I thought about that guy," Shane said and then asked, "What about him?"

"I just got confirmation from a source of mine that two days ago, Troy's younger brother, Jacob, was attacked by three other prisoners at the Joyceville Institution in Kingston," Chioma explained. "They had homemade knives and stabbed Jacob multiple times. He died before they could get him to the hospital."

The Finn brothers ran a motorcycle repair shop on West Street, but it wasn't their main source of income. They were drug dealers; middlemen between those who only sold by quantity and Finn's so-called employees who sold at the street level.

"You and Inspector Stabler were responsible for Jacob being in jail," Chioma said. "Troy could be seeking revenge for his brother being killed in custody."

"It's a strong possibility," Shane responded. "They were very close and Troy was very protective of his younger brother, who was not too bright and was very impulsive."

"I never understood how you got involved with the Finn brothers in the first place," Chioma said. "Who was the firm's client you were working for?"

"No client," Shane said. "I did it as a favour for someone."

Shane then explained.

Chapter Eleven

It was six months ago. Shane received an encrypted text message from Doobie MacArthur asking for a meeting.

MacArthur was his confidential source for virtually any information he needed.

Doobie lived in a wheelchair accessible basement apartment on Wellington Street, where he spent virtually all of his time working magic on a keyboard facing four wide-screen monitors wired to a vast array of servers. Doobie was a world-class gamer and a brilliant hacker. There were very few places connected to the internet that he couldn't get into.

Doobie's real name was Randy, but he had been known as Doobie since elementary school because of the simple fact that if you didn't see him smoking a marijuana joint, it was because he was rolling one. Doobie was the dictionary definition of a pot-head.

There was a time when Doobie graduated to using hard drugs, and it nearly killed him. He was a diabetic and because he didn't look after himself, he eventually had to have both his legs amputated from the knee down. Doobie managed to kick his cocaine habit, but a joint was still ever present.

Shane paid generously for the information that Doobie somehow managed to get from hundreds of both government and private sector data banks, and from the dark web. But the two men were friends and there had been a number of occasions when Doobie had given Shane a heads-up on something important at no charge. That included the time when serial killer Adam Talino had secretly paid a hacker to get past the VPN on Shane's phone and embed child pornography in an attempt to ruin his life.

After Shane got his text message, he went to see Doobie at his apartment, a spacious, one-room affair with very little in the way of furniture. There was a single bed, a small kitchenette and a massive work area set up on two long tables.

"What's going on, Doob?" Shane asked as the two men sat facing each other; Shane in an old folding metal chair and Doobie in his high-end electric wheelchair, which had a cup-holder attached to one arm and an ashtray on the other, currently containing the ends of smoked joints and a roach clip. Roach was the slang term used for joints that were smoked until they were too small to hold with your fingers, so you used the metal clip to hold them.

When Shane saw it in the ashtray, he said, "I didn't think anyone bothered using a roach clip anymore."

"It's an old habit of mine, but you know what they say, 'waste not want not'," Doobie said with a smile that exposed his darkly stained teeth.

Doobie was somewhere in his fifties and had a heavily-lined face, shoulder-length hair and scraggly beard, both streaked with gray. MacArthur always reminded Shane of the late country music star

Waylon Jennings during the years when Jennings was a member of the so-called outlaws, along with singer/songwriters Willie Nelson and Chris Christofferson.

"I need a personal favour," Doobie said.

"I owe you one or two. What do you need?" Shane asked.

"There are two brothers here in town, drug dealers, Troy and Jacob Finn. Have you heard of them?" Doobie asked as he pulled a fresh joint out of the front pocket of his faded denim shirt and lit it with a disposable lighter from the other pocket.

"I know them by reputation, but that's about it," Shane said.

"Where ever they're getting their stuff from, it's really bad shit, or else the brothers are making it bad shit before it hits the street," Doobie said with some intensity. "The coke's been stomped on so much it's almost all baby powder or whatever else they're cutting it with. The pills have somehow been reconstituted with some kind of shit added, and the weed is laced with fentanyl."

"Why are people still buying weed on the street and not legally in the cannabis store where it's safe?" Shane asked.

"Have you ever been in a weed shop, Mister Straight Lace?" Doobie asked in frustration.

"No, not really," Shane said sheepishly.

"It's not cheap," Doobie said and then quickly added, "But that's not the point. The shit the Finns are selling has made a lot of people very sick and has put at least two people I know, including the daughter of a good bud, in the hospital, in a coma, and on life support."

"I'm sorry to hear that, Doob. Have the cops gotten involved?" Shane asked.

"You know how that works," Doobie responded. "Nobody wants to talk to the cops. They've been around to the usual locations, talking to people to see if maybe they'll give up the name of the source, and warning people there's dangerous shit around."

"What do you want from me, Doob?" Shane asked.

"Listen, it would be easy for me not to give a fuck. I got the money to buy my weed legally, and my hard drug days are long over," Doobie said. "But people are going to start dying and the Finn brothers couldn't give two shits. They need to be shut down."

"So, use your magic fingers on your keyboard and find a way to get the Finn's name to the cops," Shane said. "Should be child's play for someone for you."

"No can do," Doobie said adamantly. "I need to keep completely out of it. You have to understand that, as good as I am, and I am the best, everything I do online leaves a signature. I've been told by a reliable source that the Finns get their bulk stuff from some very heavy hitters. People in that category tend to spend a ton of money on people like me who do nothing else but closely watch the regular online traffic and the dark web for anything that might be of interest to their bosses. They use algorithms to develop very sophisticated programs that search for keywords and phrases or online signatures, and for sure, the name Finn would pop."

"It's the same thing you do to gather and sell information, Doob," Shane commented.

Doobie dropped what was left of his joint into the ashtray before he burnt his fingers and then said, "Again, not the point. We need to do this the old-fashioned way. Set the Finns up for a bust."

"Doob, I admire your desire to put the Finns out of business, so why don't I just go and whisper in the ear of one of my contacts in the police service?" Shane said.

"No," Doobie said firmly. "I want your help, but I need you to come up with a way to keep our names out of it, if at all possible. Don't think for a second that the Brantford Police Service doesn't leak like a sieve. I don't trust the cops."

"Well, Doob, there's a very good reason for that. The local cops have been working with the Mounties for years to find you and shut you down," Shane said.

"Yeah, yeah, I know. Can you help or not?" Doobie said impatiently.

"Do you know which of the brothers is the least intelligent? Perhaps more ambitious and greedy?" Shane asked.

"That's easy. Jacob," Doobie answered. "Some people think maybe he's got a screw loose. Jacob does the bulk of the heavy lifting for the Finn's drug business. Troy has final say on everything, but he prefers to run the bike repair shop and let Jacob take the risks involved in selling at the street level. Troy does the deals with the major supplier and looks after the cash, likely laundering it through the business."

"Is it possible that Troy doesn't know that Jacob's been messing with the product before his sellers hit the streets?" Shane asked. "The stuff would go farther, which means a lot more money, and maybe Jacob is only handing Troy what he's expecting and then pockets the rest."

"Dude, I think you could be right on with that theory," Doobie rasped out as he held the smoke in his lungs from a newly lit joint.

It always amused Shane that while Doobie was a very intelligent man, his use of words like 'dude', put his language skills stuck in the 1990s.

"Up until now, the Finn brothers, mainly Troy, were known as straight shooters," Doobie said after he exhaled. "You got what you paid for."

"Okay, I have an idea, but its success rests on two key things," Shane said. "Number one is that our assumption that Jacob is messing with the product without Troy's knowledge is true. And number two, while I know you don't want to leave any kind of online trail, you have to find out the name of the person selling in bulk to the Finns. I need to have that to make my plan work."

"I can get that, Amigo," Doobie said. "I've got a couple of burner phones around here somewhere. I can make some calls and get that name."

After his meeting with Doobie, Shane stopped shaving for three days. Because of his heavy beard, if he used an electric shaver in the morning, he would have to use it again in the afternoon if he was going out somewhere. By the night of the third day, he had the start of a good beard, albeit one streaked with gray. Emma didn't think much of it.

"Please tell me this isn't permanent," she complained. "And why do you have your hair slicked back? You look like a gangster in a Grade B film."

"It's for surveillance I have to do tonight and there's a chance the people I'm watching will recognize me if I'm clean shaven," Shane told her.

Shortly after 9 pm, Shane drove in the Charger to a strip mall on Colborne Street, south of the downtown, and parked in front of a closed bakery shop. From there, he walked to Bing's Restaurant and Tavern, the largest tenant of the mall.

While Bing's apparently did serve food, Shane wasn't sure if anyone actually ate it. Bing's was your basic dingy bar with four pool tables, a large open area with the traditional small round tables and chairs, and a small stage for local bands to grind out some music on Friday and Saturday nights. The long bar along one wall was busy with customers, all of the stools were in use, as were quite a few of the tables. The lighting, such as it was, was provided by shielded bulbs hanging from the girder-exposed ceiling. The place reeked of stale beer and body odour, and Shane could still pick up the smell left behind on the walls from when it was legal to smoke in bars.

Shane was wearing a dark blue suit, the best one he owned, and a very light dress shirt with no tie. This was before he had his new high-tech knee brace, so he had his cane with him, but that was the plan anyway. Shane owned several different kinds of canes. This was a traditional one, made of wood, with a curved handle, but Shane had purposely modified it by filling part of the handle with lead, which made the cane a lot heavier.

Shane knew that by using a cane, it made him appear vulnerable. To certain people, like the young man Shane was in the bar to see, Shane wouldn't be considered a threat because he was obviously disabled.

Shane spotted Jacob Finn sitting with another young man at a table near one of the corners of the room. Both had a glass of draft beer and a shot glass of whisky in front of them. Before he approached, Shane stood at the bar, ordered a bottle of beer, and watched as a steady stream of both men and women stopped at Jacob's table to say a few words, bump fists or whisper in his ear. This is where Finn holds court and makes contact with his various street level dealers,

Shane thought. This is his environment, so I need to be careful how I do this, he realized.

After he walked over to the table, leaning heavily on his cane for the benefit of Jacob's colleague, who was probably his bodyguard, Shane said, "Hello, Jacob Finn, mind if I sit down?"

"Who the fuck are you?" Jacob asked in an irritated voice.

Both men looked each other over as Shane sat down. Jacob was thin to the point of being considered scrawny. He was wearing a striped golf shirt and both his arms and his neck were heavily tattooed; some new and colourful, and others faded. He had a wide leather band on one wrist and an expensive sports watch on the other. Finn had clear green eyes, his face had high cheekbones and a rough complexion dotted with old, deep acne scars. His hair was thin and long, pulled back and tied at the back. His attempt at a moustache was sparse across his upper lip, as was the goatee hanging from his chin.

When Jacob looked at Shane, he would see what Shane wanted him to see; a tall man in an expensive suit jacket that pushed against a muscular upper body, but disabled because he had a cane. A scraggly black beard and slicked back hair. Shane knew Finn would also take note of the top half of a colourful tattoo on his right neck, showing just above his shirt collar and a small, faded teardrop tattoo beside his right eye. Both temporary markings had been added by a makeup artist Shane knew. The teardrop tattoo means different things to different people, but Shane was confident Finn would interpret it as meaning Shane had spent time in prison, was perhaps a member of a gang, or had murdered someone.

In answer to Finn's question, Shane said, "My name's Mike and I'm here on behalf of Mr. Duncan."

"I don't know a Duncan, so fuck off," Jacob said to the amusement of his colleague at the table.

"Mr. Finn, Jacob, let's not waste each other's time," Shane said in a calm voice. "I drove over an hour to get here and I don't want to be here any longer than I have to, so cut the bullshit so I can deliver Mr. Duncan's instructions."

"As I said, I don't know any Duncan and I sure as shit don't know you," Jacob responded.

"Fine," Shane said as he took his phone out of the inner pocket of his jacket. "I'm going to call Mr. Duncan and give you the phone so you can ask him about me, but trust me, he won't be happy to hear from you. And then, no doubt Mr. Duncan will turn around and call your brother, the Finn he actually deals with, and ask him why the perfectly fine Duncan product is turning to shit in Brantford and putting people in hospital, which is drawing some very unwanted attention."

This was a tense moment for Shane. He was hoping that his bluff about calling MacKenzie Duncan, the name of the Finn's wholesale drug dealer that Dobbie came up with, would work. Otherwise, he would have to call Doobie, who would impersonate Duncan, and hope like hell that it was Troy who handled all the communications with Duncan and Jacob had never talked to him directly.

"Okay, okay, Mike, or whatever the fuck your real name is, what does your Mr. Duncan want?" Jacob asked, emphasizing the word 'Mister' in a sarcastic tone.

"Not in here, out back," Shane said and then got up and walked toward the tavern's rear exit door.

Even though a sign said it was alarmed, when Shane pushed the metal bar to open the door, he knew there would be no alarm because he had already checked out the alley behind the building and had seen people standing by the door smoking. The proprietor would have disabled the alarm a long time ago, or it would be going off all the time.

When he got outside, with Jacob and his colleague right behind him, Shane was glad to see the back alley was currently empty. There was a light over the door, but with a low-wattage bulb, so its coverage area was very small and the shadows were deep.

The three men stood in a fairly close semi-circle. Jacob said, "So, Mike, just so you don't get any ideas," and then he nodded at his colleague, a wide, overweight man with a shaved head. The man turned to his right and lifted the back of the light jacket he was wearing to expose a handgun he had jammed into the top of his jeans at the small of his back. He dropped his jacket back over the gun and turned to face Shane with a smile on his face.

Stupid, Shane thought. If you're going to threaten someone with a gun, you don't leave it stuck in the back of your jeans. How quickly are you going to be able to retrieve it? Especially if you're a guy with a beer gut who has his belt notched extra tight to hold the gun in place, plus keep his pants up.

Shane, who had casually moved his hand halfway up the shaft of his cane as he walked out the back door of the bar, suddenly slammed the lead-filled handle of the cane into the big guy's crotch. The man howled in pain, grabbed himself with both hands, and bent over at the waist as he slowly began dropping to his knees. Shane reached over, pulled the handgun out of the man's belt and pointed it at Jacob's forehead.

Jacob immediately held his arms up and exclaimed in a panicked voice, "I'm not armed! I don't carry, I leave that to Paxton!"

Now Shane knew Jacob's bodyguard's name for future reference. He then made a circle motion with the gun and Jacob lifted his jacket and slowly turned all the way around to show he had nothing in his belt.

"Pull up the bottom of your jeans," Shane demanded. Jacob obeyed, showing Shane that he didn't have an ankle holster.

"So, Jacob, this is how this is going to work," Shane said. "I didn't come to Brantford alone. There are two associates of mine parked nearby in a van. You're going to take me to where you keep your stash and where you've been messing with the quality of the product to the point that you're eventually going to kill a bunch of people, which is obviously bad for business. The men in the van are going to take away everything you have and destroy it. We will then leave you a new, but small, fresh supply as a test run to see if you can behave yourself in future. How does that sound so far?"

"Yeah, sure," Jacob said, but Shane saw defiance in the young man's eyes.

"Jacob, I don't think you're bright enough to realize the gravity of your current situation," Shane said. "Depending on your level of cooperation, instead of taking your shit drugs away, I have the option of having my two colleagues take you and Paxton away in the van instead. You would not be coming back. Does your drug-addled pea brain understand that?

"Yeah, yeah, I got it," Jacob muttered.

"The only reason you're not riding away in that van right now is because Mr. Duncan likes and respects your brother. They've done business together, successfully, for a long time and Mr. Duncan considers Troy to be one of his best and most loyal middlemen. He's sure that Troy would have no part in putting bad product on the street. That leaves you. And you'll have to deal with your brother, who will undoubtedly be very unhappy with you."

Now Shane only saw resignation in Jacob's eyes.

The back door of the bar suddenly burst open and two couples came out, laughing and talking excitedly, everyone reaching into a pocket or purse to pull out a package of cigarettes. Shane quickly turned to face them, holding the gun behind his back. He hoped Jacob wouldn't do anything stupid. When the four people saw Shane, Jacob and Paxton, who was still on his knees, bent over in pain, they stopped talking and stared. Shit! Witnesses are the last thing I need, Shane thought.

"Our friend here got a little carried away with the beer and shots," Shane called out with a smile on his face.

One of the women shook her head, then all four resumed talking and laughing, and walked to another area of the back alley to light up their cigarettes. Shane turned back to face Jacob while moving the gun to the front of his body, where it would be hidden from the smokers.

"Let's go get your vehicle and you can drive to where your lab and drugs are. The van will follow," Shane said.

"I don't think I can walk!" Paxton managed to get out in between taking rapid breaths. "I need a hospital! I think this motherfucker has broken my balls!"

"We'll pull the car into the alley and help you get inside," Shane said. "You can go to the hospital later. Until then, you can suffer for threatening me with a gun."

It was no small feat getting a big man like Paxton up off the ground and into the front seat of Jacob's SUV while he moaned loudly in pain. Shane sat in the back, and while Jacob drove, he secretly took his phone out of his pocket, pulled up a tracking app and hit the icon to engage it.

Three days prior to confronting Jacob, Doobie had provided Shane with information he needed about MacKenzie Duncan, a Hamilton area a drug importer and wholesaler. Shane then decided on a plan, stopped shaving, and called Mark Stabler, who was still a Sergeant at that time.

"I need your help with something," Shane had told Stabler.

"I don't do help, especially for you, Daniels, because it always seems to end up being a very bad piece of highway," Stabler replied in his usual grumpy manner.

"I beg to differ," Shane said lightly. "I seem to recall recently solving a murder and letting the Brantford Police Service, and specifically you, take credit for it."

"What do you want, Daniels?" Stabler asked.

"I would like you to prepare one of your confidential informant registration documents for me and then I'm going to come in and sign it today," Shane said.

"And why would I do that? I'm almost afraid to ask, but what the hell have you gotten yourself into, Daniels?" Stabler asked.

"I'm sure you're aware that some bad drugs are currently being sold in the city, which are making a lot of users very sick. There's at least one person in the hospital, in a coma, and not expected to make it," Shane explained. "I have a way to hand you both the supplier and his supply so you can get the stuff off the streets. You'll be called a hero, and who knows, you might even get a promotion."

"There you go again, Daniels, acting like you're still a cop, which you are not," Stabler said tersely. "Give me what you got and we'll take it from there."

"I can't do that, not this time. I have it on good authority that your place has someone leaking information. If I give you what I know and you move on this dealer, he'll know well in advance, and you'll get nothing," Shane said.

"Bullshit!" Stabler reacted in a stronger tone than he normally used. "On whose good authority is there a leak? Is it one of your low-life street informants?" he asked.

"I can't say. He's in a vulnerable position because of what he's told me," Shane said. "But you have to trust me that this guy is solid." Shane had no intention of giving up Doobie MacArthur's name.

Saying it was absolutely against his better judgment, Stabler finally agreed, and Shane signed the papers to become a registered confidential informant. In Canada, the legal principle known as informer privilege prevents informants from being publicly identified or called to testify at a trial. There are some exceptions, like the concept of 'innocence at stake', which allows a judge to order the disclosure of an informant's identity if it's essential for a fair trial.

Jacob drove his SUV to a mostly unused industrial area south of Colborne Street East and wound his way along a series of lanes fronting old, rusty metal-sided warehouses of various sizes and shapes.

While Jacob was driving around, Shane wiped down the handgun he took off Paxton and put it on the floor in front of his seat. He had hoped to pull off his con without weapons and violence, but he was prepared for it. Shane always felt a bit of nausea after the adrenaline from a physical confrontation wore off. He knew it was necessary because Paxton was armed, but Shane regretted hitting the young man and hoped he didn't suffer any permanent damage.

Jacob eventually pulled his SUV along the front of a medium-sized warehouse with a large roll-up door and a regular one beside it.

"This is it," Jacob announced as he shut off the engine and released his seat belt. He then said, "If you're still suffering, you can stay in the vehicle, Paxton."

"No Shit," Paxton spat back. He had been moaning and swearing during the entire drive. "Just hurry up and do what you gotta do, so I can get to the hospital. Fuck!"

Shane got out of the SUV and followed Jacob to the door beside the roll-up. The overhead light fixture was not turned on, so the front of the building was in the dark, the only illumination was coming from a street lamp on the other side of the lane. Jacob unlocked and opened the door, reached into the left, hit three switches, and a bank of fluorescent lights hanging from the ceiling flickered on. As Shane walked into the large, inside area, he had to blink rapidly several times as his eyes adjusted to the suddenly brightly lit warehouse.

Four fold-up plastic tables were sitting end-to-end in the middle of the floor. Their surfaces held white plastic pails, boxes of clear plastic sandwich bags and yellow rubber gloves, several three-burner hot plates with stainless steel pots on them, metal mixing bowls, ceramic mortars and pestles used for crushing pills, and what looked like two instruments used to press powder into pills.

Also on the tables, Shane saw bags of pills he assumed were fentanyl, jars marked caffeine and Lidocaine Powder, which is an anesthetic, and bags of baby powder. They were all items he knew were used to cut drugs. There were some other chemicals Shane didn't recognize, and he assumed that, as bad as the other cutting agents were, these were likely the ones making users very ill.

"This is quite a set-up you've got, Jacob," Shane said, but then added, "Mr. Duncan does expect that his dealers will step on his product a little bit before it hits the streets, but what I'm seeing here goes dangerously beyond a little bit."

Jacob didn't respond and Shane noted a bit of a smirk on the young man's face.

"Where's your supply of original product?" Shane asked.

Jacob led Shane to a corner of the warehouse where there was a pallet covered by a blue tarp, which he pulled off. There was a small stack of cocaine wrapped in bricks and four open cardboard boxes filled with plastic bags of pills.

"Where's the shit that you're selling?" Shane asked, putting some irritation in his voice.

Jacob went to a second pallet and pulled the tarp off. There were four more boxes, each filled with tiny plastic bags containing either pills or white powder. Also on the pallet were two large, clear plastic garbage bags filled with marijuana.

"Why are you selling weed? It's a legal product," Shane asked.

"It's a small side business I have because not everyone can afford the cannabis store prices," Jacob said.

"And don't tell me, let me guess, it's laced with fentanyl," Shane said.

Jacob didn't say anything; he just shrugged his shoulders.

Shane was counting on Sergeant Stabler and some backup to be on time and in place, so he said, "You can keep the original product, Jacob, but everything else in this warehouse is going into my van parked outside and it's all going to be destroyed. You're going to find another location and you will not be setting up another shit factory like this one. Do you understand my instructions? I need to hear you say it."

"Yeah, I understand," Jacob said impatiently.

"People are seriously ill because of what you've done, Jacob, and some may die," Shane said. "The cops are going to be pulling out all stops to find the drugs and to find you. You need to lay low for a while, and I will leave it to you to explain that to your brother, who I'm sure is not going to be pleased."

Jacob again didn't say anything, but Shane could tell from the expression on Finn's face that he was thinking about his options because he was about to lose tens of thousands of dollars in profit. Please don't do anything stupid, Jacob, Shane thought. Finn would have realized that Shane no longer had the gun.

Got to get aggressive and bring this thing to an end quickly, Shane decided. So, in the most menacing voice he could muster, he said, "Don't get any ideas, Jacob, or I'll beat you to a pulp with my cane and then I'll burn this warehouse to the ground with you in it. The cops will rummage through the rubble and they'll be satisfied that the bad drug problem, and the man behind it, have been solved. Now open the sliding door for my guys in the van!"

Jacob hesitated for a moment and stared intensely at Shane, but then turned, walked to the main door, bent over, grabbed the handle, and started rolling it up.

Please be there! Shane pleaded to himself.

When the door was fully open, there was a white van with its sliding door facing the opening. The van door rolled back and four police officers in tactical gear, armed with semi-automatic rifles, jumped out and moved inside the warehouse. One of them yelled, "On your knees! Hands on the back of your head! Do it now!"

Both Shane and Jacob quickly obeyed, and while two of the officers held them at gunpoint, the other two put them in handcuffs behind their back. Then Sergeant Stabler, in a suit but wearing a tactical vest, walked into the warehouse.

Stabler gave no indication that he knew Shane. He said, "Jacob Finn, you, your colleague Paxton Strong who is sitting in your vehicle for some reason, and whoever this person beside you is, are all under arrest for the possession of illicit drugs for the purpose of trafficking. I expect there will be further charges as well. I have told you why you're being arrested. You have the right to remain silent. You have the right to retain and instruct a lawyer without delay. If you cannot afford a lawyer, you will be instructed on how to access legal aid. Do you understand what I've told you, Mr. Finn?"

"Yeah, yeah," Jacob muttered, his head down. Shane figured Jacob would be in a panic about what will happen when his brother finds out what he's been up to and that he's been arrested.

"What's your name?" Stabler asked Shane.

"Mike," Shane replied.

"Mike who?" Stabler said impatiently.

"Smith," Shane responded.

"Well, Mr. Smith, if that's your real name, do you understand the rights I have told you?"

"Yep, got it," Shane said.

"You're now going to be transported in separate cruisers to the Brantford Police Station for formal processing," Stabler said and then nodded to the tactical officers, two of whom grabbed Shane and Jacob and pulled them to their feet. Jacob was led out of the warehouse door and to the right to an awaiting cruiser, its strobing rooftop emergency lights bouncing brightly off nearby buildings.

Shane was taken out the door and to the left, where Stabler's dark, unmarked SUV was parked, the emergency lights behind the front grill flashing. On the way, Shane saw Jacob's vehicle with all four doors open and two officers searching inside with flashlights. There was no sign of Paxton, who was probably already on his way to the police station, or maybe the hospital, Shane thought.

Once they were on the passenger side of Stabler's vehicle, the tactical officer removed Shane's handcuffs and walked away without a word.

Stabler then approached and said, "I'm sure you're proud of yourself, Daniels, but you had no business getting involved in something this dangerous."

"Maybe so, but we just saved some lives by stopping those drugs from going on the street," Shane said.

"Yeah, there is that," Stabler replied flatly.

Chapter Twelve

When Shane finished telling Chioma about his involvement with the Finn brothers, she looked at him for a moment and then said, "I agree with what Inspector Stabler told you that night. You had no business going undercover like that. What if Jacob was smarter than you thought and he didn't buy your story about you being there to represent his supplier? You could have been killed."

"I did it as a favour for Doobie MacArthur and, more importantly, I wanted to get some bad drugs off the street before a lot of people died," Shane said.

"Come on, Shane," Chioma admonished. "MacArthur doesn't trust the cops, but you trust Stabler. You could have gone to him and he could have put an undercover narcotics officer in place. But not you. You had to get directly involved in what was a dangerous situation. As I said, you're a law firm investigator who doesn't know how to stay in his lane. I don't know how Emma puts up with it."

She's not putting up with it right now, and not in the future, Shane muttered to himself.

"Anyway…," Chioma dragged out, "If Troy found out it was you who set up his brother's bust, and his brother has now been killed serving a prison sentence you were responsible for, he has plenty of motive to seek revenge on you and Inspector Stabler."

"I agree," Shane responded. "Troy could very well have become so unhinged by his grief and anger that he would kill and dismember two people to send us a message about his plans for revenge."

"We need to get all of this information to Sergeant Franks," Chioma said.

"I will, but not right away. I want to check further into Troy Finn first," Shane said.

"There you go again, Shane, doing things you need to let the police handle," Chioma said with exasperation in her voice.

"I will talk to Franks, Chioma, but before he decides to descend on Finn because he fits the profile, I need to confirm something first, okay?" Shane asked.

"Fine. And don't forget you've got to tell Jason what's going on," Chioma stated.

"I will, see you later," Shane said as he got up from his chair and started out the door of the office.

As he was leaving, he looked at the young man sitting behind a desk in one of the cubicles in the center area of the law firm. He stood thinking for a moment, then turned and went back into Chioma's office, closing the door behind him.

"What do you know about the new Law Clerk, Tin Tran?" Shane asked Chioma.

"I would have to look at his personnel file for anything detailed," Chioma answered. "Why are you asking?"

"I'm positive Inspector Stabler is the same way, but I've always been extremely protective of where I live," Shane said. "You can't search and find my home address anywhere on the internet, and I even pay Doobie to check from time to time so it stays that way. It's one of the precautions I took when Lan moved in with us and was still a possible target of the Vietnamese-Canadian gang she and her family tried to escape from. It's possible that whoever sent the package with the heart in it got my address from someone in this firm."

"And what? You now suspect Tin Tran because he's Vietnamese?" Chioma asked in surprise. "Isn't that some kind of racial profiling on your part?"

"Think about it, Chioma. The Law Clerk who Tran replaced, Sherrie Morrison, is a hard worker who never missed much time as far as I know, suddenly gets ill with a mysterious illness," Shane responded, "And along comes Tran."

"I think you might be getting paranoid," Chioma said.

"I need to be a bit paranoid and consider every possibility because something bad is going to happen and I need to stop it," Shane declared in a firm voice. "The criminal organization that was a threat to Lan has been dismantled, and its leader, Hong Phuong, deported to Vietnam where he's supposed to be in jail. It's possible some remnants of the organization still exist and Phuong has a long reach. Can we find out if he's still in prison? And can you do a deep dive on Tran? And I know it will involve you going into online databases

I'm not supposed to know about, but it's important. Or I can ask Doobie to do it."

"No, that's fine, I can do it," Chioma said.

When Shane returned to his own office, on an impulse he didn't understand, or maybe he did and didn't want to admit to it, he sent a text to Amelia Martin asking if she wanted to get together for that coffee they talked about. They agreed to meet at the Tim Hortons on the first level of the Brantford General Hospital.

Shane drove to Terrace Hill Street and parked the Charger in the parkade off a steep street that ran down the side of the hospital. The garage was right next to a busy entrance to the lower levels of the BGH, and the coffee shop was just inside the sliding glass doors across from the reception area for day surgeries.

Shane didn't see Amelia, so he lined up, bought two medium coffees and sat at one of the nearby small round tables with two chairs. He spotted Amelia approaching from down one of the nearby hallways. Shane immediately realized that he was right back when he first met Amelia and had speculated the pathologist had a great body under the loose hospital scrubs she was wearing at the time. Today, she was wearing form-fitting jeans, a light pull-over top over full breasts, and had let her hair down so that it flowed over the top of her shoulders.

"Hello, Shane Daniels," Amelia said in a soft voice as she sat down.

"I didn't know what you took in your coffee, so I just grabbed some creamers and sugar packets," Shane said and realized he sounded like he was nervous.

"Just black is fine," Amelia said with a smile as she took the plastic takeout lid off the top of her coffee. "I'm glad you decided to meet. I was going to ask you how the case was going, but I decided we should talk about something else rather than work."

"Are you getting settled into your condo?" Shane asked.

"I don't have much in the way of furniture yet," Amelia answered. "A bed and dresser, a couch and TV, a small table and chairs, and kitchen utensils. That's about it. You have to come and see it."

Shane didn't react to the invitation and instead asked, "Do you have any family here in Ontario or are they all back east?"

"A few distant cousins in Nova Scotia, that's it," Amelia said. "Both my parents are dead. How about you?"

"Both my parents are dead as well," Shane answered. "My Mom died when I was young and my father died in prison while he was serving a life sentence for murder." Shane had absolutely no idea why he had just shared that information with a woman who was basically a stranger.

"I'm sorry to hear that," Amelia said as she reached across the table and put her hand on top of Shane's, who felt the temperature of his body start to climb. "That must have been very traumatic for you."

"Yes, it was," Shane said simply.

Amelia withdrew her hand, which made Shane happy because of the thoughts that had gone through his head when it was on top of his.

"I've been checking you out, Shane Daniels," Amelia said. "It seems, according to the information that came up online, that you're rather famous for solving some high-profile cases. And you were recently involved in the arrest of a serial killer, Adam Talino. I'm impressed."

"Mainstream and social media tend to blow that stuff up out of proportion," Shane said.

"Something tells me that isn't true," Amelia said with a smile, and Shane had to catch himself from staring too long at her beautiful face.

"It sounds like you have an exciting life," she said, "I would love to get more deeply involved in some murder cases."

"Do you mind if I ask if you're married or have a significant other?" Shane asked, changing the subject.

"No, I don't mind," Amelia said with a smile, "And no, it's just me. I guess you could say I'm married to my career and don't have time for any long term relationships."

"But I imagine a beautiful woman like you gets asked out a lot," Shane stated and regretted the words the second they were out of his mouth. What are you doing? Shane berated himself. Why would you say something like that? Why are you even here? Why are you allowing yourself to be tempted like this?

"And what about you?" Amelia then asked, "I noticed you don't have a wedding ring."

"I have a partner. Her name's Emma," Shane said and then quickly stammered out, "And an adopted daughter, Lan."

"Well, just so you know, Shane Daniels," Amelia said as she put her hand back on top of Shane's. "You having a partner won't worry me when we're together. Will it bother you?"

Oh shit! Shane thought as he realized he was aroused by what he had just heard Amelia say.

"I..uh…have to think about that," Shane stammered.

"You do that, Shane Daniels," Amelia said softly.

In a panic, Shane reached into his pocket, pulled out his phone, looked at the screen and said, "I had this on vibrate while we were having our coffee, but I've been monitoring my messages closely because of everything that's going on with the body parts. I'm sorry to cut our coffee short, but something important has come up and I have to go."

"I understand, Shane Daniels," Amelia said. "I'm sure we'll see each other again soon. And don't forget if you need anything, give me a call."

"Thanks, see you, bye," Shane said nervously and then got up and walked quickly to the exit. When he looked back briefly, Amelia smiled and waved.

As he drove home from the hospital, Shane started to get a stress headache. He couldn't understand why he was acting this way. Why would he consider, for even a second, about betraying Emma with another woman? He still loved Emma deeply. Was it because he suspected Emma no longer felt the same way about him? Was it because Emma threatened to end their relationship if he didn't stop getting so deeply involved in his cases and let the police handle them instead? Emma had basically said that a human heart being delivered to their house, and being seen by Lan, was the last straw.

Amelia Martin was an enigma to Shane. The mutual attraction was obvious and for Shane, it was almost totally physical. He prided himself on his ability to read people, to tell when they were being sincere, deceitful, or outright lying. He just couldn't get a read off Amelia.

In high school, Shane loved studying Greek mythology, in particular Homer's Odyssey and Odysseus's great adventures. Odysseus had an encounter with the Sirens, creatures often depicted as half-woman and half-bird, who lured sailors to their death with their enchanting songs. Odysseus was warned about this, so when he sailed by the rocky cliffs where the Sirens lived, he had his men put beeswax in their ears. But Odysseus wanted to hear the Sirens' song and survive, so he had his men lash him to the mast. Once he heard the Sirens, Odysseus begged to be untied, but his crew ignored him and they sailed to safety.

The Sirens were considered a symbol of temptation, the danger of desire and the allure of the unknown. Shane decided that Amelia Martin was a Siren.

Once he got home, Shane walked around the empty house and thought about how much he missed Emma and Lan. He went into the kitchen, looked through the fridge and rummaged through the cupboards looking for something to eat, but he didn't find anything appealed to him. He settled on a can of Diet Sprite and then called Emma. It was Lan who answered.

"Hi Dad, we knew it was you, Mom let me answer, guess what I did today?" Lan said excitedly, all in one quick sentence.

"I'm betting you went to the beach," Shane said, his spirits improved thanks to hearing Lan's voice.

"I sketched some seagulls and I can hardly wait to show you," Lan said. "And I built a huge sandcastle. Mom helped. And even though it was really hot, the water was really cold."

"Lake Huron doesn't get very warm, even in the summer," Shane said. "When I was a kid, the water at the beach was always shallow and cold, and you had to walk out a long way before it was even up to your waist."

"I'm having a lot of fun, I got lots of books to read, but I'm missing out on my camp," Lan complained.

"I know, but hopefully you can come home in a few days and the camp will still be going," Shane said.

"Here's Mom," was all Lan said and then she was gone.

"Hi," Shane heard Emma say.

"Hi. Sounds like Lan's having fun. How about you?" Shane asked.

Emma ignored the question and instead asked, "Have you found out who sent a heart to my house, and have you had them arrested?"

"Not yet, but I've got some good leads and Mark Stabler has a team of detectives working the case," Shane replied. "I think something should break soon."

"I hope so," Emma lamented. "As nice as it is here, I want to come home. I can't afford to miss too much time off work, and as you heard, Lan is pretty disappointed about missing her camp."

"Emma, I'm so sorry this has happened," Shane said. "I'm sorry I get myself so involved in cases and it results in some sick individual seeking revenge. I would never want anything to happen to you and Lan because of something I did."

"I know you're sorry, Shane, but as I told you before I left, this is a result of who you are," Emma said emotionally.

"I don't want to lose you, Emma. There has to be some kind of compromise," Shane pleaded.

"I love you, Shane. Please let me know when I can come home to my house," Emma said and then ended the call.

Shane stood in the kitchen and just stared at his phone for a moment. His thoughts were all over the place, spinning around in his head with no clarity. The headache he had developed on the way home had gotten worse, to the point where it was a constant pounding behind his temples. He decided to go to the bathroom cabinet and get a couple of ibuprofen capsules, but on the way there, the doorbell sounded.

Shane walked to the front door and activated the small monitor on the security system control panel mounted on the wall beside it. He saw on the monitor that his friend, Ben Chen, was standing on the front step holding a small box in his hands.

Shane opened the door and said, "Ben, what are you doing here!?"

"You want to tell me why the fuck you sent me two fucking human eyeballs?! Ben exclaimed.

Chapter Thirteen

After ending her call with Shane, Emma Carstairs set her phone on the wooden coffee table in front of the sofa where she was sitting, leaned forward on her elbows, and put her hands over her face.

Tears formed in her eyes as she thought about how everything that was good in her life was suddenly turned upside down.

Except for Lan.

Realizing she didn't want her daughter to see her upset, Emma quickly wiped her eyes with her hands and looked over to the kitchen area where Lan was sitting at a table, concentrating on her sketch pad. She didn't notice, that's good, Emma thought. Lan had already asked a lot of questions about why they were staying at the cottage in Port Elgin for an undefined period of time, without adding to it if Lan saw that Emma was upset.

Emma flushed with pride as she watched Lan working on her latest sketch. Her daughter was both smart and a gifted artist for such a young age. What made it even more extraordinary was the fact that Lan did incredibly detailed charcoal sketches using a prosthetic right hand, a high-tech model which worked seamlessly with involuntary commands from her brain through the nerves in her arm.

That Lan was even here with her still sometimes surprised Emma. When she and Shane first got together, they decided they didn't want to have children. Emma was rebuilding her career as a surgical nurse after leaving the Canadian Forces following the loss of her leg in a landmine explosion in the Balkans, and she was completing the necessary academic credentials to become a counsellor for recent amputees.

Shane's reason for not wanting children was more complicated and Emma had always considered it sad and a bit troubling. Shane was convinced he would be a lousy father because of genetics. Shane's father, the man he had adored, turned out to be a chronic liar and, even worse, a killer, responsible for the murder of a young woman. And Shane's Uncle Max, the uncle he didn't even know he had because his father lied about his existence, murdered Shane's mother on behalf of his father.

Emma must have told Shane a hundred times that his unwillingness to be a parent was nonsensical; he would never turn into a man like his father, or his uncle, because he hated them for what they did. Unlike them, Emma would tell Shane, you are a good and honest person who goes out of his way to do what is right.

For Emma, everything changed regarding children when she fell in love with Lan the first time she saw her in the Children's Surgical Ward at the Brantford General Hospital. Emma was asked by Social Services to try and talk to the young amputee, who was mute as a result of the shock she suffered over the deaths of her parents and the loss of her right hand. Emma managed to get Lan talking again and realized just how precocious the little girl was. The two of them quickly became very close.

Thinking back now, Emma realized, and not for the first time, that her determination and, if she was honest with herself, selfishness about not being separated from Lan, had put them both in danger. What Lan knew about it, even at such a young age, was a threat to the Vietnamese-Canadian criminal organization that her parents had been forced to work for. But Emma had steadfastly refused to allow the RCMP to take Lan to a safe house located in another city. She was traumatized enough already, Emma had argued, and putting her with strangers would make it worse. Lan insisted she wanted to stay with Emma and Shane, and got very emotional at the thought of being separated from them. Emma had insisted that she and Shane could keep Lan safe.

But that didn't turn out to be true, and Emma blamed herself for not listening to the police. A visiting social worker betrayed her and gave the security code for the house to the gang, who then sent two of its members late one night to kidnap Lan. Emma managed to fight one off and shoot the other. She was very lucky that night, but by that time, her love for Lan had grown to the point that she still refused to allow the young girl to be taken to a safe house. There was another attempt to kidnap Lan while she was walking from her school to the bus, but Ben Chen was luckily nearby and successfully intervened, although he suffered a terrible beating.

As she sat on the sofa watching Lan working diligently on her sketch, Emma smiled at the thought of just how much she had changed from the woman who didn't want children. And Shane had also changed. At first, he had accepted Lan into their lives because he knew that's what Emma wanted. But Shane also fell in love with Lan and the two of them had become very close; Lan was always full of curiosity about his cases.

Shane Daniels. What's the future of our relationship going to be now that I've given him an ultimatum about how he handles his work for Jason Burke? Emma asked herself.

Just like she did with Lan, Emma fell in love with Shane the first time she met him after he sat down beside her at a group therapy session run by her psychiatrist friend Charlene Anderson. He was tall, well-built physically and very good looking. And obviously very uncomfortable about being at the meeting as he shifted around in his seat, a tight grip on the wooden cane in his hand. When they introduced each other, Emma saw sadness in Shane's eyes and pain in his expression, the same look she had seen countless times on people who had suffered career-ending injuries. She often saw the same thing on her own face when she looked in the mirror.

By the time Shane moved into Emma's house, his deep depression was gone, and his life was rejuvenated as he found a new career working for Burke and Associates. They were deeply in love and had trouble keeping their hands off each other. Shane built a reputation, much to the chagrin of some cops, as an investigator who could solve cases they couldn't or that they had gotten wrong.

There had several occasions when both Emma and Shane found themselves in very dangerous situations as Shane chased killers and con artists, and she got herself deeply involved in her client's lives. There was no question that they fed off each other's excitement and adrenaline rushes, and the sex after a successful outcome was always incredible. It was a great life. But now Lan was in the picture, and as far as Emma was concerned, it was a complete game-changer. They were responsible for a young girl who was destined to do some great things in her life and they had to make sure they were both around to see that happen.

Emma was well aware that it was not going to be easy for her not to get personally involved if there were any unanswered questions surrounding how or why one of her clients became an amputee. The need to know was part of her nature, just as it was with Shane.

And then there was Shane. Emma knew that he was aware that this latest incident, someone sending him a human heart as part of a sick revenge plot, was too much for her to handle with Lan in the house. Just what was this person capable of? Was Lan, who had already spent so much of her young life under the threat of a criminal gang, in danger because of some case Shane had been involved in?

But the push back from Shane when she told him he had to stop delving so deeply into cases that the police should be handling was putting an obvious strain on their relationship. She had to admit to herself that perhaps Shane's love for her and Lan might not be strong enough for him to change who he believed he was: a disabled man who was robbed of his chance to carry a gun and a badge; to be a police detective solving murders. Instead, he's making up for what he lost by solving crimes, including murder, as a private investigator. Maybe Shane will begin looking for someone who won't ask him to stay behind his desk at the firm. Emma had never seen Shane take a second look at another woman, but maybe that will change. Maybe he'll find a beautiful woman who still has both her legs.

Why am I being so insecure? Emma berated herself. That's not me! I'm an intelligent, confident and independent-minded woman who is more than capable of looking after herself. I'm just asking the man I love to make a compromise for the sake of our daughter's safety.

"Are you okay, Mom?" Lan suddenly asked from the kitchen. "You look sad. Is everything okay between you and Dad?

Unbelievably perceptive, this little girl of mine, Emma thought.

"Everything's fine, sweetheart," Emma replied.

Chapter Fourteen

Well, my friends in the freezer, our time together has come to an end. And I have some exciting news to tell you.

But before I get to that, I'm afraid that I also have some bad news for you. I had told you that I would incinerate you and scatter your ashes so that your life ended with some dignity. But I'm sorry to say that was wishful thinking on my part. I now have to do some further indignities to your bodies so that you'll fit in several garbage bags that I can lift into the trunk of my car.

Getting you here was easy with a promise of a hot meal and some cash as you accepted me as a Good Samaritan who was working in the homeless community. You quickly said yes when I offered to give you a ride to a brand new hostel where you could stay as long as you wanted and get quick access to medical and dental care, which you both were in desperate need of.

However, once I ended your life, getting your bodies out of the trunk of my car, dragging them in here, and then lifting them into the freezer was very difficult physically. It's not how they make it look in movies. So, I've decided that I will turn off the freezer, wait until you thaw and then dismantle you in the freezer so I can lift you out a piece at a time. Pretty smart, right? Of course, I'm going to need a reciprocating saw, big sheets of plastic, a clear face shield and a heavy duty mask for the smell.

Anyway, none of that's your concern anymore.

Let me tell you the good news. Thanks to pure luck, or maybe God, if there is one, my revenge on those who hurt me is off to a successful start.

Tonight, I was watching the Inspector's house, trying to figure out a way to get inside undetected. There was a police cruiser parked out front. I expected that, so I was planning to circle around to the back of the house and look for a possible entry point, maybe an unlocked or open window.

I assumed there would be a security system and I knew there was a personal care worker in the house. I was thinking that if there's a sliding door, I could knock on it, hold up the fake badge I bought online, and tell her I'm there to do a quick security check. Otherwise, I would have to do a forced entry, get inside and do what I needed to do, and then get out before the no-doubt sleepy cop gets out of his cruiser and in the front door. He'd automatically rush upstairs first to check on the Inspector's wife, so I could hide someplace downstairs and then walk out the front door.

Anyway, I was considering all of this when suddenly the cruiser pulled away from the front of the house! Did the Inspector decide to pull the security detail? I wondered. Or maybe it was a shift change and the cop decided he didn't want to wait around for his replacement. It was a lucky opportunity, so I moved quickly before the next cruiser showed up.

It was pretty simple after that. I rang the doorbell and showed my badge to the camera over the door. The Personal Care Worker let me in, and I stabbed her, I don't know, six or seven times, and then went upstairs to the Inspector's wife's bedroom. She was propped up in her bed reading a book. Her name was Mary, same as you, Mom. Isn't that ironic? She didn't look too good. She had reading glasses sitting on the end of a nose on a very pale face. She was wearing a fancy kerchief and I could tell she was bald underneath it. She put her book down and asked me, "Who the hell are you?".

I said, "My Mom's name was also Mary, but she was much more beautiful than you."

"What do you want?" she asked me and I could tell she was terrified. I said…and you're going to like this, Mom,…I said, "I am revenge."

She tried to get up, but she was weak and slow, so I just walked over, held her down with my left hand, and slit her neck with the blade in my right hand.

I didn't have time to wait around and see the final result. She put her hand over the slice, but blood was rapidly pumping out of her body and I knew it wouldn't be long.

When I got downstairs, I took a peek through the curtains in the front window and saw that another cruiser had shown up. I went to the back of the house and found a sliding patio door onto a deck and left that way.

The backyard was fenced in, but there was a gate to a lane that I walked down to an adjoining street, then around the corner and back to where I parked my car.

From there, I drove to Shane Daniels' house in East Brantford. I had already been there a couple of times and confirmed that Daniel's girlfriend and their Vietnamese kid must have gone somewhere. So, they're out of my reach, for now.

But, my freezer friends, don't despair, because there's even more good news!

When I got to Daniels' place, there were two police cruisers in front, along with a dark blue van that I assumed was from Forensics.

That means that Daniels' friend, Ben Chen, did exactly what I thought he would do when I sent him a package containing eyeballs that one of you kindly donated. Instead of calling the cops in the small town where he lives, I knew Mr. Chen would get in his vehicle and drive right here to find out why his friend sent him the box.

So, my freezer friends, that's my exciting news.

And now that Ben is in town, I don't have to worry anymore about where Emma and her kid ran off to because I have a target whose death will cause as much pain for Shane Daniels as he did for me.

Chapter Fifteen

The morning after Ben arrived at Shane's house, Jason Burke was sitting in the office of Justice Morley Crowder, along with Crown Attorney Evan Gregory, his legal assistant, and Jason's second chair, Susan Cartright.

Judge Crowder had been on the bench for over thirty years; a tall, thin man with a hawk-like nose, a prominent forehead, thin lips and a full head of trimmed, steel gray hair. He was the Senior Justice for the district and was well known for his no-nonsense approach to courtroom demeanour.

"Ladies and Gentlemen, I'm sure that you join me in being saddened by Justice Oliver Wendal's sudden death," Crowder said. He had a deep voice and Jason knew from experience that Crowder used it to full effect to command respect in the courtroom.

"Justice Wendal had been battling health issues but was determined to carry on his duties," Crowder said. "I understand his death was caused by a sudden, massive heart attack."

"I have to mention, your Honour, with all due respect, that it was obvious Judge Wendal was under severe medical distress right from the beginning of the trial," Jason said. "I tried to point that out to him several times, and I feel bad that he refused to listen, because he might still be alive if he had agreed to recluse himself from the trial and seek medical attention."

"I was told by the Clerk that you did raise some concerns," Crowder said.

"The thing is, your Honour, and I say this with the greatest respect for Judge Wendal and his highly regarded career on the bench, I believe his illness may have impacted his judgment on several key issues in the trial," Jason said. "His ruling in voir dire that what my client said to the two officers the night Olivia was killed would be allowed under the 'excited utterance' exemption was flawed because an examination of the officer's statements clearly showed the lead detective forced his subordinate to change what she heard that night."

"Your Honour, that was an accusation made by Mr. Burke during the trial and has nothing to do with Judge Wendal's ruling in voir dire!" Gregory exclaimed.

"Hang on, Mr. Gregory, you'll get your chance," Crowder said and then asked Jason, "What else, Mr. Burke?"

"I raised questions over what appeared to be an attempt by the Prosecutor and the Pathologist to downplay, perhaps even overlook, a bruise on the victim's wrist, which clearly proves there was, in fact, a struggle over the knife between my client and his wife."

"That's simply untrue and you know it, Jason!" Gregory protested.

"Despite your feeble attempt to discredit him, the Pathologist was quite clear that he noted the discolouration on Mrs. Tremblay's wrist and could not say one way or the other if it was a bruise caused by someone grabbing it."

Crowder ignored Gregory's outburst and asked Jason, "What is it you're after here, Mr. Burke?"

"I believe there's enough grounds for you to call a mistrial, your Honour," Jason responded. "I think my client deserves a fresh jury that's not tainted by questionable hearsay testimony from the lead detective in the case and a less than forthcoming pathologist. Plus, I believe the presiding Judge's attention was impaired or, at the very least, distracted because he was ill."

"I strongly disagree, your Honour," Gregory said. "When you review the transcripts, you'll see that Judge Wendal was in complete control of the trial. He gave Mr. Burke ample opportunity to cross-examine witnesses and make his points to the jury."

"I have reviewed the transcripts," Crowder stated. "I'm sorry, Mr. Burke, I don't see enough grounds to call a mistrial. The jury has been patiently waiting in the courtroom this morning. I'm going to dismiss them for today to allow me the rest of the day to further review what has occurred to date. We will resume the trial tomorrow morning."

"However," Crowder continued, "I'm wondering if there's not some kind of compromise that can be reached here. I understand, Mr. Gregory, that Mr. Burke previously informed you that his client was willing to plead guilty to manslaughter, even though he insists he didn't mean to kill his wife and acted in self-defence when she tried to stab him. Would you consider a plea deal?"

"Your Honour, there was no struggle. Noah Tremblay murdered his wife in cold blood because he was fed up with her refusal to take her bipolar meds, and he was furious that she got pregnant. I'm well on my way to proving that in the trial," Gregory said with conviction.

"I know that my colleague is always supremely confident," Jason countered sarcastically, a thin smile appearing on his face. "However, I understand that he has three witnesses left to call. First is Olivia's psychiatrist, who will testify that Olivia had anosognosia, a condition under which she had trouble accepting she was bipolar and, as a result, would not take her medications. The psychiatrist will also testify that even with her mood disorder and anosognosia, he didn't believe that Olivia was prone to severe anger issues or violent tendencies."

"But I will counter with testimony from Doctor Monique LeBlanc, considered one of the leading authorities on mood disorders," Jason continued. "And she will tell a different story based on her review of Olivia's file, interviews she conducted with Noah and a police report. Officers had previously been to the Tremblay's house on a noise complaint made by a neighbour. They found that Olivia, in a rage, had smashed most of the glasses and dishes in the kitchen, and had torn up some furniture."

"So, we can expect duelling psychiatrists that will confuse the jury," Crowder said.

"No, because I'll point out that Doctor LeBlanc is a professional witness, hired by the defence, who had no personal contact with the victim," Gregory said defensively.

"But it will raise a lot of reasonable doubt," Jason countered and then said, "Mr. Gregory plans to call my client's best friend, Jamie Willcott, to testify that Noah expressed anger to him about how Olivia, against his wishes, stopped taking her birth control pills in order to get pregnant, and that Noah was going to demand she get an abortion. But it's the worst kind of hearsay, and Judge Wendal should not have ruled during voir dire to allow it. However, I will get Willcott to admit he and Noah were drinking heavily the night that Noah apparently made the comments, so how good was his memory of exactly what was said? Plus, it turns out that Jamie and Olivia were dating and broke up when she started seeing Noah, so he may have still been carrying a torch for Olivia. More reasonable doubt for the jury to consider."

"And finally," Jason continued, "My colleague has Olivia's mother, Charlotte Crombie, on the witness list. She will undoubtedly testify, as any mother would, that her daughter had issues, but was a good girl who wouldn't hurt anyone. And as much as I don't wish to cross-examine a grieving mother, I will have no choice but to question the validity of her testimony, especially given her open animosity toward her son-in-law."

"As usual, your Honour, my colleague's ego makes him believe the Crown has no chance against his courtroom skills, when, of course, that's not the situation in this case," Gregory said. "The facts already presented to the jury are quite simple and clear: Noah Tremblay stabbed his wife in cold blood. End of story."

"What would you be looking for in a plea agreement?" Crowder asked Jason.

"Olivia's death was the result of a tragic set of circumstances," Jason responded. "But Noah does realize that, under the law, he faces consequences for what happened. He'll plead guilty to manslaughter. He's already spent a year in pretrial custody. In my opinion, I don't think Noah should be sentenced to any more than two years less a day in a provincial institution." .

"I can't agree to that! The man brutally murdered his wife!" Gregory shot back.

"Well, then, I guess the trial will resume," Crowder said with some impatience evident in his voice. "But, Mr. Gregory, you do have the rest of the day to discuss a plea agreement with your boss at the Crown Prosecution Service and either reconsider or make a counteroffer."

"I can't see it happening," Gregory said flatly. Jason just shook his head.

Chapter Sixteen

While Jason was meeting with Justice Crowder and Evan Gregory, Shane was approaching the front door of Inspector Mark Stabler's home.

Three marked police cruisers, two unmarked Ford sedans and a Forensics van were parked in front of the house, and a uniformed officer was standing at the front door. Shane gave his name, the officer looked at the tablet he was holding, nodded to permit Shane to enter, and then handed him white Tyvek coveralls, boot covers and disposable surgical gloves to put on.

Sergeant Franks had called and awakened Shane early that morning to tell him Inspector Stabler had returned to his house last night and found that both PSW Jalissa Dale and Stabler's wife, Mary, had been murdered. It took a moment for Shane to clear his head and process the news. He had been up until the early hours dealing with the aftermath of Ben showing up at his house with a box containing two human eyeballs. Like the packages Shane and Mark Stabler received, Ben's had a note, but his one read:

YOUR FRIEND WILL SOON SEE HOW I FEEL.

"What the fuck's going on, Shane?" Ben had asked after Shane let him in the door and they went into the kitchen, where Ben put the box on the table.

"Christ, Ben! Why did you drive here all the way from Port Elgin? Why didn't you just call the cops? You know I wouldn't have sent you something like this, right?" Shane asked Ben in rapid succession.

"I didn't know what to fucking think, Okay!?" Ben shot back. "I fucking panicked! At first I thought it was a joke, you sending me fake eyeballs, and then I decided that's not something you would do. Then I took a closer look and realized the fucking things were real!"

"But if you didn't call the cops, why didn't you just call me?" Shane asked.

"As I said, I fucking panicked!" Ben shot back. "I thought maybe you had some big case underway and these fucking things were sent to me as a warning to get you to back off from whatever you were investigating. I didn't know who to trust. I thought that maybe I was under surveillance or someone was monitoring my fucking phone calls!"

"Really, Ben?" Shane said with exasperation in his voice.

Ben had always been an over-the-top kind of guy with a real flair for the dramatic. He easily bought into conspiracy theories about how either the government or maybe some nefarious international cabal was monitoring everything we do.

"I hope Michelle wasn't home when this arrived," Shane said. Ben's girlfriend lived with him at his house in Paisley.

"No, she's at some fucking artist's thing in Collingwood," Ben said.

"That's good," Shane said. "I don't need both of you in a panic."

Shane had then called both Inspector Stabler and Sergeant Franks, and within half an hour, there were multiple cruisers and a Forensics van parked in front of his house and his kitchen was jammed with investigators who were either examining the box with the eyeballs or taking statements from Shane and Ben.

Now, the next morning, Shane entered Inspector Stabler's house, weary from lack of sleep and saddened that whoever was behind the threats had managed to breach Stabler's security precautions and strike in a deadly fashion.

Just inside the door, Shane saw a trail of dried blood on the floor that curled to just inside the dining room area to the left. It led to a body lying on the hardwood floor, covered in a white sheet. Three forensics officers in white Tyvek suits were working in various areas of the room, one of them was taking photos with a high-end digital camera.

Shane knelt and pulled back the sheet covering the body. The woman was on her back, the front of her light blue nurse's uniform completely soaked in blood. Her face was frozen in a look of shock; her mouth open in a circle, and her eyes wide and fixed on nothing.

"Her name's Jalissa Dale. She was Mrs. Stabler's personal support worker," Shane heard Sergeant Franks say behind him.

"Where's Mrs. Stabler?" Shane asked as he turned to face Franks.

"In an upstairs bedroom. Her throat was cut," Franks said flatly.

"How the hell did this happen!?" Shane asked angrily.

"The officer posted out front got impatient because his shift was over and he had plans, so he left before his replacement arrived," Franks said. "The killer must have been watching, saw the cruiser leave and used the opportunity to enter the house."

"I can't believe the stupidity of an officer who would leave his post early knowing there was a threat against the wife of an Inspector, his superior officer," Shane said in frustration.

"He's been suspended pending further disciplinary action," Franks stated.

"So, Mrs. Dale let her attacker in the door," Shane stated.

"We can only speculate that either Dale knew the person or they showed her some kind of official identification," Franks said. "She was under strict instructions to keep the alarm system on and not let anyone in the house except for police officers."

"Then it was someone with a fake ID or perhaps Dale's connected somehow," Shane concluded.

"I'm betting on the fake ID," Franks said and then added, "Speaking of identities, we know the names of the victims where the hearts, and now eyeballs, came from."

Franks unzipped his Tyvek coveralls, retrieved his notebook from his suit pocket, and after flipping through a few pages said, "The woman was Annabelle Swanson, age fifty one, and the male was Wilson Peak, age sixty two. Although they mostly lived in one of the homeless encampments, they had been residents, off and on, at the

Salvation Army Hostel and were frequent users of their hot meal program. No one had officially reported them missing, but when my officers checked the Hostel, the staff said Swanson and Peak hadn't been in for a meal for well over a week and that was highly unusual. I had some plainclothes officers scour the encampments and anyone who was actually willing to talk to them said they hadn't seen the two for at least a week. They found one empty tent and a cardboard box structure with some personal belongings. DNA was collected to confirm, but we're sure it's them."

"They were, sadly, easy targets," Shane said as he thought about the victims of the serial killer Adam Talino, the young women living in homeless encampments in Hamilton and Toronto.

"I assume the eyes that were sent to my friend Ben were from one of them," Shane said.

"Probably. I'm going to go see the Pathologist after I'm finished here," Franks said.

"Can I meet you there?" Shane asked.

Franks gave Shane a stern look and he expected the Sergeant to say no, but instead he said, "Fine. You're involved, so you're supposed to stay away from the investigation, but I'm obviously wasting my breath telling you that. And besides, the way you and Doctor Martin were looking at each other suggests you would just go back later and she would tell you what you wanted to know anyway."

Shane didn't respond and instead asked, "Where's the Inspector?"

"He's upstairs in the bedroom," Franks answered with sadness in his voice. "His wife's body has been removed, but the Inspector hasn't left the room."

"Do you mind if I go up and see him?" Shane asked.

"Sure, but I don't know if he'll talk to you," Franks answered. "He's said very little to anyone. His son, Wyatt, and his fiance, Rachel, are on their way from Toronto."

"He never discusses his family, his personal life," Shane commented. Shane left Franks in the living room and walked up the nearby staircase to the second floor. There was a bathroom directly across from the landing and a hallway to the left and right. There were two doors along the hall to the left, both closed, and one open to the right, so that's where Shane headed.

Inside the master bedroom, there was a large dresser and mirror along the wall to his left and on his right, an opening to a walk-in closet and a door Shane assumed was for an en-suite bathroom. The light was dim in the room; the curtains were closed and a small bedside lamp was on.

The blankets on the queen-size bed were pulled down, the bottom sheet and two pillows dark with blood stains. Beside the bed was a pole stand on wheels holding a vital signs machine and a nightstand, its surface covered with various prescription bottles.

The Inspector was sitting on a wooden chair beside the bed, slightly bent over, his head looking down in thought, his hands resting on his knees.

"Mark, I am so sorry," Shane said softly.

Stabler looked up. The grim expression on his face and the sadness in his eyes hit Shane hard emotionally, leaving him feeling helpless.

"She was going to make it, you know," Stabler said softly. "Mary had breast cancer that had spread, but she was responding to treatment. I told her I was going to take a leave or maybe even retire so we could spend more time together, but she didn't want that. She said I wasn't ready to stop being a cop."

"We'll find who did this, Mark," Shane said firmly.

"You won't, Daniels, because you're not a cop, you're actually a victim and not supposed to be involved in the investigation. But, of course, I might as well be saying that to a brick wall," Stabler said.

"I wish I had met your wife, Mary," Shane said. "It sounds like she was a fighter."

"I'm done talking, Daniels," Stabler said, put his head down again and stared at his hands.

"Alright, I understand. Again, I'm really sorry," Shane said, and then left the bedroom and went back downstairs, where he stopped near the front door and removed his Tyvek suit, booties and gloves, and put them in a clear plastic disposal bag sitting nearby.

Sergeant Franks walked out of the living room, a tablet in his hands, which he was using for notes, and asked, "How's he doing?"

"About as expected," Shane answered and then said, "As you know, he's not an emotional guy, but he looks crushed. I really didn't know what to say to him."

When Shane got back in the Charger, which he had been allowed to park near the cruiser that was blocking the street, he called Ben, who was still at Shane's house.

"You doing okay?" Shane asked when Ben answered.

"Fuck, no," Ben said. "I keep seeing those fucking eyes looking up at me from the box. That's never going away."

"I'm sure it will eventually," Shane said, trying to sound encouraging, but he knew how Ben felt because the sight of the human heart in the box sent to his house still lingered with him.

"It's pretty fucking quiet at your place. I'm used to hanging out with Lan and seeing Emma give me disapproving looks for my language." Ben complained.

"Yeah, it does feels empty without the girls. Hopefully, I can get them home soon," Shane said.

"So what's the plan?" Ben asked. "What're we going to do to catch the fucker behind this?"

"I'm going to the office and talk to Jason, fill him in on what's going on and then I'm going to the hospital to meet Sergeant Franks and talk to the Pathologist about the eyes," Shane answered.

"You, my friend, are just going to hang out at the house, for now," he said. "Maybe figure out what we're going to eat. There's no food in the house."

"Fucking boring," Ben whined. "Maybe I'll find a grocery store and grab some stuff so I can cook us something decent. Then I'll call Michelle and see what she's up to."

Chapter Seventeen

When Shane arrived at Burke and Associates, he stopped at the reception desk to say hello to Office Manager Jill Langley and check for messages.

He knew something was up by the look on Jill's face and the fact that she was looking at him over the top of her reading glasses, which she never did unless there was some kind of problem. Shane thought Jill looked like a school teacher who had just caught one of her students with their hands hidden under the desk, texting on their phone.

"Jason's trial has been dismissed for the rest of today and tomorrow, so he's in the office catching up on things, and he's been talking to Chioma," Jill said, still looking at Shane over the top of her glasses. "And he just got a call from a contact at the Brantford Police who told him Inspector Mark Stabler's wife has been murdered."

"I see," Shane responded. With his large network of contacts, Shane assumed Jason would've heard about Mary Stabler's murder, and Chioma must have ratted him out about the body parts sent to him, Stabler and now Ben.

"Is Jason in his office?" Shane asked.

"Yes, he is," Jill answered.

"I'll go see him," Shane said.

"Good idea," Jill responded, still looking at Shane over the top of her glasses. I feel like I've been sent to the Principal's office, Shane thought.

Jason Burke had a spacious corner office befitting the founder of the firm. It contained a conference table, a large mahogany desk, a meeting area with a sofa, three plush armchairs and a coffee table, and a small kitchenette along one wall.

Jason was working on a laptop when Shane knocked softly on the door, walked into the office and sat in one of the two chairs facing Jason's desk.

"What the hell, Shane! Why would you keep me in the dark about a threat against you and Mark Stabler involving human hearts sent to your homes? As head of this firm, and as your friend, I should've been told immediately," Jason said, the irritation in his voice very evident.

"You've started a murder trial, Jason. The last thing you need is this kind of distraction," Shane said defensively. "I would've briefed you when the time was right. I know you, Jason. If you were told what happened, it would have seriously affected your concentration in the courtroom. I couldn't do that to you."

"I'm more than capable of judging what is or is not a distraction," Jason snapped back.

"Speaking of judges, I hear Judge Wendal dropped dead at the trial," Shane said, hoping to calm Jason down by changing the subject.

"He did, tragically. It came as a shock to a lot of people, but I knew he was trying to preside over a trial when he was too ill to be doing it," Jason said. "Evan Gregory knew it too, but he wouldn't admit it and didn't back me up when I suggested to Judge Wendal that he should recuse himself."

"Sounds like Gregory," Shane commented.

"The trial is now on hold for at least a day until Justice Crowder gets himself up to speed," Jason said and then changed the subject back to what Shane knew Jason really wanted to discuss.

"I talked to Chioma this morning," Jason said, "When I asked her if anything important was going on, she told me what was happening."

"I had asked her to keep everything confidential for now," Shane said.

"I knew something was up by the look on her face," Jason said. "Chioma couldn't lie even if her life depended on it. She's the most honest person I know."

Jason then leaned over the top of his desk and said, "Chioma told me a lot, but I want the details from you."

So, for the next fifteen minutes, Shane talked and Jason listened without interruption. When he finished, Jason said, "The news that Mark Stabler's wife had been murdered came as a shock, obviously, and I'm still quite upset about it."

"Have you had a chance to talk to Mark?" he asked.

"Briefly," Shane answered. "I was at his house earlier this morning to look over the scene. The Inspector was sitting in the bedroom where his wife was killed and had very little to say, which is not surprising. He was heartbroken."

"I will followup to see if there's anything we can do for him," Jason said sincerely and then added, "Mary Stabler's murder has now moved what started out as threats to a very dangerous new level."

"I'm aware of that," Shane responded flatly. "I need to find whoever is behind this before someone else is attacked."

"Do you suspect Troy Finn is behind this because of his brother's murder in prison?" Jason asked.

"It's possible, but only if Troy somehow found out that I was the informant who set Jacob up to be busted," Shane said. "It's also possible Jacob was shanked in prison on the orders of McKenzie Duncan, the Finn's supplier, in retribution for Jacob messing with his product and getting caught. Troy would know that."

"Is there any way to quietly confirm whether Troy knows you were the undercover informant involved in his brother's arrest and, if he does, if he's the person seeking revenge?" Jason asked.

"I have an idea," Shane said, but didn't offer any details and instead said, "There's a strong possibility that Adam Talino's behind this, paying someone to carry out his sick idea of revenge."

"I figured you would automatically suspect Talino because of the history between you two," Jason said. "And before you try to defend yourself, I do agree it's a possibility."

"I need to talk to him, to look him in the face, and then I'll know if he's behind it," Shane said. "He's a narcissistic psychopath, so it will be nearly impossible for him not to gloat."

"But if you suggest why you're there to see him, he might try and take credit for it, just to mess with you," Jason said.

"I realize that," Shane responded.

"What about Emma and Lan? How are they doing?" Jason asked with concern in his voice.

"They seem to be fine. Lan doesn't appear to have been traumatized at all from seeing the heart in the box and, in fact, much to Emma's horror, wanted to look at it again," Shane said with a bit of a smile on his face but then it quickly disappeared when he added, in a serious tone, "Emma is not very happy with me right now because she believes this is the result of me getting too involved in cases."

"I'm sure you two will be able to work it out," Jason said. "And it's good to know they're someplace safe."

"Speaking of safe, there's something else I haven't told you," Shane said.

"What a surprise," Jason said facetiously.

"When Stabler and I received the human hearts and started working on the theory that this was someone seeking revenge for a case we both worked on, we wondered if it was just us," Shane said. "Maybe we weren't the only people involved. So, as a precaution, I now have people from our security firm watching you, Gillie, and your house."

Jason's wife's actual name is Gillian, but she's been called Gillie for as long as Shane has known her.

"I haven't noticed them, so they're good at it," Jason responded. "I appreciate your concern, especially for Gillie."

Shane and Jason discussed the situation for another fifteen minutes before Shane left to allow Jason to return to his preparation for the resumption of the Tremblay trial. On his way past Chioma's office, Shane poked his head through the doorway and said with a smile, "So, you ratted me out to Jason."

"Had to happen," Chioma said with a smile of her own. "Besides, my telling Jason what was going on first softened how he was going to react when he did find out what you were withholding."

"Thanks…I guess," Shane tried to say with a straight face, but then they both chuckled.

Shane left Burke and Associates and drove to the hospital, where he met Sergeant Franks in the reception area and they took the elevator to the Pathology Department on the hospital's lower floor. As they approached the stainless steel automatic doors into the autopsy suite, Shane saw someone he knew leaning against the wall beside the entrance.

Maria Galendez had worked as a Clerk in various departments in the hospital for over thirty years and was highly sought after for her experience and competence. A short woman, dressed in hospital scrubs, Maria was dark-complexioned, with brown eyes and gray hair pulled into a bun at the back of her head. Shane knew Maria through Emma when the two women worked together on the surgical ward.

Maria was looking at a tablet in her hands and shaking her head when Shane walked up and said, "Hi, Maria, you look troubled."

"Oh, hi Shane," Maria said as she looked up from the tablet. "It's this new Pathologist we got. I realize it takes time to get acquainted with everything, you know, like the computer systems, things like that, but nothing's getting done. We've already got several autopsies waiting to be performed and now there are two more, which I assume you're here about. Doctor Martin is a nice lady, seems smart and is very beautiful. All of the male interns are finding an excuse to come down here. But, I'm not sure if she knows what she's doing."

"I'm sure it's like you said, she's just taking some extra time to get acquainted," Shane said, not sure why he felt the need to defend Amelia. Or maybe he did know why and just didn't want to admit it to himself.

Maria walked away, her head back down studying her tablet, while Shane and Franks entered the autopsy suite where they found Amelia, dressed in blue scrubs, standing behind two stainless steel hospital gurneys lined up in front of her. Each gurney held a body covered by a white sheet.

"You're back. Same case," Amelia said.

"Sadly, yes," Shane said, while Franks remained silent.

"I only met him once, but my heart is broken for Inspector Stabler," Amelia said.

"What do you have for us?" Franks said, obviously impatient to get down to business.

"Okay…" Amelia responded and Shane could tell she was taken aback by Franks' bluntness.

"First, the eyeballs sent to Shane's friend," she said. "The blood type matches one of the hearts, the female, now believed to be Annabelle Swanson. We're waiting on DNA results, and unless, God forbid, there's a third victim, the eyes are probably hers."

Amelia then pulled back the sheet on the gurney in front of her to expose the top half of Jalissa Dale's body. Shane was surprised she did this, considering he was not a cop and was there only on Franks' good graces, a very unofficial capacity.

"Mrs. Dale, Jalissa, was stabbed six times, probably in very quick succession and with deadly accuracy," Amelia said. "Twice in the area of the liver, twice in the stomach and twice upward, under the sternum and likely into the heart. I'll be able to confirm that during the postmortem. The wounds are deep, so it was a long-bladed knife. No ragged edges on the entries, so very sharp."

"This person knew what they were doing," Franks commented in a flat voice.

Amelia pulled the sheet back over Jalissa's body and then moved down to the next gurney and pulled the sheet back from Mary Stabler's body, but this time only to the top of her shoulders. A sadness came over Shane as he thought about the devastated Inspector sitting alone in the dimly lit upstairs bedroom in his house. His wife's body had been removed, leaving Stabler beside an empty, blood soaked bed.

"As you can see, Mary Stabler's throat was slit," Amelia said. "The cut is very deep, again suggesting a very sharp knife, and made with precision. Both carotid arteries were severed. Mary was in bed at the time, so the person who did this probably approached on her left, grabbed Mary by her hair, pulled her head back, and sliced all the way around her neck. Vicious overkill. It would have been a right handed person."

Amelia pulled the cover back over the body and then said, "I will need a few days to complete the postmortems and get the report to you, Sergeant."

"Sooner rather than later would be preferred," Franks said firmly and without another word, turned and walked out of the suite.

"A direct man of few words," Amelia said to Shane.

"The threat against the Inspector was bad enough, but now his wife has been brutally murdered. So, for every member of the Brantford Police Service, this is now very personal," Shane said.

"And how's your friend? Ben? Is that right?" Amelia asked.

"Ben, yes, and he's still suffering a bit of shock, but he's fine," Shane said. "We've been through a lot over the years. He's a tough guy."

"Is he still in the city?" Amelia asked.

"He's staying at my house, at least for now," Shane said. "I expect he's currently out buying groceries."

Amelia came out from behind the gurneys and stood very close to Shane's side. He could feel her breasts against his arm, and it sent a shot of arousal through his body.

"So, Shane Daniels, I apologize for being direct, but when can we get together again for coffee, or maybe even dinner?" Amelia asked in a soft voice, her lips very close to Shane's ear.

Shane was frozen in place and could feel the heat rising in his body.

"As much as I would enjoy that, I think I did tell you that I have a partner," Shane said, determined to get his physical reaction to the woman holding his arm under control.

"You did, and you remember that I said it didn't matter," Amelia whispered. "You can't deny that, whether it's right or wrong, there's a very strong physical attraction between us. You just have to decide if you want to act on it."

Amelia then put her hand on Shane's chest and said, "And the way your heart is racing tells me you already know the answer is yes."

"I've gotta go, Amelia, there's too much going on for me to deal with this right now," Shane managed to say and was frustrated that he stuttered over the words.

"Okay, no pressure," Amelia said with a smile, reached up and kissed Shane lightly on the cheek, and then walked away toward the gurneys. "You know where to find me, Shane Daniels," she said over her shoulder.

Shane left the autopsy suite quickly and stopped in the hall just in front of the doors to get his head around what had just happened. Sergeant Franks, who was standing in front of the elevator doors talking on his phone, gave Shane a look of curiosity.

Amelia Martin is a Siren from Greek mythology, Shane decided, and I just nearly crashed myself on the rocks. I don't know what's going on with me, he thought. I have never been tempted by another woman since the day I met Emma. He knew that Amelia was right; he was very physically attracted to her. I'm acting this way because of the current tension between Emma and me, that's all, Shane decided, but he knew he hadn't completely convinced himself.

Shane's thoughts were interrupted when his phone rang. When he pulled it out of his pocket, the caller ID said it was Chioma. When he answered, she said, "You need to come back to the office right away."

"What's going on?" he asked.

Shane listened as Chioma explained and when she was finished, he said, "I'm on my way."

Franks, who had completed the call he was on, was standing in front of the doors waiting for the elevator. When Shane walked up and stood beside him, Franks asked, "None of my business, but is there something going on between you and Doctor Martin?"

"You're right, it's none of your business, Sergeant, but the answer is no," Shane said.

"Listen, I get it, she's a knockout, but based on what that lady told us when we first arrived, Doctor Martin needs to start doing her job and not be distracted by good looking gentlemen such as yourself," Franks said in a facetious tone as he stared at the numbers above the elevator door, waiting for them to start counting down.

Shane ignored the comment and instead said, "You need to come with me to make a possible arrest at my firm. We believed that whoever was behind this must have had access to inside information about where Stabler and I lived, and the cases we worked on together. The researcher at my firm may found who's responsible."

Chapter Eighteen

Sergeant Franks followed Shane as they drove in separate vehicles to the Burke and Associates office on King Street.

They went immediately to Chioma's office, where she was behind her desk and Jason Burke was sitting in one of the guest chairs.

"I'll get another chair," Jason offered, but Franks declined, saying he would rather stand.

"Okay, it turns out that our new Law Clerk, Tin Tran, was not completely truthful on his application for employment or during his interviews," Chioma said. "Potential employees are specifically asked if they have had any previous criminal convictions or if they have any known connection to a criminal organizations. The background we performed, including a police check, showed Tran was clean, and his academic credentials were excellent, so we hired him."

"But, when I dug a lot further into Tran's background, with the help of Doobie MacArthur, who has substantially more resources than I do, we found something which could connect him directly to the threats using the body parts," Chioma said.

"Who the hell is Doobie MacArthur?" Franks asked.

"He's just a confidential resource I use from time to time," Shane said nonchalantly, hoping that would satisfy the Detective.

"And if I called Cyber Crimes, would I be told that this 'Doobie' is on their radar as a known hacker?" Franks asked. "Which would mean that anything he found regarding Tran would've been illegally obtained and would never make it to court."

Shane, who wished Chioma had not mentioned MacArthur's name in front of Franks, said, "Forget about Doobie, Sergeant, forget you ever heard his name. Can you do that? As far as you're concerned, everything you're hearing was collected legitimately by Chioma."

Shane, who knew Franks would be a by-the-book cop or Inspector Stabler wouldn't have him on his team, watched as the Sergeant thought it over.

"If you want to get the person who murdered Stabler's wife and Jalissa Dale, you have to let this go," Shane said.

"Fine. I've never heard of Doobie MacArthur," Franks decided and then asked Chioma, "What've you got?"

"Let me begin by telling you that three days ago, Hong Phuong, the leader of the Vietnamese-Canadian criminal organization that was dismantled by the RCMP, was murdered in his cell at a prison in Hanoi," Chioma said.

Following his arrest for criminal activity in Canada, Phuong had been deported to Vietnam under an agreement that he would not be executed by the Vietnamese for crimes he had committed in his native country.

"I thought Phuong was being held in isolation in a high-security section of the prison?" Jason asked.

"Apparently not secure enough," Chioma responded. "Someone got to him, perhaps a member of a rival gang who paid off the guards."

"So what does that have to do with your Law Clerk, Tin Tran?" Franks asked.

"Phuong was Tin's uncle," Chioma stated.

"You're shitting me!" Jason exclaimed. "How the hell did he get on my staff without someone knowing this!?"

"He's covered his background with some very professional help," Chioma said. "His mother is Phuong's sister, but unlike Vietnamese tradition, she took her husband's last name, Tran. It appears that she has taken extensive measures to separate herself, and her son, Tin, from the Phuong name, either because she doesn't want to be connected to Phuong's criminal organization or perhaps to hide from the authorities the fact that she's involved."

"So, if Phuong's organization in Canada is not totally dismantled like the Mounties would have us to believe, and members of his family are still involved, they would be looking for revenge for his death," Shane said. "And it's possible the family here in Canada would put some of the blame on the person responsible for accelerating the investigation that led to Phuong's deportation."

"Your daughter, Lan," Jason said.

"Lan maybe the target," Shane said, "But also anyone connected to her. Emma and I, obviously. Ben, because he's close to Lan and prevented her from being kidnapped, and Inspector Stabler, because he was the public face of the joint Brantford Police-RCMP task force that shut down the cannabis resin labs the gang was running out of various homes in the city. Phuong's organization was well known for its viciousness regarding its enemies; in particular, cutting up bodies and sending parts as a warning."

"I don't know, it seems a bit far-fetched that the Phuongs would blame Lan, and those close to her, for their leader's murder in a Vietnamese prison and would seek revenge in this fashion," Franks said. "Wouldn't it be more likely they would seek retribution from the people who actually had him killed?"

"I agree, it does," Shane admitted. "But that would be assuming we're dealing with a logical mind. Think about it. Tin Tran's uncle is murdered in Vietnam and he's in Brantford, half a world away. He's devastated and angry, and wants someone, anyone, connected to his Uncle's deportation to pay for what they've done."

"Well, the only way to find out is to ask him," Franks said and then asked, "Where is he now?"

"He's in court helping one of my Associates," Jason said.

"I'm going to have him picked up for questioning about falsifying his employment application," Franks said, "But at this point, we have no reason to hold him if he doesn't wish to cooperate. Does he live in the city?"

"He said he was living with his parents in Hamilton until he got a place of his own," Chioma said.

"So now we know where Phuong's sister is, that's good," Franks said. "I've had past dealing with one of the Crown Attorneys in Hamilton who I'm sure can get a search warrant issued quickly for the Tran's residence. I'll have to coordinate with the Hamilton Police Service."

"What about the Mounties?" Shane asked. "They need to be told the Phuong organization is still active, perhaps now being run by the sister out of Hamilton."

"Let's not get ahead of ourselves until I have a chance to talk to Tran," Franks responded.

"I have to say that even though he lied about his background, I can't see Tin being involved in dismembering bodies in order to threaten people," Chioma said with conviction in her voice.

"I've talked to him dozens of times since he started with the firm. He's a very pleasant, soft spoken young man, very enthusiastic about landing his first clerking position, and is trying hard to fit in," she added.

"I know from experience that many evil, disturbed people are very good at hiding their true nature," Shane said. "Look at Adam Talino; young, handsome and very charming. He had everyone fooled. He had lunch with the Mayor once a week, and he gave away hundreds of thousands of dollars, which made him a hero in the city. But in reality, Adam Talino is a psychopath who was hiding in plain sight and murdering vulnerable young women.

Chapter Nineteen

Well, my friends in the freezer are gone now, so I'll have to talk to you, Mom, even though I know you're not really here.

I miss you so much! I miss you every hour of every day! You were the most important person in my life. So loving and caring, such a gentle soul who always gave of herself and never asked for anything in return but love.

Mom, you were so old-fashioned and I loved you for it. Baking cookies and muffins in the kitchen, wearing a dress and an apron like you were in some 1950s television show.

It didn't matter who it was or why they were there, as soon as someone walked in the door of the house, you were off to the kitchen to make coffee and load up a tray of baked goods.

That even happened the day that Shane Daniels, the man who ruined our lives, came to the house to accuse my disgusting stepfather of murdering some young woman he was banging. I wasn't there, but I can picture you standing there with a tray of coffee and cookies when Daniels said that Inspector Mark Stabler, another man who ruined our lives, was waiting outside to arrest the man I despised, but you loved for some reason.

That was the beginning of the end for you, Mom, and it broke my heart and shattered my soul.

I tried to tell you, Mom, that the man you married after my father died was untrustworthy and rotten inside. He took advantage of your good nature and treated you like his personal housekeeper. When you found out he was having an affair with a woman young enough to be his daughter and that he murdered her, you couldn't deal with it, and I lost you.

I can't get to my evil stepfather because he's in prison. But Mom, I want you to know that I am getting revenge. I'm making the people responsible for taking you away from me feel the same grief and pain I do.

I'm not done yet, but the cop is now a heartbroken widower because I slashed his sick wife's throat. Daniels has hidden his wife and kid from me, but today I got to his best friend. It didn't work out exactly as I planned, but I'm pretty sure he's dead.

I knew Daniels wasn't home, but there was a big, black pickup truck parked out front belonging to Daniels' friend, Ben Chen, who had done exactly what I thought he would do when I sent him the eyeballs; he headed straight here to Brantford.

I watched as Chen left the house and got in his truck. I followed him to a grocery store and waited in the parking lot until he came out carrying two bags jammed with stuff. I trailed him back to Daniels' house and watched him carry the bags into the house. I waited a few minutes, pulled down the brim of the ball cap I was wearing to obscure my face, walked to the front door, rang the bell and held my fake badge up to the security camera.

I stood very close to the door and when Chen opened it, I said, "Bye, Ben," and then started stabbing.

Somehow, as I was jamming the knife in and out of his body as quickly as I could, Chen managed to push me away and close the door.

I heard the deadbolt being engaged, but I also heard a thump, likely Chen banging into the door before he fell to the floor. I don't know for sure if he's dead, but he probably bled to death before anyone found him.

I know, Mom, that I should be leaving the city immediately because I think it's only a matter of time before Daniels figures out who I am.

But I need to be around to see the hurt and pain on Daniels' face when he finds out his best friend is dead.

And I want to find a way to see the cop's pain and grief.

I want to witness them suffering what I suffered every day since I lost you, Mom.

Then, I promise, I'll disappear.

Chapter Twenty

They put Shane in front of a small monitor, wearing headphones, at a desk facing a wall inside a common office area at the Brantford Police Service headquarters on Elgin Street.

On the other side of the wall was an interview room and on the monitor, Shane could see Tin Tran sitting by himself at a metal table, his hands clasped in front of him.

Tran looked nervous and agitated, but that didn't surprise Shane. It was understandable considering that two cops showed up in the courtroom where Tran was sitting with an lawyer from Burke and Associates, and asked him to come with them.

In the headphones, Shane heard the sound of the door to the interview room opening and watched on the monitor as Sergeant Franks, carrying a tablet, and a woman in a dark pant suit entered the room and sat at the table across from Tran.

"Mr. Tran, I'm Sergeant Greg Franks and this is Detective Constable Tara Jones. I appreciate you coming in to speak with us."

"I really didn't have much choice. Two officers pulled me out of a courtroom. It was rather embarrassing," Tran said, the irritation in his voice quite evident.

"I apologize for that, but we have some rather urgent questions to discuss with you," Franks said. "You're not under arrest; however, you do have the right to speak to legal counsel if you wish, before we continue."

"Well, first I'd like to have some kind of idea about why I'm here," Tran said.

"Mr. Tran, can you tell us why you lied on your application for the position at Burke and Associates?" Franks asked. "Specifically, in the background section, it asked if you had any known relationship or association with a convicted felon or a criminal organization."

"I didn't lie on the application," Tran answered forcefully, but even watching on a monitor, Shane could easily tell Tran was not being truthful by the way the young man's eyes quickly looked down and back up, how the expression on his face froze in place, and because he gripped his hands tighter together.

"Actually, you did, Mr. Tran," Franks said. "Tran is your mother's married name, which she kept after the divorce from her second husband. Her maiden name is Phuong. She's the sister of Hong Phuong, who was the head of a Vietnamese-Canadian criminal organization until he agreed to be deported back to Vietnam rather than face a long list of charges here in Canada."

The look on Tran's face changed to one of both surprise and resignation.

"I said 'no' on the application because my mother and I never had anything to do with my Uncle and his businesses!" Tran exclaimed.

"We hate him. We disowned him. He dishonoured the Vietnamese people who came to this country to live a better life."

"Not surprisingly, given his criminal activities, there were thousands of police surveillance photos taken of your Uncle over the years," Constable Jones said, speaking for the first time.

Jones was in her mid-forties, a medium-built woman with a plain face, frame-less glasses and dark hair pulled up in a bun at the back of her head. She took the tablet she had brought with her, touched the screen and then turned it to face Tran.

"I went through a lot of them and I found this," Jones said as she pointed to a photo on the tablet. Isn't that you and your mother standing beside your Uncle?"

"I'm like twelve or thirteen years old in that picture!" Tran protested. "I think it was a family funeral that we were obligated to attend by tradition. We would not have been there otherwise!"

Shane, looking at the monitor, and listening through the headphones, saw that Tran was becoming increasingly emotional as he answered the questions, but the signs that he was being deceitful were no longer evident.

"Mr. Tran," Franks began in a serious tone, "Shane Daniels, whom you know from your firm, was involved in bringing down your Uncle's criminal enterprise. He and his partner adopted the young girl whose parents were murdered on your Uncle's behalf. She witnessed your Uncle collecting money from a cannabis resin lab house where she and her parents were forced to live. A friend of Mr. Daniels, Ben Chen, guarded this young girl's life and even prevented an attempted kidnapping. Inspector Mark Stabler of my Police Service was a key member of the joint task force that took down your Uncle and his organization."

"Each of these three people received a human body part and a threatening note shortly after your Uncle was murdered in a Hanoi prison a few days ago," Franks continued, "And now Inspector Stabler's wife and her personal support worker have been viciously murdered. Did you know about your Uncle's death?"

"My mother was notified, but we didn't care," Tran replied. "My Uncle was a very evil man who was responsible for countless deaths because of the drugs he sold and for the murder of many members of the rival gangs. Good riddance."

Shane saw the signs of strong conviction on Tran's face; a tightening of his jaw and neck muscles, an intensity in his eyes.

"That's fine, but there are still a few things we're wondering about," Franks said to Tran. "The person behind the murders, and the threats, had access to closely guarded information about where Mr. Daniels and Inspector Stabler live. The threatening notes are of a personal nature, suggesting one person seeking revenge. You work at Burke and Associates, so getting those addresses would be easy. And maybe you're lying about your relationship with your Uncle. Perhaps you were actually very close. Maybe you and your mother were actually deeply involved in the family business, hiding under the illusion that you were estranged. You don't blame whoever actually stabbed your Uncle in the Vietnamese prison; you blame the people responsible for putting him in that jail in the first place. So, you get a position at Burke and Associates, under false pretenses, so that you can be close by to get revenge."

"We're also curious about what happened to Sherri Morrison, the Clerk you replaced," Jones said. "She's off work with a mysterious illness. Did your family do something to make her sick so there would be an opening at the firm for you?"

"Absolutely none of this is true!" Tran exclaimed and then calmly said, "I would like to consult with a lawyer now."

Shane watched on the monitor as Franks and Constable Jones picked up their tablets and left the interview room.

When they came out, he removed the headphones, turned off the monitor, and followed the two officers to Franks' office, located along the same wall. Once they were inside, Franks sat behind the desk, Jones took a chair in front and Shane remained standing.

Franks looked at Shane and asked, "What do you think?"

"It's not him," Shane responded. "I think he's being sincere when he says he hated his Uncle and wanted nothing to do with him. His body language and facial expressions betrayed him when he tried to deny that he lied on his employment application about his connection to the Phuong criminal gang. But that was not the case when he said he didn't care about his Uncle dying in prison."

"It doesn't have to be him directly killing people and cutting up bodies," Franks argued. "He can sit there and say truthfully that he had nothing to do with it because he had other people do it for him. We know from past experience that members of the Phuong gang are more than capable of cutting up and disposing of the bodies of their enemies."

"And maybe Tran can also say truthfully, 'it's got nothing to do with me' because it's his mother who's calling the shots," Franks added.

"Well, we can't hold him without some tangible proof," Jones said.

"After he's had an opportunity to talk to a lawyer, I will ask him for precise details of his whereabouts over the past three days and we'll check what he tells us very carefully," Franks said. "And we'll also see what turns up when we execute a search warrant at his mother's place in Hamilton."

"I know you wanted to wait, but I think you should bring the Mounties in on this right away," Shane said. "Specifically, a Sergeant Gurdeep Singh of the Organized Crime Division. He was involved in dealing with Lan's situation right from the beginning and he led the Task Force that eventually dismantled Phuong's organization. I don't remember Singh ever mentioning any of Phuong's siblings being involved in his criminal enterprises, but he might have some intelligence on the sister, Tran's mother. I have Singh's card in my wallet. I'll leave it for you."

"Okay, fine," was the only response from Franks.

"Any word on how the Inspector's doing?" Shane then asked.

He had been having a tough time getting the image out of his head of a dimly lit bedroom and Stabler sitting in a chair beside his wife's empty, blood-stained bed.

"He tried to come in today and work on the case, but the Chief saw him and made him go home on bereavement leave," Franks said. "The Inspector was not happy, but the Chief insisted."

"I can imagine," Shane responded and was going to ask something else when his phone started vibrating and making a pinging sound. It was the distinct signal that a security alarm had gone off at his house.

While he touched the system's icon on the home screen of his phone, Shane said to Franks and Jones, "My friend, Ben Chen, the guy who got sent the eyeballs, is staying at my place. He's either forgotten to turn off the security system or someone has broken into my house."

When the image from the camera over the front door came up on Shane's phone, he couldn't believe what he was seeing. The front door had been broken open and two firemen in full gear were on the front step, looking into the house.

Shane switched to the camera covering the area inside the front door and was shocked to see two paramedics working frantically on a man on the floor. He couldn't see past the paramedics, but he recognized the lower half of the man on the floor.

It was Ben!

No, no, no! Shane screamed in his head.

"I gotta go!" Shane exclaimed to Franks and Jones.

Chapter Twenty One

Waiting rooms in hospitals are all the same, no matter what city you're in, Shane thought as he sat in one on the surgical floor of the Brantford General Hospital.

The walls, painted an institutional green, had framed posters with either information on hospital policies and procedures, healthy living, or a list of conditions you might have if you have a certain disease. A wide-screen TV was mounted near the ceiling in one corner of the room, tuned to HGTV and one of its numerous home renovation shows. Chairs, plus benches which held two people, lined the walls, all with green, plastic covered cushions that looked comfortable until you sat on one for about ten minutes and then realized it had been badly broken down from years of use.

By the time Shane had driven from the police station to his house, breaking the speed limit the entire way, Ben was already on his way to the hospital by ambulance.

There were two police cruisers parked out front and a Brantford Fire Department truck was still there. Two uniformed officers were at the front door, and one of them, who was writing in his notebook, Shane knew; Sergeant Jim Flaherty, a veteran patrol officer with the Service.

When he got to the front door and looked inside, Shane's heart started to beat faster and he felt nauseous. There was a large pool of blood on the floor of the entryway and blood-soaked squares of gauze were scattered around it.

"I have the victim's wallet and his identification says he's Ben Chen of Port Elgin," Flaherty said and then asked, "Do you know him, Shane?"

"Yes, he's a friend of mine. He was staying at the house," Shane said, trying to keep his emotions under control.

"What happened?" he asked, his voice coming out sounding shaky.

"It appears that when your friend answered the door, whoever was there attacked him with a knife," Flaherty said. "It looks like, after he was stabbed, he managed to close the door on his attacker, lock it, and call 911."

"All the Dispatcher could hear was someone whispering, 'I need help'," Flaherty continued, "She used the phone's 911 signal to send paramedics to this address. When they arrived, they knocked loudly on the door, but got no response, and when they tried the door, it was locked. They spotted blood seeping out from under the door and heard someone knocking softly on the other side. They called the Fire Department, which, luckily for your friend, had a truck already in the area on another call. The firefighters smashed the deadbolt and had to push the door open to move your friend because he was sitting on the floor leaning against it."

Shane had a huge lump in his throat and was afraid to ask, but he did. "Was Ben still alive when they finally got in?"

"Barely," Flaherty answered. "He lost a lot of blood, and at first, the paramedics couldn't find a pulse. They worked frantically on him, got some IVs going and managed to pick up a heartbeat, but they weren't sure if he was going to make it to the hospital. I'm sorry, Shane."

"Do you need me here? I gotta get to the BGH," Shane said, his thoughts going in several different directions.

"I understand Sergeant Franks and Constable Jones from CID are on their way, along with a team from Forensics," Flaherty said. "I'm sure they'll want a statement since you know the victim and you own the house."

"I just left them at the station. They can come to the hospital when they need to speak to me. Right now, I have to go and check on Ben," Shane said impatiently.

"Is this connected to the murder of Inspector Stabler's wife and that other woman at Stabler's house?" Flaherty asked. "Because I know Franks was working on that, and I heard you were connected to the case somehow."

"Yes, but please, I gotta go," Shane said quickly. "Call or text me when you're ready to clear the scene and I'll have someone come and fix the door."

Shane walked away without waiting for a response from Flaherty, got in the Charger and drove to the hospital.

On the way, he called Ben's girlfriend, Michelle, on his hands-free phone, and after he told her what happened, she cried out, "What the fuck!" and Shane had to wait as he heard her sobbing. After a few moments, she suddenly said, "I'm on my way," and hung up.

Next, he called Emma and gave her the news. She was, at first, just as emotional as Michelle and then she was angry.

"Ben was almost beaten to death trying to protect Lan and now this!" she exclaimed. "Four people have been murdered, including Frank Stabler's sick wife! Lan and I are under threat, but we don't know why! I don't know how much more of this kind of shit I can take, Shane! You have to find out who's doing this and put a stop to it!"

"I'm trying, Emma," Shane said softly.

"Lan and I are going to leave for Brantford right now," Emma said in a much calmer voice.

"You can't do that, Emma, it's not safe," Shane pleaded.

"We'll stay in a hotel, no one will know where we are. I need to be there for Ben," Emma said, and like Michelle, she hung up before Shane could respond.

After he got to the hospital and parked the Charger, Shane went to the Emergency Department but was told that Ben was already in surgery.

That was why he was now sitting in the surgical floor waiting room and had been for almost three hours with no details on what was happening with Ben. He had already asked several times at the nurse's station, but all they knew was that he was still in surgery.

Shane was not surprised when Michelle suddenly walked into the waiting room. He knew she would have probably driven recklessly fast to get from Paisley to Brantford so quickly.

They hugged and in a very emotional voice, Michelle said, "Please tell me he's still alive! Is there any word on what's going on?"

"He's still undergoing surgery, that's all I know," Shane said as he and Michelle sat in chairs next to each other.

Michelle was taller than Ben, and back when Shane first met her, she had a Goth-like appearance; spiked dark hair, pale complexion, black lipstick, eyeshadow and eyeliner, a nose ring, and a stud just below the middle of her lower lip. Both ears had been lined with small rings.

But all of that was gone now as she went with a completely different look. The rings along her ears were gone, as well as the nose ring and lower lip stud. Currently, there was a small diamond stud in the side of her nose and in each ear lobe, likely gifts from Ben. Her hair was straight and shoulder-length with purple streaks. She wore light red lipstick, had eyelash extensions and dark eyeliner, which was currently smeared, likely because she had been crying while making the drive to Brantford. In terms of clothing, today she had torn jeans and a t-shirt featuring the alternative rock band 'The Smashing Pumpkins'.

"How did this happen?" Michelle asked as tears ran down her face.

"Ben opened the door to someone at the house either because he knew the person or he thought it was a cop. We're not sure," Shane answered. "We suspect the same thing likely happened at a police inspector's home, where a personal support worker let someone in and both she and the inspector's wife were murdered. It appears Ben managed to fight off his attacker and then close and lock the door. He's probably alive because he was able to do that."

"And this is all connected to the human eyeballs that Ben thought you sent him," Michelle stated.

"Yes, but I'm not sure yet exactly how Ben fits into all of this," Shane said. "I think someone is getting revenge for a case that Inspector Mark Stabler and I were involved with. They killed the Inspector's wife to hurt him. They must have found out somehow that Emma and Lan were in hiding, so they went after Ben to hurt me. Whoever it is, they know a lot about me if they knew Ben was my friend and where he lived."

"I feel so helpless, just sitting here," Michelle said in a sad voice.

"He's going to recover. Ben's a strong guy," Shane said, trying to sound positive.

Amelia Martin suddenly walked into the waiting room and Shane stood up. To Shane's surprise, Amelia put her arms around his neck and pressed her body tightly against his. Shane felt embarrassed as Amelia clung tightly to him with Michelle in the same room. He wasn't sure what to do with his hands. He decided to just lightly hold them against her back.

"The Department Clerk, Maria, heard your friend was brought in and is undergoing emergency surgery, and she told me," Amelia said softly. "I figured you'd be here, and I wanted to come and tell you how sorry I am and that I hope your friend will be okay."

"Thanks, Amelia, I really appreciate your support," Shane said and he assumed she would then step back, but she continued to keep her body tight against his. An involuntary sensation of arousal suddenly went through Shane, adding to his embarrassment, because he knew Michelle would be watching as he and Amelia stood tightly together for a lot longer than an normal friendly hug. Amelia moved her face from the side to the front of Shane's, their noses almost touching, and she put her right hand softly on the side of his face.

"I can see the hurt and worry on your face," Amelia said softly. "If you need anything, if I can help in any way, please call me."

"I will, Amelia, thanks," Shane tried to say casually, but it came out in a nervous stutter.

Amelia left, leaving Shane standing in the waiting room trying to calm himself.

"Who the fuck was that!?" Michelle asked.

"Doctor Amelia Martin. She's the new Regional Pathologist assigned to the hospital," Shane tried to reply calmly, but likely failed, as he sat down.

"She seems overly…friendly," Michelle said and Shane could see a mix of curiosity and suspicion on the woman's face.

"She's a nice person and was just trying to express her concern for Ben and for how I was dealing with the situation," Shane said, trying to sound matter-of-fact.

"I'm sure she was," Michelle said sarcastically and then asked, "Has Emma met this beautiful and overly friendly Doctor Martin?"

"Not yet, she just started recently at the hospital," Shane answered, ignoring Michelle's obvious dig.

"I'd like to be there to fucking see that," Michelle muttered, just loud enough for Shane to hear, then took her phone out of her pocket and started scrolling through her emails.

Shane took out his own phone and saw texts from Jason, Chioma, Sergeant Franks and even Inspector Stabler asking if there was any news about Ben. Shane was a bit surprised, and appreciative, that Stabler had reached out, considering what he was going through with the murder of his wife.

Shane answered them all by saying Ben was still in surgery and there was no update. He put an extra line in his reply to Stabler, asking the Inspector how he was making out and to let Shane know if there was anything he could do.

Shane had just completed sending the texts when Emma and Lan walked into the room holding hands.

"Dad, we're here!" Lan exclaimed and ran over to Shane, who got out of his chair and crouched down to hug the little girl.

"Is Uncle Ben going to be okay? He's not going to die, is he?" Lan asked emotionally, in rapid succession, as a few tears rolled down her cheeks.

"Ben was hurt really bad, but some excellent surgeons are trying to fix him," Shane said, trying to keep the emotions he felt out of his voice.

"They better fix him," Lan stated firmly as she used her left hand to wipe the tears from her face. She then turned to where Michelle was sitting and said, "Hi Michelle."

"Hi Lan," Michelle said, trying to put a smile on her face.

After they hugged, Lan sat in the chair beside Michelle and they held hands.

When Shane stood up from greeting Lan, he looked at Emma and said, simply, "Hi."

"Hi," Emma said back.

Then she embraced him and gave him a quick kiss on the lips, which surprised Shane, considering they weren't on the best of terms right now.

When she stepped back, she said, "You smell like perfume."

"It's from a raven-haired beauty who came in here and welded her body to Shane," Michelle said. "I can't wait for the fucking two of you to meet."

Shane looked at Michelle and was going to say something about her smart remark, but he realized she was probably acting this way because she was scared about Ben and frustrated that there was nothing she could do to help him.

"Who's this raven-haired beauty Michelle is talking about?" Emma asked.

"Doctor Amelia Martin, the Pathologist assigned to the hospital," Shane answered.

"I've never heard of her," Emma said with a bit of an edge in her voice.

"She just started. She handled the examination of the body parts sent to us, Inspector Stabler and Ben, and did the post mortem on Stabler's wife," Shane said.

"And it sounds like you've gotten very close quite quickly," Emma said skeptically.

"She's a nice person and very caring compared to most pathologists who handle dead bodies all day," Shane responded.

"I see," Emma said in a flat tone and Shane wondered if she saw something in his face that was making her suspicious of his relationship with Amelia. Was he showing a guilty conscience over his physical attraction to Amelia? Shane was an expert at reading faces and body language, but he knew Emma was very good at it too. It was one of the reasons why she was an excellent counsellor for people who had recently undergone an amputation. Many would try and put up a brave front about what had happened to them and not deal with their true feelings. Emma had a talent for spotting that.

"Can we talk out in the hallway for a minute?" Shane asked.

"Let's," was all Emma said.

After they were outside the waiting room, Shane said, "Emma, I'm happy to see you and Lan because I miss both of you a lot, but I don't think you being back in the city is a good idea, even if you stay in a hotel. Whoever is doing this seems to have a lot of information about both us and Mark Stabler. Maybe they've been following us, and if that's the case, they might know you're here, and that makes it too dangerous for you to stay."

"You know I'm not helpless, Shane. I'm quite capable of defending myself and Lan," Emma said, raising her voice slightly. "I'm not going anywhere until I know that Ben is going to live. We should also be making sure that Michelle is safe."

Emma then pointed her finger at Shane's chest and said, "And what about you, Mister? Shouldn't you be in hiding or in a police safe house while the cops find out who's doing this? Oh, wait, you can't do that, can you? You're Shane Daniels. You can't help yourself, you have to stay involved and solve the case because nobody else can, even when you're actually one of the victims."

Shane was stung by Emma's words. He knew he couldn't just accept them as Emma being angry and upset about the threat she and Lan were under, and the life threatening attack on Ben. It was also about their relationship going forward and the changes she wanted to see him make in how he handled his cases.

Shane was about to respond when he saw a doctor approaching and hoped it was a surgeon with news about Ben.

The physician was a dark-complexioned, short and thin man, wearing blue scrubs, a surgical cap, and had the mask he had been wearing lying open on his chest.

"Hi Emma," the doctor said when he reached where Shane and Emma were standing. Emma was a surgical nurse, so she would know all of the doctors who worked in the department.

"Hi, Doctor Khan," Emma responded.

"I'm looking for Ben Chen's family," Khan said.

"We're as close to family Ben has," Emma said. "Both of his parents are deceased and any relatives he has all live in China."

Michelle, who spotted the doctor standing with Shane and Emma, came out of the waiting room to join them after telling Lan to stay in the waiting room. Lan, disappointed she was not going to be included, did as she was told, but crossed her arms and scrunched up her face so everyone knew how she felt about it.

"Doctor Khan," Emma continued, "This is my partner, Shane Daniels, Ben's oldest and closest friend, and beside him is Michelle Watson, Ben's partner. Shane and Michelle, this is Doctor Zahir Khan, the Chief Surgeon here at the BGH and the absolutely best we have."

"I appreciate you saying that, Emma," Khan said.

"You operated on Ben?" Emma asked anxiously.

"I did, and I wish I had more encouraging news for you," Khan said. "Ben lost a lot of blood before he made it here to the hospital. The paramedics got him on an IV at the scene, but Ben was barely alive when he was brought into Emergency. We had to get him stabilized before we could do surgery. He was stabbed in the left lobe of his liver. We removed a small section of it to avoid infection, but luckily, the liver is the one organ that will rejuvenate itself."

"He was also stabbed in one kidney, which we had to remove, but he other one is functioning normally," Khan stated.

"He was stabbed twice in the lower intestine, fairly close together, so we did a bowel resection. Whoever did this used a long, narrow bladed, very sharp knife, and knew where to stab to cause maximum damage."

Doctor Khan hesitated briefly before he continued. "While the work we did to repair Ben internally was successful, that's unfortunately the only encouraging news I have at this point. When we were just completing the operation, his heart stopped, likely because of the severe trauma his body has suffered. We managed to shock his heart into working again, but had to put him on life support.

Khan hesitate again and then said, "I'm afraid the prognosis for Ben surviving the night is not very good. I'm sorry it's not the news you wanted to hear."

Tears started running down Michelle's face, her mouth fell open in shock, and she ran back into the waiting room, where she sat with her hands covering her face, her shoulders going up and down as she sobbed silently.

Tears were also running down Emma's face, but Shane knew she would be fighting to stay calm for Michelle and Lan. Lan, who saw Michelle crying and that Emma was upset, ran out of the waiting room and hugged Emma tightly around her waist. Shane was also trying to put up a brave front, but the huge lump in his throat told him that keeping his emotions under control was going to be very difficult.

"And if Ben survives the night?" Shane managed to calmly ask the surgeon.

"If that happens, I believe he has a fighting chance," Khan answered encouragingly. "He's carrying extra weight, but I could tell that prior to the attack, Ben was in very good health. If there's even a slight improvement in his vital signs over the next few hours, he could survive."

"Thanks, Doctor Khan, I know you and your team have done the best you can for Ben," Emma said softly.

"Emma, there's nothing you can do for Ben right now. Why don't you, Shane and Michelle go and try to get some rest for the next couple of hours?" Doctor Khan said sympathetically. "I promise I'll call if anything changes."

Khan nodded at Shane, turned, and started walking toward the double doors at the end of the hall that led to the operating theaters and intensive care rooms.

"Doctor Khan is right. You and Lan have had a long day, including the drive from Port Elgin," Shane said to Emma. "Why don't we go and get something to eat, and then you go to your hotel and get some rest. Michelle can come with us and I'll book her a room."

"I'm not going anywhere," Michelle called out from the room. "I'm going to be here when they tell me Ben's going to be okay."

Lan, who was still holding tightly to Emma and had tears running down her cheeks like everyone else, said, "I can stay with Michelle. She's scared about Uncle Ben and I am too."

"That's a nice and very brave thing to offer to do, Lan, but you need to eat and rest," Shane said. "And I think Emma would appreciate you being with her for support."

"Okay, I can do that," Lan said, and Shane could see that his daughter was torn up emotionally over what had happened to Ben. Shane knew the death of her parents in the car accident that she survived was still a vivid memory for Lan, but she was surprisingly a well-adjusted young girl considering what she had been through.

But she adored Ben for reasons Shane never did quite understand, given his friend's penchant for foul language, outrageous conspiracy theories and questionable fashion choices. She laughed at almost everything Ben said, much to his delight. Shane was very concerned about the emotional impact on Lan if Ben died.

Shane had to be honest with himself; he wasn't sure how he was going to handle it if Ben died. They had been friends for so long and had been through a lot adventures together. He didn't know if he could deal with the emotional fallout if he lost Ben.

Shane could feel the anger building inside him.

He had to find out who did this.

Chapter Twenty Two

Jason Burke knew he should ask for another delay in the resumption of the Noah Tremblay trial, given that he was mentally distracted by what was going on outside of the courtroom.

But in the aftermath of Justice Wendal's sudden death, he knew that Justice Crowder was anxious to resume the trial out of fairness to the jury and witnesses.

Shane had called Jason first thing in the morning to tell him that his friend, Ben Chen, had survived the night and while he was still on life support, the doctors were cautiously optimistic that Ben would survive.

Jason was relieved to hear the news. He knew how much Ben meant to Shane and he was concerned about the emotional impact it would have on Shane if Ben died. He had a temper, which Jason knew Shane tried to keep suppressed, but he wasn't sure what would happen if Ben died and Shane found out who was responsible.

Human body parts being sent to Shane, Ben and Inspector Stabler, the murders of Stabler's wife and her personal support worker, and now the near fatal attack on Ben were all wearing heavily on Jason's mind.

If this was a revenge plot, both he and Shane weren't sure who all it encompassed. Jason was being cautious and in addition to private security guards, Sergeant Franks had now assigned a police officer to keep an eye on his home and his wife, Gillian.

Jason had considered deferring at least the next witness to Susan Cartright, his second chair, but because he was trying to maintain a relationship with the jury, he decided that introducing someone else might change the dynamic. He just needed to focus.

"Are you alright, Mr. Burke?" Jason suddenly heard Judge Crowder ask. "The Prosecutor has completed his questioning of the witness and we're waiting for you."

"Yes, I'm sorry, your Honour," Jason said, embarrassed that his thoughts had completely drawn his attention away from the trial.

The witness was Jamie Wilcott, supposedly Noah Tremblay's best friend, but he was far from that during the testimony he had just finished.

Under questioning by Prosecutor Evan Gregory, Wilcott said Noah had a hair-trigger temper and in the days leading up to Olivia's death, all of Noah's anger was directed at her. Wilcott claimed that the night before Olivia was murdered, Noah told him that Olivia had tricked him and had purposely allowed herself to get pregnant. Wilcott said that Noah was very angry and told him that he was going to make Olivia have an abortion, one way or the other.

Jason got up from behind his table and stood in the area in front of the witness box. He gave Wilcott a bit of a smile and then asked,

"Mr. Wilcott, you testified that all of the angry stuff Noah said about his wife took place the day before she died, correct?"

"Yes, it was the Friday night at the start of the long weekend last August," Wilcott said in a confident voice.

"And this conversation took place in a bar here in Brantford, the Ox and Hound," Jason stated.

"Yes, that's right," Wilcott replied.

"You and Noah ended up having quite a bit to drink that night, didn't you?" Jason asked.

"We were blowing off some steam from the week at work, and it was the start of the holiday weekend, so we had three days off," Wilcott said.

"You blew off some steam to the tune of six large glasses of draft beer over about a two hour period, correct?" Jason asked.

"I don't remember how much beer we had," Wilcott said, shrugging his shoulders.

"I'm not surprised, given how much you had to drink," Jason said sarcastically.

"Objection, your Honour!" Gregory said as he stood up behind his desk. "My colleague is making derogatory comments and not asking a question."

"Objection sustained," Judge Crowder ruled. "Stick to questions, Mr. Burke."

"Your Honour, the defence has already submitted into evidence the receipt from the Ox and Hound from the night in question, which shows Mr. Wilcott paid for six large drafts with a credit card," Jason said. "We have also submitted a receipt which shows my client paid for the same number of beers on his own credit card."

"The receipts are in the official court documents, and the Prosecutor has a copy, that's correct," Judge Crowder said.

Jason nodded at the Judge, turned back to face Wilcott and said, "So, Mr. Wilcott, we do know how much you had to drink that night and it was a lot. You didn't drive home, did you?"

"No, I only live a few houses up the street from Noah, so we shared a taxi," Wilcott said.

"We are all glad to hear that, I'm sure," Jason said, and before Gregory could stand and object, Jason turned to the Judge and said, "Sorry, your Honour."

"Move on, Mr. Burke," Judge Crowder admonished.

"Before she started dating Noah and they eventually got married, you went out with Olivia Tremblay, correct?" Jason asked Wilcott.

"We dated during high school and for a little bit after," Wilcott said.

"What happened to end your relationship?" Jason asked.

"Nothing big. Olivia decided she liked Noah better and had fallen in love with him. It happens," Wilcott said in a very casual manner.

"Mr. Wilcott, I need you to be very honest with me when I ask my next two questions," Jason said. "And please remember that you're testifying under oath at a trial which will decide the future of the man who considers you his best friend."

"I understand that. Ask your questions," Wilcott said defensively.

"Even after Olivia broke up with you and married Noah, did you still have strong feelings for her?" Jason asked.

Wilcott shifted nervously in his seat and took a quick glance at Noah sitting at the defence table.

"Yeah, I still had feelings for her," Wilcott said. "I thought we were getting along really well and that she loved me. I admit I was hurt when she started seeing Noah. However, I got over it and Olivia and I remained friends."

"Now, here's my second question and, again, I ask that you give this court an honest answer," Jason said. "Do you believe Noah when he says he didn't mean to kill Olivia and that he acted in self-defence?"

Wilcott shifted in his seat again and Jason saw the man's face cloud over with indecision on what he was going to say. He looked at Noah and said softly, "I'm sorry," and then turned to Jason and said firmly, "I don't think it was an accident. I think Noah killed her."

The comment caused a vocal stir to ripple through the spectators' area in the courtroom until Judge Crowder said, "Quiet, please."

After the rumbling of voices subsided, Jason said, "Mr. Wilcott, let's summarize what we now know from your testimony. You still had strong feelings for Olivia. On the night before she died, you and Noah drank a lot of beer, which means anything you thought you remembered hearing that night would not be reliable because you were inebriated. Olivia dies, and you think Noah did it on purpose. He killed the woman you still loved. In revenge, you decide to concoct a story about Noah threatening Olivia because the only reason you remained Noah's friend was so you could stay close to Olivia. But now you've been caught in your lie because you were drunk when you claimed Noah made the threat."

"Your Honour! Once again, Mr. Burke is making a statement and not asking a question!" Gregory exclaimed.

Before Judge Crowder could react, Jason said, "I'm finished with this witness, your Honour," and walked back to his table and sat down.

"Re-direct, your Honour," Gregory said as he remained standing at his table.

"Go ahead," Crowder said.

"Jamie, were you being truthful when you testified that Noah Tremblay threatened his wife on the night before she died?" Gregory asked.

"Yes, I was," Wilcott said in a firm voice.

"Thank you," Gregory responded and then turned to the Judge and said, "Your Honour, the Crown has completed presenting its case."

"Mr. Wilcott, you may step down," Judge Crowder said to Jamie.

After Jamie left the witness box and took a seat in the spectator area, Jason stood up and said, "Your Honour, in light of the serious credibility issues with both the testimony of this witness and the investigating officers, the indecisive forensic evidence, and the fact that no one witnessed what happened the night Olivia Tremblay was killed, I ask for a directed verdict of not guilty."

"Your request is denied, Mr. Burke," Judge Crowder ruled and then asked, "Would you and Mr. Gregory please approach the bench?"

When both men were standing in front of him, Judge Crowder said to Jason, "Mr. Burke, I denied your motion because I believe the Crown has presented enough compelling evidence that the case should go to the jury to decide."

"Thank you, your Honour," Gregory said.

Crowder looked at Gregory and said, "I don't think you should be thanking me because I agree with the defence that your case has cracks in it. Mr. Burke is correct when he says there are credibility issues with your witnesses, which means he has successfully raised a lot of reasonable doubt for the jury to consider. So, I ask again if there's not some kind of compromise that can be achieved. Mr. Burke says his client is willing to plead guilty to manslaughter in exchange for a sentence of two years less a day."

"Your Honour, as I have stated before, that sentence does not match the severity of the crime Noah Tremblay committed," Gregory said firmly. "There needs to be a message sent that if you stab and kill your wife, you will be severely punished. However, in the spirit of compromise, I would accept a guilty plea on manslaughter with a prison term of twelve years."

"Twelve years, Evan, really!?" Jason responded in frustration, trying to keep his voice down so he wouldn't be heard by the rest of the courtroom. "Noah has already been in jail for over a year and you would have him serve at least another nine years before he's eligible for statutory release? We can't agree to that."

"And you want him to spend two easy years in provincial jail for murder?" Gregory shot back.

"Is this about serving justice, or is this about your ego, Evan?" Jason asked as he glared at Gregory. "Is this perhaps because after several failed prosecutions, you're desperate for a win?"

"I resent that!" Gregory said loud enough that it drew the attention of everyone in the courtroom.

"That's enough, gentlemen," Judge Crowder admonished. "Please step back. We'll take a short a recess and then, Mr. Burke, you can begin presenting your defence."

Jason and Gregory returned to their respective tables and Judge Crowder called the break. After the jury left and the spectators started heading for the door at the back of the courtroom, Jason turned to his left to speak quietly with Noah sitting beside him and with Susan Cartright next to Noah.

"The Judge tried again to get Gregory to accept a plea deal for manslaughter, but the prosecutor refuses to accept reasonable jail time," Jason told Noah and Susan. "So, after the recess, we will begin our defence."

Noah, who had remained silent for most of the trial, didn't say anything. He looked thin in the suit Jason had provided him and there were dark circles under his eyes. Jason remained concerned about his client's state of mind.

"I think you did a good job undermining Jamie Wilcott's credibility," Susan said to Jason. "Several members of the jury were writing notes to themselves and even though I'm not nearly as good as you at reading faces, I could tell they were skeptical about his testimony."

"I thought he was my friend," Noah said in a soft, shaky voice.

"I'm sorry about the way things turned out between you and Jamie," Jason said sympathetically.

"Am I going to testify?" Noah suddenly asked.

It was extremely rare for the suspect in a murder trial to testify in their own defence. Lawyers were reluctant to put their clients on the stand and expose them to aggressive questioning by the prosecution. If the defendant didn't come across as truthful and sincere to the jury, it would go a long way in their decision to convict.

Jason had been mulling over whether or not to put Noah on the stand for weeks. During his long discussions with Noah, Jason noted that Noah had adamantly stuck to his story that he loved Olivia and was trying desperately to disarm her when she attacked him with the knife. Noah said knew it wasn't her fault; it was her bipolar disorder causing her to act that way. In the end, he had no choice but to defend himself, but Olivia suddenly came right up against him and the knife went deep into her body.

Jason was convinced that Noah would come across to the jury as a brokenhearted man who did a terrible thing because he thought he had no choice. However, the issue was whether or not Noah could withstand Gregory's cross-examination, which would include Noah's criminal record and the past domestic disturbance calls to his house.

Jason felt he had raised a lot of reasonable doubt in the minds of the jury regarding Noah's intent in the confrontation with his wife. But was it enough?

Only one person knew exactly what happened that night, and there was no escaping the fact that Olivia Tremblay died when her husband stabbed her in the heart. Could Noah convince the jury he was not guilty of second-degree murder? To Jason, putting Noah on the stand was the equivalent of a Hail Mary pass in football. But did he have any choice?

"I'm going to put you on the stand," Jason answered Noah. "We need to start getting you ready right away."

Chapter Twenty Three

Mom, you're not here physically, but I can feel your presence and it does ease my pain over losing you a little bit.

I want you to know, Mom, that I have seen pain and anguish on the people I blame for you taking your own life.

The cop will never be the same. He's all alone now just like me.

I'm sorry that I failed to kill his best friend, but Shane Daniels is in emotional pain and afraid that Ben Chen is going to die.

I feel a great deal of satisfaction.

I know you think I should go now, Mom, and you're right.

But I do want to wait and see if Chen dies. If he doesn't, then I'll have to go and help him along.

Then I get to see even more hurt in Shane Daniels' eyes.

Chapter Twenty Four

While Jason was doing his cross-examination of Jamie Wilcott at the Tremblay trial, Shane was walking through the Intensive Care area of the Surgical floor at the Brantford General Hospital.

He found Michelle, along with Emma and Lan, who were holding hands, all looking intently through the window of one of the ICU units.

Beside the sliding glass door into the unit, a uniformed Brantford police officer was sitting on a chair studying his phone.

When he approached the girls, Shane asked, "How's he look?"

"Better than what my imagination had me fearing," Emma said, not taking her eyes off the window.

Shane looked inside and saw Ben on the bed in the room, with only his arms outside of the white sheet covering his body. One hand had a multi-port catheter on it with tubes running to at least four IV bags hanging on a nearby pole. A set of wires ran out of the top of the blanket and was attached to vital signs monitoring equipment on a rolling rack beside the bed.

Shane got a lump in his throat seeing his friend in the room as some of the emotions that he had tried, sometimes unsuccessfully, to keep under control over the past twenty four hours started to surface.

Everyone stood silently looking through the window as Doctor Khan and a nurse, both dressed in medical gowns with hoods, along with masks and booties, studied Ben's vital signs on the monitors. Khan made some notes on a medical chart.

"I knew Uncle Ben was not going to die," Lan suddenly announced. "He'll be back trying not to say the "F" word in front of me before you know it. Right, Mom?"

"We'd better wait and see what the Doctor says, sweetheart," Emma told her.

Doctor Khan and the nurse exited the room via the sliding glass door and while the nurse walked away to attend to another patient, Khan stopped, pulled back the hood on his gown, let down his mask and pulled off his surgical gloves.

"As you can see, Ben is no longer on life support; we were able to remove him from that several hours ago," Khan said with a pleased look on his face. "He's breathing normally on his own and all of his vital signs are good. This is excellent news."

Tears started running down Michelle's and Emma's faces. Michelle covered her face with both hands and said, "I can't believe it."

"While I'm now confident Ben has a good chance of recovery, we aren't out of the woods yet," Khan said. "He's in danger of infection, which is why we're taking so many precautions and the reason why, unfortunately, I can't let you in to be with him yet."

"We understand. Whatever it takes," Shane said, but he had trouble getting the words out as he was overtaken by the emotional relief that his childhood friend would live.

Lan walked over and hugged Michelle around the legs and said, "I told you he would be okay."

"Yes, you did," Michelle said emotionally and then crouched down and hugged Lan tightly.

"I'll be around to check him every couple of hours," Khan said and walked away toward the nearby nurse's station.

Shane and Emma stood silently looking through the glass at Ben. After a few moments, Emma said, "Given everything that happened, I can understand why you didn't get a chance to shave yesterday, but I see you didn't shave this morning. You're looking a little scruffy, Mister. And why are you wearing a suit?"

After leaving the hospital late last night, Shane went with Emma and Lan to the hotel where they had booked a room. Michelle refused to leave the hospital and said she would sleep in the waiting room if she had to. Lan got a bit upset, wondering why they couldn't just go home and stay there. Emma had made it a practice not to lie to Lan, but she didn't want her to be frightened.

"There's a bad person somewhere in the city right now that we don't want to know where we are," Emma explained to Lan. "So, until the police catch this person, we'll stay in the hotel where it's safe. Plus, it means we can stay in the city so we can visit Ben in the hospital."

"Does this have to do with people coming after me again because of what I saw at my old house?" Lan asked. Shane and Emma were constantly amazed at how highly intuitive their daughter was.

"We're not sure, but we don't think so," Emma answered. "Please try not to worry. We're safe."

"I'm not worried because I know that Dad will solve the case like he always does," Lan stated confidently.

"I'm trying, Lan," Shane said, aware that his daughter's faith in him was unshakable.

Shane then left Emma and Lan at the hotel and stayed at the house for the night. Jason had insisted on getting someone from the security firm he had on retainer to stand guard outside Emma and Lan's hotel room, which Shane really appreciated.

Now, as they stood outside Ben's hospital room, Shane answered Emma's question about his appearance.

"I'm going to a funeral because a man will be there that I want to see if he recognizes me," he said. This is how I looked when I was undercover, although my beard was longer."

"Is this connected to that Finn brothers thing you got yourself tangled up in because of Doobie MacArthur?" Emma asked in a low voice so that Lan and Michelle, who were standing nearby, couldn't hear.

Before Shane could say anything, Emma said, "Don't answer that yet," and then turned to Michelle and asked, "Could you and Lan maybe go and get us some coffee from the Tim Horton's on the main floor? And a hot chocolate for Lan?"

"Donuts?" Lan asked with a hopeful look on her face.

"And donuts," Emma answered with a smile.

"Let's go, Michelle! I want chocolate dip with sprinkles!" Lan said excitedly, and she and Michelle headed down the hallway to the elevators.

When they were out of earshot, Emma said to Shane, "Okay, go."

"Jacob Finn's body has been transported back to Brantford from the prison where he was killed," Shane said. "His funeral is today. As far as I know, his brother, Troy, was never aware of who was involved in setting Jacob up for arrest on drug manufacturing and distribution charges."

"The same thing applies to MacKenzie Duncan, the drug kingpin from Hamilton, who was their main supplier," Shane continued. "However, if Troy did find out it was me, he could be responsible for everything that's happened to us and to Inspector Stabler, who arrested Jacob. Troy could be seeking revenge, blaming us for putting his brother in jail, where he was killed."

"You never should've gotten involved with the Finn brothers in the first place," Emma said, and Shane knew she was getting upset.

"Emma, I did it as a favour for Doobie and, more importantly, because Jacob Finn was putting drugs on the street that were putting people in hospital and would eventually kill someone," Shane said.

"You should've told Doobie 'no' and let the police deal with it," Emma argued. "This is a perfect example of what you can't be doing anymore. You have a young daughter to think about now."

"I realize that, Emma. You've already made your feelings known about how you want things to change," Shane said with frustration in his voice.

 "And I think you're saying a lot of this because, right now, you're scared," he added

"Don't tell me how I'm currently feeling, Shane!" Emma snapped back. "I've been reconsidering a lot of things since Adam Talino had someone beat me up and leave me on the sidewalk right near the place where I go to work every day because he wanted to get back at you."

"But Emma, you need to recognize the fact that everything that has happened, the heart sent to our house, the murder of Stabler's wife and the attempted murder of Ben, could all be connected to the little girl you brought into our lives," Shane responded angrily and then immediately regretted it.

"Don't you dare put this on Lan," Emma hissed back.

"Emma, can we please not discuss this now?" Shane pleaded. "I love you and I want to talk all of this through, but first let me find out who is threatening us."

For a moment, Emma just stood and looked Shane in the eyes, the look of anger gone from her face, replaced by a calm expression.

Shane was trying to think of something else to say when Emma suddenly embraced him, held him tightly, and whispered in his ear,

"I love you too. Yes, we'll talk later. Go and find out who's this to us. But please be careful."

After they released each other, Shane said, "Just so you know, after I attend the Finn funeral, I'm going to Milton to see Adam Talino."

Chapter Twenty Five

Saint Mary's Catholic church, a century old red brick landmark, was located, not surprisingly, on Church Street, just north of Brantford's downtown.. The street was aptly named because it was also home to Saint Mark's Anglican and the Fairview United church.

The large parking lot at the back of Saint Mary's was already full when Shane arrived and he had to drive up and down the lanes a couple of times to find a spot.

When he walked to the front of the building, he saw several small groups of people still milling about on the sidewalk, and in the area just in front of the steep concrete steps to the huge wooden front doors, which were sitting open.

Shane spotted a dark Ford sedan parked across the street from the church with a man and woman inside, and he realized that they were cops keeping an eye on who was attending Jacob Finn's funeral. They would be using a high-end digital camera with a zoom lens to take photographs of everyone attending the funeral, looking for men and women suspected of being part of the Finn's organization.

And as a bonus, they were likely hoping to get photographs of drug Czar MacKenzie Duncan and whoever arrived with him to pay their respects to Troy over his brother's death.

In addition to his drug business, Duncan was also suspected of being in partnership with several Southern Ontario bike gangs.

It was a safe bet that Duncan was, in fact, in attendance for the funeral when Shane saw a tall, muscular man in a black suit and tie, white shirt, and wearing sunglasses, standing stock still beside the front door to the church. Shane knew that Duncan's security guy would be eyeing everyone who entered the church from behind his reflective shades. When Shane passed him, he noticed the man was wearing an ear-bud, which meant there were others like him inside, all in communication with each other.

The church was packed, but Shane managed to find one space in a pew about halfway up the aisle to the altar. He looked around but didn't see anyone he knew, although he did recognize a couple of Jacob's friends that he had seen when he was in Bing's, the bar Jacob liked to hang out in. He also spotted two men sitting in separate areas of the church that he was positive were cops, either from the Brantford Police Service or from the RCMP Organized Crime Division.

Troy Finn was sitting on the first pew at the front of the church and to his right, Jacob's coffin was on a drape-covered stand. A framed picture of Jacob was sitting on the top of the coffin and the area at the front of the church was filled with huge flower arrangements.

There was a woman sitting on each side of Troy, both wearing a black dress, and although he could only see the back of their heads from his pew, Shane assumed one of the women was Troy's wife and the other, with gray hair, was his mother. Shane knew that Jacob was not married.

In the pew directly behind Troy, Shane recognized MacKenzie Duncan, who had his arm around a much younger, pretty blonde woman sitting beside him. On each side of Duncan and the woman, there were two men in black suits who could have been clones of the guy Shane saw standing at the front door of the church.

MacKenzie Duncan was a broad shouldered man who Shane knew was seventy one years of age. He had a wide face with a boxer's nose, tight curly hair and a neatly trimmed beard. The hair and beard were mostly gray now, but Shane figured that when Duncan was younger, they were fiery red.

The service took over an hour and even with the slow moving overhead fans, the church got hot and stuffy. Troy did the eulogy, which was both long and often painful to watch. He broke down into tears on several occasions and, at times, rambled as he talked about the loss of his younger brother. He said his brother was a bit wild and did have his troubles with the law, but he did not deserve to be shanked in jail.

Troy Finn was a brute of a man; his big body was trying desperately to rip open at the seams of a suit jacket that Troy probably hadn't worn since he was a good many pounds lighter. His dark hair was long, almost to his shoulders. He had a thick, bushy moustache and eyebrows that made a single line across the top of his eyes. To

Shane, he looked like a stereotypical old-school bike gang member, which he was until he opened his repair shop.

When the service ended, the family members left first, and because everyone in the church probably knew who he was, no one moved until Duncan, the woman with him, and the two bodyguards walked down the aisle.

Shane lingered in his pew as people lined up to leave. He could see that Troy was standing on the concrete landing just outside the door accepting condolences as people left. When it was Shane's turn, he shook Troy's hand and said, "I'm sorry for your loss."

"I don't believe we've met before. Were you a friend of Jacobs?" Troy asked.

"I'm a bit of a pool enthusiast and Bing's has some of the best tables in the city," Shane replied. "I got to know Jacob there. We had some good times and some very competitive games."

"Yeah, he loved hanging out at Bing's, that was his office," Troy said and then asked, "What's your name?"

"Shane," Shane said.

"Well, Shane, thanks for coming. My family appreciates it," Troy said and then shook Shane's hand again.

The entire time that he stood with Troy, Shane watched the man's face very closely for any small sign, anything at all, that indicated Finn knew who he was. There was nothing. Troy acted like Shane was a complete stranger. Sending body parts as a warning, killing

Stabler's wife, and nearly killing Ben, were the acts of someone who was sick with the desire for revenge. If it were Troy, Shane was confident that Finn wouldn't be able to keep a reaction off his face when the man he wanted revenge on was standing right in front of him.

When Shane got back to the Charger, he got a call from Sergeant Franks.

"Just as you thought, it's not Tran," Franks said. "He has an airtight alibi for both the time periods when Mary Stabler and her aide were killed, and when Chen was attacked at your house. The search of his mother's house turned up nothing incriminating or even anything that linked her to her brother's organization. She was adamant that she and her son had been estranged from her brother and were never involved in his criminal enterprises. She was, quite frankly, very convincing."

"It's not Troy Finn either," Shane said.

"And how do you know that?" Franks asked.

"I just attended his brother's funeral," Shane said. "I spoke to him and he had absolutely no idea who I was."

"Maybe that's what he wanted you to think," Franks said.

"No, I would've known," Shane said.

"You better be sure," Franks responded.

"I'm sure. Take Finn off the list," Shane said and then asked, "Have you looked into Ava Evans? Is she still on bail awaiting trial for paying her driver to kill her brother?"

"She is, and she's still wearing an ankle monitor. She hasn't been anywhere we don't know about," Franks said. "Her assets are still tied up, so unless she has money stashed somewhere we don't know about which she's using to pay someone to get revenge on you and the Inspector, it's not her. I also understand that her use of social media and her bank accounts are being monitored closely."

"Okay, we take Ava Evans off the list," Shane said. "Now I need to see Adam Talino."

"You don't need to see anyone, Daniels," Franks said, and Shane could hear the exasperation in the cop's voice. "We've been over this several times. You're a victim in this case, not an investigator. I'm not like Inspector Stabler, who tells you 'no' but then lets you go ahead and do stuff on your own anyway. You're supposed to be under protection because you're life is in danger. What part of that don't you understand? You don't go to funerals, and you don't see Adam Talino. Either go home or go to your office and stay there!"

Franks ended the call without saying anything else. Shane loosened his tie, unbuttoned the top button of his dress shirt, started the Charger and then began the drive to the Maplehurst Correctional Complex in Milton to see serial killer Adam Talino.

Chapter Twenty Six

Jason was really encouraged when he looked at the expressions on the faces of the jurors after Doctor Monique LeBlanc had taken the stand.

He had already talked for ten minutes and still hadn't completed reviewing LeBlanc's academic credentials when Evan Gregory stood up and said, "Your Honour, there's no need to waste any more of the court's time. The Prosecution accepts that Doctor LeBlanc is an expert in her field."

Jason could tell the jurors were impressed with what they heard about LeBlanc's extensive work in the field of mood disorders. And he was sure LeBlanc's credibility was enhanced by her appearance; a tall, thin, attractive, well-dressed woman in her sixties with short gray hair, frame-less glasses and an almost regal bearing.

"Doctor LeBlanc, even though you never had the opportunity to meet Olivia Tremblay prior to her death, you were given access to, and spent many hours, reviewing her file. As well, you listened to the audio tapes of her sessions with her Psychiatrist, Doctor Mason Clement. Is that correct?" Jason asked.

"Yes. It gave me a complete picture of who Olivia Tremblay was and the lifelong struggle she had with being bipolar," LeBlanc answered.

"You also spent a significant amount of time talking with my client, Noah Tremblay, about Olivia. Why was that?" Jason asked.

"Noah would have known Olivia the best. And hearing about both his experience living with her and being a witness to her battle with her mood disorder helped give me an even better insight into her condition," LeBlanc said.

"What about Olivia's parents, Jim and Charlotte Crombie?" Jason asked. "Did you speak with them? I imagine they would've provided some helpful insight into their daughter."

The Crombies had attended every minute of the trial, sitting stoically on the bench directly behind the prosecutor's table.

Charlotte had wept openly when photographs of her daughter's body, taken at the crime scene, were shown on the courtroom monitor and during the Pathologist's testimony about her daughter's autopsy.

Jim had shown no emotions, but there had been several occasions when Jason saw him staring at Noah with a look of contempt on his face. Jason knew the Crombies had always disliked Noah and were against Olivia marrying him. He had Shane talk to some of the Crombies' neighbours, who were also their friends, and they told him Charlotte had often expressed her disdain for Noah and her wish that Olivia had married Jamie Wilcott instead.

"I tried on a number of occasions to speak to the Crombies, but I'm afraid they weren't very cooperative, which I understood because they knew I was working for the lawyer of the man they believed murdered their daughter," Leblanc responded to Jason's question.

"Did you get a sense that they were in denial about the seriousness of Olivia's mood disorder?" Jason asked.

"When I tried to interview the Crombies about Olivia, her mother, Charlotte, said there was nothing to talk about, that her daughter was doing just fine with or without her medications and that Noah murdered her."

"Do you think the Crombies knew that Olivia had been diagnosed with anosognosia, the neurological condition that made her often unaware she was bipolar?" Jason asked.

"Noah told me that Olivia was very close with her parents, especially her mother, and that they doted on her," LeBlanc answered. "So, yes, I think they knew."

"I guess we know why the Crombies didn't testify, even though they were on the prosecution witness list. They undoubtedly would've been purposely untruthful about their daughter's condition and her relationship with her husband, Noah," Jason stated.

"Objection, your Honour!" Gregory exclaimed.

"Mr. Burke has just made a statement with no basis in fact and is speculating on testimony that hasn't been heard!" Gregory said. "He has, quite frankly, insulted the parents whose daughter has been murdered."

"I agree," Judge Crowder ruled, then turned his attention to Jason and said, "As an experienced solicitor, you know better, Mr. Burke. I should hold you in contempt, but I will let you off this time with a very stern warning. Next time will be different."

Crowder then looked at the jury and said, "Members of the jury, you will disregard Mr. Burke's speculation about the victim's parents."

Crowder turned back to Jason and said, "You may continue with your witness, Mr. Burke, but stick to what Doctor LeBlanc knows."

"I understand your Honour," Jason said, but he knew he had made his point with the jury that Olivia's parents were aware that their daughter wasn't taking her medication, and that made her vulnerable to major mood swings.

"Doctor LeBlanc, I had already mentioned to the jury earlier in the trial that Olivia had a neurological condition called anosognosia. Her psychiatrist, Doctor Clement, had reached that conclusion during his original sessions with Olivia. Do you agree with that diagnosis based on a review of Olivia's file and Doctor Clement's recordings?"

"I do," LeBlanc answered simply.

"Could you provide us with more information about anosognosia?"

"Certainly," Leblanc responded. "In simple terms, people with anosognosia don't recognize they have a problem or that their condition is serious. Olivia fell into the latter category. She was well aware she was bipolar, but didn't think it was a problem. Even after she had a manic episode, she would either forget it ever happened or act as if it wasn't a big issue. While it resembles denial, anosognosia is a neurological issue and not a mental defence mechanism. It's commonly seen with people who are schizophrenic and can lead to treatment non-adherence."

"In other words, someone like Olivia wouldn't take the medications she needed for her bipolar condition," Jason said.

"Exactly," LeBlanc responded. "And her awareness would come and go."

"And Doctor LeBlanc, would individuals like Olivia with bipolar disorder exhibit violent behaviour?" Jason asked.

"I want to make it clear that violent behaviour is not a defining characteristic of the disorder," LeBlanc answered. "But during manic episodes, some individuals experience heightened irritability and aggression, which can increase the likelihood of violent behaviour. That's likely what happened the night Olivia died."

"Objection," Gregory interrupted. "Doctor LeBlanc was not present the night Olivia Tremblay was murdered, so she has no first-hand information on what happened and therefore should not be allowed to speculate."

In response, Jason said, "Your Honour, the prosecution has been allowed to put forward the theory that my client killed his wife in cold blood based on inconclusive forensic evidence, an incomplete post mortem and the discredited testimony of a man who admits he was in love with the victim. So, I should be allowed to present a theory of what happened based on the findings of an acclaimed expert."

Judge Crowder hesitated for a moment while he thought it over and then said, "Objection overruled. You may continue, Mr. Burke."

But Gregory was not giving up.

"Your Honour! The defence is using a highly speculative theory about the circumstances on the night Olivia Tremblay was killed to try and raise reasonable doubt around what the evidence clearly shows happened; Olivia was stabbed in the heart by her husband."

"You can present that argument during your closing remarks, Mr. Gregory," Crowder said. "Your objection has been noted."

"Doctor LeBlanc," Jason continued, "When you held your sessions with Noah, did he talk about some of Olivia's violent outbursts?"

"Yes, he said that he had to replace glasses and dishes on several occasions because Olivia had smashed them in a rage, and on one occasion, he came home to find one of the dining room chairs had been broken after being slammed repeatedly on the floor," LeBlanc said.

"Did Noah say if he witnessed these rages?" Jason asked.

"He said he normally discovered the damage when he arrived home from work," LeBlanc answered.

"And what would Olivia's explanation be?" Jason asked.

"Your Honour, I think we're now getting into hearsay," Gregory objected.

"I agree," Crowder ruled. "Mr. Burke, if your client wants to testify to what his wife said, then he'll have to take the stand."

"Fine, your Honour, but I would ask for a little leeway on my next question because it introduces physical evidence," Jason pleaded.

"Go ahead, Mr. Burke, but carefully," Crowder said.

"Was there anything in Doctor Clement's notes or recordings that indicated Olivia discussed violent outbursts with him?" Jason asked LeBlanc.

"He asked Olivia on several occasions if she ever felt anger or rage and acted out physically and she told him she didn't have that problem," LeBlanc answered.

"So did you take that as another indication of the anosognosia on Olivia's part?" Jason asked.

"Yes," LeBlanc answered simply.

"Did Noah mention to you anything about public outbursts by Olivia?" Jason asked.

"On at least one occasion in a grocery store," LeBlanc said.

Jason knew Gregory was going to object again on the grounds of hearsay, so he quickly said, "Your Honour, I would now like to show the jury defence exhibit D-03."

Gregory was on his feet and was going to say something, but Judge Crowder waved with his hand to indicate that the Prosecutor should sit down and then said, "You may proceed, Mr. Burke."

Jason nodded at the Clerk, who was sitting in front of a laptop at a desk directly below the Judge's bench, and a video came up on the large monitor.

It was black and white, and grainy. It was shot from an overhead camera facing an aisle in what was obviously a grocery store because of the shelves of products on each side. It showed a young man and woman standing in the aisle. He's holding the handle of a shopping cart, which is about half full of groceries, and the woman is in front of the cart, waving her arms wildly. It appears that she's yelling something, but the surveillance system didn't capture audio.

The man walks around to the side of the cart and holds up his hands in an attempt to calm the woman down. She stops yelling but walks to a shelf and uses one arm to angrily sweep boxes of cereal onto the floor.

She then stomps off in the direction of the camera, and at that point, the video freezes. While the quality of the recording had made it difficult to make out the faces of the couple when they were at their shopping cart, the woman was now much closer to the camera. It was Olivia Tremblay. The video resumed playing and then stopped again when the man came into view. Noah Tremblay.

"Doctor LeBlanc, does this video, captured by a supermarket surveillance system three months before Olivia's death, provide proof of your theory that Olivia did have fits of rage as part of her bipolar condition?" Jason asked.

"Yes, it does," LeBlanc said.

"So it's possible that, in a fit of rage, Olivia attacked her husband with a knife on the night she died, correct, Doctor?" Jason asked.

"Objection, your Honour!" Gregory exclaimed. "Speculation!"

"Sustained," Judge Crowder said. "Move on, Mr. Burke."

"I have finished questioning this witness," Jason said, pleased with the way it went. He felt he had introduced more reasonable doubt about the prosecution's theory that Noah murdered his wife.

"Do you have questions for Doctor LeBlanc, Mr. Gregory?" Judge Crowder asked the prosecutor.

"I most certainly do, your Honour," Gregory said as he jumped to his feet and walked with determination to the area in front of the witness box.

"Doctor LeBlanc, I would like you to make something very clear to the jury because both you and my colleague, Mr. Burke, engaged in speculation and innuendo about Olivia Tremblay's bipolar disorder. You weren't there, so you have no idea what happened the night Olivia was murdered, correct?"

"Yes, that's correct," LeBlanc answered.

"Olivia's psychiatrist, Doctor Mason Clement, who actually knew her, testified that although she was sometimes in denial, Olivia was taking her meds most of the time and was basically well adjusted," Gregory said. "I noticed you didn't mention that when you were testifying about your review of Doctor Clement's notes and tapes.

Were you perhaps paid to come here and discredit Doctor Clement's treatment of Olivia?"

"Objection, your Honour," Jason said as he stood up at his desk. "Mr. Gregory has made an accusation with no basis in fact and is trying to impugn a highly regarded medical professional."

"Gentlemen, please approach the bench," Judge Crowder said.

After Jason and Gregory were standing in front of him, Crowder leaned forward and spoke in a quiet voice so he wouldn't be heard elsewhere in the courtroom.

"Gentlemen, I believe I've been very lenient since I took over the trial in terms of how you each have approached the questioning of witnesses. I have done this to allow the trial to continue in a timely manner after the disruption caused by the tragic death of Justice Wendal, and to avoid getting bogged down by procedural disputes. But both of you have taken advantage of this in a most egregious manner, acting at times as if you're in an episode of 'Law and Order' where you can toss out your theories to the jury and assume it's okay because you tacked a question on at the end."

"That is not proper decorum in a Canadian court of law and I blame myself for allowing it to happen," Crowder said. "You've both been guilty of purposely getting something on the record you hope can be a basis for an appeal if the jury doesn't rule in your favour. The obvious animosity between you two has prevented a compromise, which I believe would have served justice in this tragic case and avoided the continuation of the trial after Justice Wendal's untimely death. I have already warned Mr. Burke about contempt of court, and now, Mr. Gregory, I'm issuing you the same warning. You may resume cross-examining Doctor LeBlanc, but tread carefully.

"Yes, your Honour," Gregory said.

"You can both step back now," Crowder said, and Jason could tell from the expression on the Judge's face that Crowder had been struggling to keep his anger under control. But he also knew the Judge was admonishing himself for allowing him and Gregory to get away with statements they made for the benefit of the jury without a basis in fact or without corroboration from a witness.

Jason returned to his table and Gregory went back to stand in front of the witness box. The sound of indistinguishable chatter among the spectators echoed through the courtroom, no doubt everyone wondering what the Judge was telling the lawyers and why it was taking so long. Crowder tapped his gavel once and the courtroom quickly quieted.

"Doctor LeBlanc, you were paid by the defence to review Olivia's file, interview the defendant and testify here today. Is that correct?" Gregory asked.

"Yes, I was paid for my consultation and analysis, and to testify about my findings," LeBlanc said.

"You do that a lot, don't you? Testify at trials on behalf of the defence," Gregory asked.

"I would not categorize it as a lot," LeBlanc answered, and Jason was glad to hear that the psychiatrist did not change from her calm, authoritative demeanour as Gregory tried to get a defensive reaction from her.

"I'm already quite busy with lecturing, research and my own private practice," LeBlanc added.

"But I see you made time to testify at four separate trials over the past year," Gregory said. "So wouldn't it be fair for the jury to consider you as basically a professional expert witness?"

"No, that would not be fair," LeBlanc answered flatly.

"I have no further questions, your Honour," Gregory announced.

Judge Crowder said to the psychiatrist, "Thank you, Doctor LeBlanc, you may step down."

He then turned to Jason and said, "You may call your next witness, Mister Burke."

"Your Honour, the defence calls Noah Tremblay," Jason responded.

Chapter Twenty Seven

The Maplehurst Correctional Complex is a huge, sprawling facility surrounded by high fencing topped with razor wire and sits on over one hundred acres of property in Milton.

It holds fifteen hundred prisoners and employs over eight hundred people. It's a combined security detention centre for remanded prisoners who are awaiting court appearances, and both a medium and maximum correctional centre for offenders sentenced to less than two years.

After Shane found a spot for the Charger in the visitor's parking lot, he called Emma to check on Ben. He knew that she, Lan and Michelle were currently at the hospital.

"He's still not awake, but that's not unusual considering he's heavily sedated," Emma said. "Doctor Khan is operating this morning, but another very good surgeon I work with, Doctor Richardson, was just in and checked Ben over carefully. He says there's no sign of infection, so far, and Ben's vital signs remain stable."

"That's good news, but I hope Ben wakes up soon," Shane said.

"I know from experience that we can't be anxious when it comes to post-operative patients who have undergone extensive procedures," Emma said. "Ben will wake up when he's ready."

After telling Emma he would stop at the hospital when he got back to Brantford and saying goodbye to her, Shane entered Maplehurst through the visitor's door, gave his name to the Corrections Officer at the reception desk and went through the detailed identification process required to visit an inmate.

Shane knew before he talked to Sergeant Franks on the phone after the Finn funeral that Franks would be dead set against him going to see Adam Talino.

But Shane had already called his old friend, Police Chief Charlie Oak, and asked him to smooth the way with the Warden at Maplehurst so Shane could have a face-to-face meeting with Talino and not in a booth with a plexiglass shield between them. Oak did ask Shane if Franks was going to be okay with him meeting with Talino. Shane told the Chief that Franks didn't want him doing anything other than providing a list of possible suspects, but he was not going to just sit at his desk and do nothing when Emma and Lan may be in danger, and Ben was almost killed.

"Sergeant Franks is not going to be happy when he finds out you went to see Talino and you went over his head to get help to do it," Oak had said to Shane. "And I don't blame him. You know that you're an irritating lone wolf, Shane. Mark Stabler has complained to me about that so many times I've lost count. The only reason it's tolerated is because you've been successful in solving some murders, including some that may never have been cleared. I will smooth things over with Franks, but be aware I'm not very happy I have to do that, so you'd better make this visit with Talino worthwhile."

"Chief, I know Talino better than anyone else," Shane told Oaks. "I chased this guy when no one else believed he was a serial killer of young, vulnerable women. Everyone saw him as this handsome, charming, rich entrepreneur and philanthropist. But I knew there was something off about the guy the first time I met him. He's a narcissistic psychopath. When I ask him if he's behind a plot against me and Stabler involving sending us body parts, having Stabler's wife murdered, and the attempt on Ben's life, his ego will not allow him to hide his involvement. He won't be able to help himself. I will see it all over his face."

"But his hate for you because you caught him, and his ego, could have him taking credit for what's happened even if he's not behind it," Oak told Shane.

"I'm confident that when I talk to Talino and look at him in the face, I'll know if he's involved," Shane said to Oak. "I might lie about a few things and if Talino agrees with them, it'll confirm it's not him."

Shane and ten other people, all women, who had been milling about the reception area at Maplehurst, were escorted by a Corrections Officer down a long hallway and into the inmate visiting area; a large, square, brightly lit room with painted concrete block walls. There were small round metal tables with two metal chairs on each side, all bolted to the floor. There were also much larger tables with a curved bench on each side to accommodate families.

The women who entered the room with Shane scattered to various tables where prisoners were already sitting and waiting for them. Shane found an open table, sat and waited.

After about ten minutes, a side door opened and Adam Talino was brought in by a Corrections Officer. Talino was in an oversized orange jumpsuit with a white t-shirt visible through the open top buttons and was wearing pull-on flat-bottom sneakers. He was handcuffed in front and would remain that way while talking to Shane. It was something the Warden had insisted on when he agreed to an open visit, plus a Corrections Officer would be posted closely by the table. Talino had not been deemed as dangerous, but he was a high-profile inmate accused of multiple murders and the Warden would be cognizant of public perception.

Shane watched Talino as he approached the table. He was rail thin, almost to the point of looking emaciated. This surprised Shane since he knew that Talino had been a dedicated member of a local fitness club where he did a lot of bodybuilding. He assumed Talino would have kept up some kind of physical routine in jail. Or it may be that Talino couldn't, or wouldn't, eat the food they served. Talino had let his dark hair grow down to his shoulders and he had grown a beard almost to the middle of his chest.

Talino sat down across from Shane and said, "Shane Daniels. I was quite intrigued when I was asked if I would meet with you.

I thought, what would Daniels want when he's already screwed me? I said 'yes' right away."

While he looked pale and sickly, Shane noted that one thing about Talino had not changed; his eyes were clear and focused, and Shane saw the same malevolence in them that he saw the first time they met.

"You look stupid with the long hair and beard, Talino," Shane said. "You look like Charles Manson, but without the swastika tattoo on your forehead or, better yet, Grigori Rasputin, if you know who that is."

"The crazy mystic who befriended and influenced the royal family just before the Russian revolution," Talino said. "I studied history, same as you, Daniels."

"Is this look of yours part of what I'm hearing about you going with a not-guilty by reason of insanity defence?" Shane asked. "Because success in doing that in a multiple murder case is extremely rare in this country, Talino, so if you're hoping to spend your sentence in a cushy psychiatric facility, it's not going to happen. You're going to do hard time in a federal prison where you will have to watch your back every minute of every day."

"You seem to forget, Daniels, that I still have a lot of resources at my disposal," Talino said with a smirk on his face. "They're trying to seize my assets, but none of them were acquired through illegal means. I'm still able to get the best defence team money can buy."

"But when they complete the psych evaluation, experts will testify that you knew exactly what you were doing when you murdered those women," Shane shot back. "That you carefully planned and carried out each one, and even wore a disguise when you were doing it."

"Your high-priced boss, Jason Burke, uses paid expert witnesses all the time," Talino responded. "And my lawyers will have no problem finding psychiatrists willing to say I have a split personality or maybe that I went into mental fugues, unaware of what I was doing and had no memory of it afterward. Maybe they can blame it on my dear, departed mother, who was cold and distant, and on my uncaring, abusive father. I'm sure they'll come up with something."

Talino then leaned forward in his chair, put his handcuffed hands on the table and said, "You know, Daniels, you have to realize that I still have a lot of influential friends in Brantford who do not believe I'm a murderer. They remember all of the good things I've done for the city and, more importantly,they still appreciate the money I put in their pockets, especially the politicians. They believe I'm being framed by an overzealous private investigator with the help of corrupt cops who needed a scapegoat because they couldn't solve the murders themselves. An obsessed investigator, that would be you, Daniels, fixated on ruining the life of a very successful man."

"I look forward to testifying against you, Talino, and telling them everything I know about you," Shane said with contempt in his voice.

"I think my defence team will tear you apart on the stand," Talino countered and then, after leaning back in his chair, asked, "But this discussion about my trial is not the reason you're here today, is it? I heard someone sent you a body part. I was also told that someone murdered Inspector Mark Stabler's wife and another woman in his house, and stabbed a friend of yours to death. I would feel bad for Stabler but I can't, because he was the stooge cop you used to have me arrested."

"For a guy in a jail a long way from Brantford, you're well informed, Talino, although you're wrong about my friend. He's alive," Shane said.

"As I said, I still have a lot of good contacts in the city, maybe even some in the Police Service, you never know," Talino said, the smirk returning to his face.

He leaned forward, hands on the table again, and said, "You're here because you want to know if I'm behind the body parts and the murders. That from here, behind bars, I hired someone to do these things as my revenge on you and a crooked cop."

"Did you, Talino? Hire someone to do these things?" Shane asked as he studied Talino's face very closely.

"Sadly, no," Talino answered, but the smirk remained on his face. "But I am enjoying the situation from afar."

Shane believed him.

He knew that Talino's ego was such that if he was involved in any way, his face, his eyes or his body language would give him away. He wouldn't be able to help himself; he would be like a little kid with a secret he was desperate to tell someone. Talino was a psychopath who could be charming and believable, which is how he became a successful businessman and a popular figure in Brantford.

But in reality, he didn't care about anyone but himself. If he were involved in what was happening, Talino's self-satisfaction would show involuntarily and Shane would see it; a change in facial expression, such as a slight movement of Talino's eyebrows or lips. His eyes would look away and back quickly or lose focus, for just a second, on Shane's face. Shane had seen these things in previous encounters with Talino when he knew the killer was lying, but not this time.

"Goodbye, Talino. I look forward to you rotting in prison," Shane said, nodded at the nearby Corrections Officer to indicate he was finished, and then stood up and started walking for the exit.

"That's it, Daniels!?" Talino called out. "Shouldn't you be asking more questions about what I know? Aren't you just a little bit curious about who I know inside the Brantford Police? Maybe my network of contacts can get me some information I can share with you. Maybe I'm lying and I'm actually behind what's happening to you and Stabler! You're walking away now, Daniels, but I know you'll be back!"

Shane ignored Talino and made his way out of the building and back to the Charger. He had to fight not to show it to Talino, but talking to the serial killer made Shane nauseous and anger burned at the back of his mind; anger that had made him want to go across the table and choke the life out of Talino.

Shane took some deep breaths to calm himself and took a long drink from a bottle of water he had on the console beside him. His phone was on a hands-free cradle attached to the dashboard and he opened it to check for messages. There was a voice message from Chioma Abiola: "Shane, I assume you're still at Maplehurst. You need to get back to the office as soon as you can. I know who's behind everything! I don't want to explain on the phone. Just get back here!"

Chapter Twenty Eight

Jason's colleague, Susan Cartright, had suggested she purchase a better fitting, more expensive suit for Noah Tremblay to wear during his testimony. However, Jason decided that Noah should take the stand looking like the same thin, sickly man in ill-fitting clothes who has been sitting beside him the entire trial.

Although they would've been able to see Noah when he was sitting beside him at the defence table, Jason waited for a moment before beginning his questioning so the jurors could get a good look at Noah as he sat in the witness box. People, by nature, made quick judgments about other people just based on their appearance. Jason wanted to give the jurors enough time to stare at Noah. He hoped they saw a broken man.

After positioning himself directly in front of the witness box, Jason began his crucial questioning of a man who faced the possibility of spending at least the next twenty five years of his life in prison.

"Noah, I think we should get to the most important question right off the top," Jason said. "Did you intentionally kill your wife?"

"No, I did not. I loved Olivia," Noah answered. His voice was weak and raspy, sounding as if he were just recovering from laryngitis. Jason considered it a good thing because it added to the impression he was trying to give the jury that Noah was not a well man, even a year later, as a result of his wife's death.

"Can you tell us how you met Olivia and eventually married?" Jason asked.

"It was just like Jamie…Jamie Wilcott said when he testified," Noah said. "He and Olivia were going out and I was friends with both of them. But the more time we spent together, the more Olivia and I realized that we were really attracted to each other. I know Jamie was really hurt when Olivia broke up with him so she could be with me, but we had fallen in love and wanted to get married."

"Tell us about Olivia," Jason said.

"She was a beautiful, passionate woman, and very smart," Noah said. "I know that everyone here is getting the impression that everything in our marriage was bad because of Olivia's mood disorder, but it wasn't like that. We had a normal life for long, long periods of time. We worked, did projects around the house together, and spent time with our friends."

"But your marriage was not without its troubles," Jason said.

"I have a bit of a temper, I admit that, and Olivia was diagnosed as bipolar, although she was constantly insisting that it wasn't true, that it was something her parents came up with, and that she was just a moody person," Noah said. "But Olivia's highs and lows could be extreme. When she was happy, she would bounce around, full of energy, singing along with songs on Alexa, making big plans for our future and dreaming up designs for the interior of the house. When she was like that, we were so happy."

"But then she would crash," Noah said with sadness in his voice. "And it was like she was a completely different person. I didn't know how to act in front of her. She would say things, sometimes very hurtful things, and I would get angry and we would argue. Then, suddenly, she would be back to herself again and act as if nothing had happened. It could be confusing and, sometimes, I admit, very frustrating for me."

"Was the frustration caused by the fact that Olivia was in denial about the extent of her mood disorder?" Jason asked.

"For sure," Noah answered. "It was a constant battle to get her to stay on her medications. Sometimes, I would get home from work and she'd be running around the kitchen, all excited about preparing some recipe she saw on Facebook. And then there would be times I would find her curled up on our bed where she'd been the whole day, in a deep depression."

"You had to be vigilant when Olivia was in her dark moods, didn't you?" Jason asked. "You had to watch for risky behaviour, correct?"

Noah hesitated before he answered, looked down at his hands, and sadness was obvious on his face.

When he looked up again, he said, "That's true. There was a time when she decided to take up smoking because she believed it would calm her nerves. Next thing I know, she's chain smoking, going through two packs a day. I managed to convince her it was going to kill her, and with the help of Doctor Clement, we got her back on her meds. It took a long time, but she eventually quit smoking."

"I always had to make sure there was no booze in the house if I wasn't going to be there," Noah continued, "If I didn't, and Olivia got depressed, she would drink whatever she got her hands on until she passed out."

"That's a lie and you know it! You're full of shit!" someone in the courtroom suddenly yelled.

Jason turned around and saw Olivia's mother, Charlotte, standing up in the gallery, her face red and twisted in anger.

"She was not like that! You're a liar!" she screamed.

Judge Crowder banged his gavel hard and exclaimed, "Mrs. Crombie, sit down and be quiet! You're not allowed to speak! One more interruption, of any kind, and I will have you charged with contempt and barred from this courtroom for the rest of the trial! Do you understand!?"

Charlotte didn't respond to the Judge's demand to sit down. Instead, she remained standing and stared angrily at Noah, but he looked away and didn't make eye contact. Her husband, Jim, finally grabbed Charlotte's arm and pulled her back down to her seat.

"A warning to everyone, disruptions will not be tolerated," Crowder expressed angrily. He turned to face the jury and said, "Members of the jury, you will ignore the outburst from the woman in the gallery which has just occurred. Your decision in this case will be based solely on evidence and witness testimony, not on the emotional opinion from one of the victim's parents. Her opinion has no bearing on the outcome of your deliberations."

Crowder then turned to Jason and asked, "Would you like a brief recess before you resume your questioning, Mr. Burke?"

Jason was deeply concerned about what had just happened. Was this just a spontaneous, emotional reaction from a grieving mother who was hearing things about her daughter that perhaps she'd been in denial about? Or, was it possible that Mrs. Crombie intentionally disrupted Noah's testimony in an attempt to turn the jury against her hated son-in-law?

Jason had to make a quick decision. Should he ask the Judge to declare a mistrial because the outburst from the victim's mother has prejudiced the jury? If it were granted, would a new trial proceed any differently with a different jury? Jason had spent hours with Noah preparing him for his testimony and he was convinced Noah would come across to this jury as sincere and believable. Would Noah be the same man on the witness stand if he spent another year in jail waiting for a new trial?

"Mr. Burke? How do you wish to proceed?" Judge Crowder asked, interrupting Jason's contemplation.

Jason glanced quickly over his shoulder and noted that Jim and Charlotte Crombie had, at least for now, left the courtroom. He then looked at Noah, who appeared to be calm after the accusation was screamed at him by his former mother-in-law.

"We will continue, your Honour," Jason told Crowder.

"Very well," Crowder responded.

"Noah, we know from previous testimony that Olivia's anger could turn to rage and she would be violently destructive," Jason said and then asked, "How bad would it get?"

"Our dishes and glassware were her favourite targets when she flew into a rage," Noah responded. "I don't know how many times I came home and found the kitchen floor covered in broken plates and glasses. She would go into the living room and grab framed photographs or ceramic figurines and smash them against the walls. One time, she got so enraged over how she looked that she went into the garage, got a hammer, and smashed every mirror in the house. It was a nightmare sometimes."

"Noah, the Prosecutor is going to ask you a lot of questions about your previous assault conviction for a fight in a bar, the domestic assault charge laid against you, and the domestic disturbance calls to your house," Jason said. "So, let's deal with them right now, starting with the assault charge."

"I was nineteen when that happened. I made a stupid mistake!" Noah said, showing the first big burst of emotion since he took the stand. "I was with some buddies in a bar and we had a lot to drink. Some guy who was in my English class in high school was mouthing off about stuff and then he made a crude remark about the girl I was dating at the time, so I punched him in the face. He fell backwards, hit his head on the floor and was knocked unconscious. They had to call an ambulance, and that brought the cops."

"The police were called to your house on several occasions because of domestic disturbance complaints by neighbours," Jason stated.

"Yes. When Olivia got angry and flew into one of her rages, the neighbours could hear her screaming, the sound of things getting smashed, and us arguing. So, they would call the cops," Noah said. "Usually, by the time the cops came to our door, Olivia had calmed down. I would explain the situation and most of the officers were understanding. They would just issue us a warning and advise us to get some help."

"However, on one of those calls, you were arrested and charged. What happened?" Jason asked.

"I really don't even remember what we were arguing about or what set Olivia off," Noah responded. "At one point, Olivia had picked up our framed wedding photo and was going to smash it. I yelled at her to stop, but she raised it over her head and was going to slam it to the floor. I was angry, and I admit that I hit her, not hard, but I did and I'm ashamed of myself for doing that."

Noah paused briefly, took a deep breath, and then said, "When the cops arrived, Olivia had calmed down and didn't want anything to happen to me, but her face was bruised. The cops said they had no choice but to arrest me." Noah said.

"Noah, I need you to give this courtroom an honest answer," Jason said, deliberately using a serious tone. "Did you get angry and hit Olivia on other occasions?"

"Never! It was just that one time!" Noah answered emotionally. "I was tired from work that day. I came home and found the kitchen in shambles. Olivia had gone into a rage over something and she had smashed plates and glasses. She had even managed to break one of the kitchen chairs. I was fed up with Olivia not taking her meds. I lost my patience with her and my temper. I felt so bad about it afterward that I was depressed for days."

"About a week before her death, Olivia informed you that she was pregnant. How did you react to that news?" Jason asked.

"I admit that I was angry and upset when she told me," Noah said. "Olivia wanted to have kids and we had talked about it countless times. But the discussions never ended well because Olivia believed she'd be a great mother and would have no problem handling a baby. But I was worried about what would happen if she had one of her dark days and I was at work. I wouldn't be there to help out. I told her I definitely wanted to have kids, but not until she started to honestly understand that she had a serious bipolar condition and needed to be consistently on her meds."

"I understand that you and Olivia did, in fact, at one point talk to your physician about having children?" Jason asked.

"We did," Noah responded. "He said it was crucial that we plan very carefully, with the help of Olivia's psychiatrist and obstetrician, in order to manage the possible risks. He said the meds could have an impact on the fetus and that there would be a higher likelihood of Olivia having mood episodes, especially after the baby was born."

"So you didn't think it was a good idea?" Jason asked.

"Not when she was in denial all the time about the extent of her mood disorder," Noah stated.

"But she got pregnant anyway," Jason said.

"She was taking birth control pills and then stopped, on purpose, and didn't tell me," Noah responded.

"Noah, I want you to tell this court, in your own words, what happened the night Olivia was killed," Jason said.

Noah looked down at his hands and Jason saw his client's shoulders go up and down as Noah took some deep breaths before he started talking.

"It was the Saturday night of the long weekend in August. Olivia had a shift at the grocery store, which she was happy about because they hadn't been giving her a lot of hours. She was in such a good mood, but not manic like she got sometimes. I thought it would be a good time to see if we could have a calm discussion about her pregnancy.

"Noah, you are aware there are people in this courtroom who will be upset, maybe even angry to hear it, but were you planning to ask Olivia to consider having the pregnancy terminated?" Jason asked.

"Yes, and if I couldn't get her to consider that, then I needed to convince her to talk to her psychiatrist, Doctor Clement, about the pregnancy," Noah said. "I had already talked to the Doctor on my own and told him that Olivia had purposely gotten pregnant, and I was, quite honestly, afraid of what would happen if she carried through with it. He said he was also concerned because of Olivia's denial about the severity of her mood disorder."

"So what happened when you tried to have this calm discussion with Olivia?" Jason asked.

"We had a nice meal, and after dinner I said I was going to have a mixed drink. I asked her if I could get her a Coke, and if we could talk before we started watching TV," Noah answered.

Jason interrupted before Noah could go any further. "Noah, this is again going to upset some people in this courtroom, but did you put rum in Olivia's Coke?" he asked.

"I made a careless, stupid mistake, I admit that," Noah answered emotionally. "But, I swear, it was just a small amount, not even a shot glass full! I thought it would help relax Olivia for what I knew was going to be a tough discussion about her pregnancy. I know how it sounds now, me giving alcohol to a pregnant woman. It was wrong, but at the time, I was desperately looking for a way to keep Olivia calm."

"Noah, the toxicology report says Olivia had a lot more than just the small amount of alcohol you said you gave her," Jason stated. "Did you mix her more than just one drink?"

"Absolutely, not!" Noah answered firmly.

Jason noted that Noah's voice was getting a lot stronger as he tried to defend his actions.

"So, tell us how you think she ended up with more alcohol in her system and what happened next that night," Jason said.

"We started talking about her being pregnant and I told her how disappointed I was that she did it without discussing it with me," Noah said. "I told her we needed to talk to our personal physician and Doctor Clement about our options. I could see that Olivia was getting upset. She asked me, 'Options? What Options are you talking about?', and before I could answer, she said she needed more Coke, and got up and went into the kitchen. She was in there a long time, so I called out and asked if she was okay. I think she was in there drinking right out of the bottle of rum.

"What happened when she came back from the kitchen?" Jason asked.

"When she returned, I said we needed to set up an appointment with the Doctor right away," Noah said. "She went from a calm look on her face to anger within seconds. She started screaming that I didn't care about her feelings, that I didn't love her, that I wanted to kill her baby, and that made me a murderer. She went back into the kitchen. I thought, okay, she's going to break a bunch of plates and glasses like she's done before, so I'll just stay in the living room and let her blow off some steam. She'll eventually calm down as she always does."

"But she didn't do that, did she?" Jason asked.

"No. She suddenly came out of the kitchen carrying one of our big knives," Noah continued, his voice now trembling.

"She had the knife over her head and was going to plunge it down into me, but I was able to grab her wrist. She was screaming, 'You want to kill my baby!' over and over, and I was yelling, 'No, no, that's not true!' and 'Stop, Olivia, please stop!'."

"I was using my left hand to hold her wrist so she couldn't use the knife, and I put my right hand on the side of her face, hoping that might help calm her down. I kept saying, 'Stop, Olivia! It's not true!', but she didn't stop screaming and started beating on my chest with her left fist."

"I was in a panic," Noah said. "I didn't know what to do. She had never been this out of control before, never! She started screaming, 'I hate you'. She was using all of her strength to hit me with her left fist and it caused me to loosen my hold on her right wrist. She got the knife free from my grip and tried to stab me again. This time, I used both hands and managed to get the knife away from her."

By this time in his story, Noah had tears running down his face and had lowered his voice to just above a whisper, but could still be heard in the courtroom because of the microphone attached to the railing in front of him. For years, courtrooms in Ontario, particularly those in centuries-old courthouses, had notoriously bad acoustics, but eventually all were outfitted with sound systems.

"I got so angry!" Noah continued in an emotional voice. "She wouldn't stop. I poked the knife at her to get her to back away, but instead she charged right up against me, and the knife went deep into her body. She stopped screaming, went limp, and just dropped to the floor. I yelled her name, got down on the floor beside her, but she wasn't breathing. Her eyes were wide open. There was blood all over her chest. I…I…I didn't know what to do to help her! I called 911."

Noah put his hands over his face and moaned, "I didn't mean to kill her."

The courtroom was completely silent. Jason noted the emotions on the faces of many of the jurors, some clearly showing sympathy.

"Does your client need a few minutes to compose himself?" Judge Crowder asked Jason, but before he could answer, Noah took his hands away from his face, used them to wipe away his tears and said, "No, I'm fine, I just want to get this over with."

"Very well, proceed, Mr. Burke," Crowder said.

"Noah, do you remember what you said to the two police officers when they arrived at your house?" Jason asked.

"Not exactly, I was in a complete panic," Noah answered.

"The officers claim you said, 'I did it, I killed my wife'," Jason said.

"I don't remember saying that," Noah said. "I do remember trying to tell them I didn't mean to kill Olivia."

"Noah, I know that you're aware that since the beginning of this trial, you've been under a suicide watch when you're in your holding cell," Jason said. "I need you to be honest with me. Have you been having suicidal thoughts?"

Noah hesitated before he said anything, and, to Jason, that was as good as him saying yes to the jury.

"I've spent the past year in a daze and, yes, in a deep depression over what happened," Noah said softly. "I was prescribed antidepressants to take, but I'm not sure how much they helped. The closer I got to the start of my trial, all I could think about was how I would have to listen to people testify about what I did to Olivia and about our baby growing inside her. I've been in a very dark place and I'm not sure if I can live with myself."

"In spite of her denial of the severity of her bipolar condition and her angry outbursts, you loved Olivia," Jason said.

"Very much," Noah said in a firm voice.

"And you didn't mean to kill her?" Jason asked.

"No, never," Noah replied.

"Your Honour, I have completed questioning my witness," Jason said to Judge Crowder.

"Mr. Gregory, it's your witness if you have questions," Crowder said to the Prosecutor.

"Thank you, your Honour, I most certainly do," Gregory said as he quickly stood up, walked around from behind his table and stood in front of Noah in the witness box.

"Mr. Tremblay, are you expecting this jury to believe that you only wanted to jab your wife to get her to back off, but the knife went deep into her body, piercing her heart, because she pushed against you?"

"That's what happened," Noah answered in a flat voice.

"So you claim," Gregory responded.

"Objection, your Honour," Jason said as he stood up. "I didn't hear a question from Mr. Gregory, only a derogatory comment to my client."

"Objection sustained," Judge Crowder ruled. "Stick with questions for the witness, Mr. Gregory.

"Yes, your Honour," Gregory said and then turned back to face Noah.

"You admit that you got angry because your wife wouldn't stop screaming, wouldn't stop accusing you of trying to kill her baby," Gregory said forcefully. "Isn't it more likely that in a rage, you deliberately plunged the knife into her so she would stop?"

"No, that's not true!" Noah responded. "I admit that I got angry, but all I was trying to do was to prevent Olivia from stabbing me with the knife and to get her to calm down. I knew she was in a rage because that's what happened with her sometimes, with the type of bipolar disorder she had. It wasn't her fault. It was all my fault. I realized that I shouldn't have used the word 'options' when I was talking about her pregnancy."

"But before the night she died, you were already very angry about Olivia getting pregnant, weren't you? You even told your friend, Jamie Wilcott, during a night of drinking, about being angry," Gregory said in an accusatory tone.

"I was upset, yes," Noah said. "Olivia should've discussed it with me first before she stopped taking birth control."

"But it wasn't just a matter of you being upset, was it, Mr. Tremblay? It was pure anger," Gregory shot back. "And you have a propensity to violence, isn't that correct? You beat up a guy in a bar, and you had previously assaulted your wife."

"I was young and drunk when I punched that guy in the bar, and the thing with Olivia was a one-time thing that I deeply regret," Noah said.

"Mr. Tremblay, forensically, your story about what happened doesn't hold water," Gregory said. "You claim your wife assaulted you with a knife, but when you were arrested, you had no defensive wounds. You say you fought off and disarmed your wife, but she didn't have a mark on her, other than a small discoloration on her wrist that your lawyer claims is a bruise, but an expert pathologist thinks otherwise. How do you explain all of that?"

"I just know what happened," Noah said softly and bowed his head.

"I think the jury knows what happened, and it's not what you claim, Mr. Tremblay. I think you plied your pregnant wife with alcohol and deliberately stabbed her," Gregory said with disgust in his voice.

"Objection!" Jason exclaimed, but before Judge Crowder could react, Gregory said, "I'm finished with this witness," and walked back to his table.

"Mr. Burke?" Crowder asked.

Jason stood up and said, "The defence rests, your Honour."

"Very well," Crowder said. "Mr. Tremblay will be taken back into custody. We will hear closing arguments starting tomorrow morning. Court adjourned."

Crowder left the bench and exited the courtroom through a side door while the jury was led out through a separate exit by a court officer. The spectators then started shuffling out the double doors at the back of the room.

Jason gestured to the two officers with the now handcuffed Noah to bring him over to his table so he could speak to him briefly.

When Noah got there, Jason put his hand on his client's arm and said, "I know Gregory's cross-examination was tough, but you did very well, Noah."

"It doesn't really matter. I know how it looks to the jury," Noah said, his head down, not making eye contact with Jason.

"Try and get some rest," Jason said.

As one officer led Noah away, Jason said to the other officer who was trailing behind, "Please keep an eye on him."

Chapter Twenty Nine

As the hours went by, Emma, Michelle and Lan remained in the family waiting room on the surgical floor of the Brantford General Hospital waiting for Ben to wake up from his surgery.

They had gone together several times to look through the window into Ben's room, where he remained unconscious, but they had been assured by Doctor Khan that all of Ben's vital signs were good and there was no sign of infection in his most recent blood tests.

"The only reason he's not awake yet is because it's his body's way of helping him heal," Doctor Khan had told them. Emma appreciated Khan's attempt to keep them confident.

Michelle, who Emma knew was trying hard to be brave and remain calm, looked exhausted. There were dark circles under her eyes and her complexion was even paler than normal. She was wearing no makeup, something she was normally quite particular about, and on several occasions, Emma had noticed tears trickling down Michelle's cheeks.

Before they had left the hotel for their long wait at the hospital, Lan had made a fuss about not being allowed to sleep in her own room and why she couldn't go back to her art camp now that they were home from Port Elgin. Emma felt bad for her, but was proud of how Lan quietly accepted Emma's explanation that they were still in danger and needed to stay together, for now.

Even after waiting so many hours at the hospital, Lan appeared to be content working on a drawing in one of her smaller sketch books, which she had sitting on her lap.

Both Emma and Michelle had been passing the time playing games and scrolling through social media sites on their phones, but Emma found she could only do that for so long before she got restless. So, instead, she paced up and down the hall, stopping to chat with some of the nurses she normally worked with in the surgical unit.

She was just about to return to the waiting room from one of her walks when her phone rang. The caller ID said it was Charlene Anderson, the psychiatrist Emma worked with, counselling new amputees who were struggling with living without a limb.

Emma and Doctor Anderson had become good friends. She felt she owed Charlene a lot because after Emma left the Canadian Forces without her left leg from the knee down, the result of an accident while clearing an old mine field, it was Charlene who helped her put her life back together. There was a long period of time when Emma was depressed about the loss of her leg, but thanks to Charlene's counselling, Emma eventually got her act together and resumed her career as a nurse.

Emma actually entered the Canadian Forces as a trained nurse and had every intention of making it her career, but after she completed basic training, she decided that spending hours practicing battlefield triage on fellow soldiers pretending to be wounded wasn't enough to fulfill her desire for danger and excitement. She wanted the same kind of adrenaline rush she got when she was under weapons fire during live round exercises. She successfully applied for a transfer to the bomb disposal unit, knowing it would eventually lead to an overseas deployment. After six months of intensive training, that's exactly what happened.

She was asking Shane to stop, but Emma was more than familiar with a penchant for getting too deeply involved in cases. She was exactly the same way, and that's why she made the decision to stop seeing clients at Doctor Anderson's practice.

Recently, she counselled a young woman, a double amputee, who Emma suspected was being physically abused by her husband. The woman denied it, but Emma kept asking until she finally admitted that her husband was hurting her.

However, to Emma's emotional disappointment, it turned out it was all a scam; the woman was injuring herself so her husband would be arrested. Once he had a criminal record, their pre-marriage contract would be voided, the woman could then get a divorce and half her husband's money.

Emma had also ended up in some very dangerous situations because of her client work. She was once kidnapped and held captive in a camper trailer by a young man who became obsessed with her.

When Emma answered her phone, Doctor Anderson asked, "How's Ben doing?"

"He hasn't woken up yet, but he's going to live," Emma answered and then added, "He's facing a long recovery and the ongoing risk that either the bowel resection won't take or his liver won't recover."

"I have my fingers crossed for him, but I know Doctor Khan, so I know he's getting excellent care," Anderson said.

"Doctor Khan has been terrific. Everybody here has been," Emma said.

"And what about you, Emma? How are you holding up?" Anderson asked.

"I'm doing okay," Emma answered sincerely. "Ben's girlfriend, Michelle, is here and I'm trying to be strong for her. Michelle's in love with Ben, so she's struggling emotionally with what's happened. Lan is with me. She loves Ben for reasons I really don't understand, and she's worried about him, but she's still a little girl, so as one would expect, she gets bored waiting here at the hospital."

"And Shane? Is he there too?" Anderson asked.

"No, Shane is out trying to figure out who attacked Ben and murdered Inspector Stabler's wife and her support worker," Emma answered.

"I hope he's being careful because whoever is behind this is dangerous and given that they killed two people and dismembered their bodies, is also likely mentally disturbed," Anderson said.

"Shane, careful? Like that ever happens," Emma said in a flat voice, almost like she was making an aside comment to herself.

"Is everything okay between you and Shane?" Anderson asked with concern in her voice.

"We're fine…really," Emma answered and then added, "We just have a few things to work out for the future."

"Any chance I can talk you into coming back soon? Your clients miss you," Anderson asked.

"I need time away from it, Charlene," Emma answered. "Shane and I, especially Shane, have continually put ourselves in situations we should be avoiding. It has to stop because we have Lan to think about now."

"You want my advice?" Anderson asked.

"Always," Emma answered firmly.

"Yes, you have Lan, and I know she has become the most important person in your life, and you would do anything to make sure she has a normal life after all that she's been through," Anderson said. "But Emma, you have a life to live too, and you can't just suddenly change it to what you believe it should look like for Lan. I guarantee you there won't be any happiness in that. And I'm not sure you can expect Shane to do the same thing. He might try because he loves you, but I think he'll eventually feel that your so-called normal life is boring and mundane. You have to be prepared for the fact that your relationship may not survive. I'm sorry if I'm being a bit blunt, Emma, but that's my analysis based on the long conversations I've had with both you and Shane. Maybe if you get a chance over the next few days, we can get together for coffee and talk some more."

"I appreciate your input, Charlene, I really do," Emma said. "I've got so many things swimming around in my head these days and my emotions are all over the place. I will need your help to sort things out. I'll call."

Emma ended the call from Charlene and had just walked back into the waiting room when the Head Nurse for the floor, Amy James, arrived and with a big smile on her face, announced, "Ben is awake and alert."

Michelle jumped to her feet from her chair and exclaimed, "Oh my God! That's great news! Can we go into his room and see him?"

"Absolutely," Amy answered but then quickly added, "However, as a precaution, for at least this time, I'm going to put you in gowns, masks and gloves. Ben is still at risk for infection."

"Me too!?" Lan asked excitedly.

"I think we can find something that will fit you," Amy said with a smile.

After the nurse got everyone prepared, they went into Ben's room, where they saw that the head of the bed had been elevated so that Ben was partially sitting up. He was still attached by catheter to several IV bags and by wires to a rack of monitoring equipment.

Emma was encouraged by how Ben looked. He'd always had a pale complexion, but she saw a bit of colour in his cheeks and his eyes were clear and alert.

As soon as they were in the room, Michelle ran over, laid her head and hands on Ben's chest, and with tears running down her face, said emotionally, "Benny! I was sick with worry! I thought I had lost you!"

Michelle had been doing it since she and Ben first started seeing each other, but Emma still couldn't get used to the idea that the Ben Chen she knew would ever allow himself to be called 'Benny', even by his girlfriend. Ben even let Michelle to call him 'Benji' sometimes, which Emma figured was even worse.

"Fuuuuuck, I hurt all over!" Ben croaked in a really rough sounding voice. "Aren't they supposed to give you a button to push to crank up the fucking pain killers?"

"Ben's back! He's going to be okay!" Michelle exclaimed, and Emma could tell, even though she was wearing a mask, that Michelle had a big smile on her face. Emma was smiling too as she felt a huge sense of relief.

"One of these fucking IVs better start giving me a lot more happy juice than what I'm getting," Ben complained in his strained voice.

"Ben, Lan is here," Emma said and stepped aside so Lan could get right to the side of Ben's bed.

"Oh. Hi, Miss Lan," Ben croaked and even though it was obvious he was in discomfort, he tried to smile. "Sorry about the F bombs."

"I think you're allowed when you nearly die, Uncle Ben. I was really scared for you," Lan said and then held up her sketch pad. "I drew a picture of you in your hospital bed, hooked up to all the tubes and stuff."

"It's excellent, as usual, Miss Lan," Ben said, and Emma could hear that his voice was already growing weaker. "I'm going to hang it in the restaurant with the rest of your sketches so everyone knows that Ben took one for the effing team."

"I need to let Shane know you're awake," Emma said as she took out her phone and typed out a quick text.

Where is he?" Ben asked.

"Running down some leads on whoever did this to you," Emma said. "He was going to a funeral and then driving to the jail in Milton to see Adam Talino."

Ben was about to try and say something when nurse Amy James walked in and asked, "How are you feeling, Ben? How's your pain level right now?"

"On a frigging scale of one to ten, I'm a goddam ninety nine," Ben tried to exclaim, but it came out as weak and raspy.

It was a small thing, but if Ben was avoiding using the word 'fuck' because Lan was in the room, Emma knew he was in fairly good control of his mental faculties.

Amy, after making some adjustments to the drip rate for one of the IV bags, said to Ben, "This should help very quickly," and then said to Emma, "Just a few more minutes and then Ben needs to rest."

"Thanks, Amy," Emma said and felt her phone vibrating in the back pocket of her jeans.

After she took her phone out and looked at her texts, Emma said, "It's from Shane. He says, 'Great News. Say hi to Ben and tell him I'll be in later to see him. On my way to the office. Chioma has a major break in the case'."

Emma put her phone back in her pocket and then asked Ben, "Do you remember anything about who attacked you?"

"Not much, it's all still kinda fuzzy," Ben rasped, and Emma noticed he was speaking a lot slower, slurring his words a bit, and his eyelids were getting heavy. The extra meds were kicking in.

"I remember someone coming to the door, " Ben said slowly. "They were wearing a ball cap, so I couldn't see their face on the security monitor. They held a badge up to the camera. Not sure about anything after that."

"You somehow managed to get the door closed before that person killed you," Michelle said softly as she put a hand gently against Ben's face. But Ben probably didn't hear her because he was now in a deep sleep.

Chapter Thirty

When Shane walked into Burke and Associates, Office Manager Jill Langley, who was sitting behind the reception desk, asked him, "Any word on your friend, Ben?"

"I just got a text from Emma telling me that Ben's awake, so that's encouraging," Shane answered and then asked, "Any word on the Tremblay trial?"

"The last time I heard from Jason, the trial was on a break, and when the court resumed, he was going to put Noah on the stand," Jill answered.

"Jason very rarely lets a client testify in their own defence," Shane said. "He must have felt he had no choice."

"Probably," Jill responded and then said, "I'm really happy to hear about Ben. Chioma is waiting in the conference room for you."

"Thanks," Shane said and made his way down the front of the office. When he passed the area of partitioned desks used by the Law Clerks, Shane thought about Tin Tran, the young man who had lied on his employment application about being related to the Phuong crime family. He wondered what Jason would decide about Tran's future with the firm.

When Shane entered the conference room, he saw Chioma sitting at the head of the long oak table with an open laptop in front of her.

Sitting on opposite sides of the table were Sergeant Franks and Inspector Stabler.

Shane sat in the chair to the right of Franks and said to Stabler, "How're you making out, Inspector?"

"I'm fine, Daniels, thanks for asking," Stabler answered with a lot more sincerity than Shane normally expected from the man. Stabler looked like he hadn't slept in days. There were noticeable bags under his bloodshot eyes, deep lines ran from the corners of his mouth, and he was in a wrinkled suit.

"I'm hoping I'll feel even better after I hear what Chioma has for us," Stabler added in a flat tone and then asked, "Any word on how your friend Chen is doing?"

"I just got a text from Emma at the hospital telling me that Ben is awake," Shane answered. "It looks like he's going to pull through, but I suspect he'll have a long recovery ahead of him."

"Did you go and talk to Adam Talino even though I told you not to?" Franks interrupted with obvious irritation in his voice.

"I did, and it's not him," Shane said.

"You're an asshole, Daniels, you know that. I've told you numerous times to stay out of the way and let me do my job. That included not talking to Talino on your own. I don't know how the Inspector puts up with you," Franks said angrily.

"I don't," Stabler chimed in. "He's like a bad cold that keeps coming back."

"Talino has both the means and the motive to get someone on the outside to do his dirty work," Franks said.

"Talino is a narcissist. All he cares about is himself and doing things that please him," Shane said. "If he was involved, he wouldn't have been able to keep from showing some satisfaction on his face, which he did not."

"If you gentlemen are finished sniping at each other, I will tell you who is probably behind everything that's happened," Chioma said.

"Sorry, Chioma, go ahead, we need some good news," Shane said.

"I've been reviewing all of Shane's cases where Inspector Stabler has also been involved and that's where I found our suspect," Chioma began, "But I'm going to put this in order so it all makes sense."

Chioma then explained that Jason defended a man named Gavin Benson, who was accused of murdering twenty two year old Paige Madison, who worked at his company. Benson was found guilty and sentenced to life in prison with no chance of parole for twenty five years. Jason felt he had a lot of grounds to appeal the verdict, but before that happened, Benson committed suicide in his cell.

"And, as I'm sure you remember vividly, Shane," Chioma continued, "You were kidnapped by Benson's son, Josh, who demanded you prove his father was innocent."

A cold chill went through Shane. He still had nightmares about his time in captivity and Josh Benson's use of drugs, bright strobe lights and ear-splitting music to torture him.

"Shane managed to escape and then went on to prove that Josh's father was, in fact, innocent," Chioma said. "Paige Madison was actually murdered by Benson's business partner, Ethan Holdaway, who had an affair with her before she became romantically involved with Gavin."

"And what does any of that have to do with my wife's murder?" Stabler asked in a grumpy tone. The Inspector was not known for his patience.

"Shane went to Holdaway's home and confronted him about Paige's murder. You were also there that day, Inspector, waiting outside in your car for a signal from Shane to arrest Holdaway," Chioma said. "Also in the house that day was Holdaway's wife, Mary, who had no idea her husband had an affair with Paige. She had to be taken to the hospital by ambulance to be treated for shock."

Shane didn't remember much about Holdaway's wife from that day, probably because he was busy concentrating on getting Holdaway to confess that he murdered Paige. However, he did remember a late middle-aged woman, wearing an old-fashioned apron and holding a coffee service tray. She was standing in the doorway to the kitchen with a look of fear and disbelief as her husband, who she had just overheard confess to murder, was arrested.

"It turns out the Holdaways had a daughter, a stepdaughter to Ethan, Jessica Tyson, who kept her mother's maiden name," Chioma stated. "Jessica went to live with her maternal grandparents in Halifax when she was sixteen because there were problems between her and her stepfather. I got that information from her Grandmother, Veronica Tyson, who I luckily managed to track down because she was still living in her own home. She told me, in no uncertain terms, that she was ninety four years old, still had her wits about her, and that she had no intentions of leaving her house until they carried her out in a box. Her husband died five years ago."

"I must say that I really enjoyed talking to her," Chioma said with a bit of a smile on her face. "Despite all that she's been through, she hasn't lost her spirit."

"Anyway," she continued, "Jessica, according to her Grandmother, was very smart, but could be moody and withdrawn, which Mrs Tyson told me was due to Jessica living apart from her mother, who she was very close to, and her hatred of her stepfather. Jessica attended university and medical school, and was in the second year of her residency at Halifax Regional Hospital when she suffered a mental breakdown, which Mrs. Tyson believes was caused by the long hours, the stress, and the emotional issues that Jessica already suffered from. After spending time at a private psychiatric facility, Jessica returned to work at Halifax General, but this time as a Physician's Assistant. That's what she was doing at the time when her stepfather, Ethan Holdaway, was arrested for murder and her mother was hospitalized for shock."

Chioma touched a key on her laptop and a photograph of a woman came up on a large monitor mounted on the wall behind her.

"This is Mary Holdaway," she said.

Mary Holdaway was a beautiful woman; an oval face, full lips and intense brown eyes. She had a flawless complexion, subtly applied makeup, and shoulder-length styled auburn hair with a few streaks of gray showing.

"Shane, I know that you and Inspector Stabler only met her once, but I'm sure that seeing Mary Holdaway's picture now will remind you of someone," Chioma said.

"What the hell!" Franks exclaimed. "She looks like an older version of the new Pathologist, Amelia Martin."

"That's what I thought as soon as I saw this picture," Chioma said and then put the photograph from Amelia's hospital identification badge on the screen beside Mary Holdaway's.

"Obviously, they're mother and daughter," Inspector Stabler said flatly.

Shane didn't say anything because he was stunned. The woman he believed to be pathologist Amelia Martin was actually Jessica Tyson, the daughter of Mary Holdaway, and the stepdaughter of murderer Ethan Holdaway. He missed the resemblance! Shane felt nauseous as he realized what this meant.

Chioma then said, "After Ethan Holdaway was arrested for murder and Mary was released from the Brantford hospital, she moved to Halifax to live with her elderly mother and, more importantly, her daughter, Jessica. She didn't return to Ontario for her husband's trial, which would be why you, Shane, and the Inspector, don't remember much about her because you never saw her again after the day you arrested Holdaway at her house."

"Mrs. Tyson told me that while Mary was happy to be in Halifax with her daughter, Jessica, she continued to have trouble dealing with her husband's betrayal and the fact that he was a murderer," Chioma continued. "Mary had a mental breakdown and ended up in the same facility that Jessica had been in. About four months ago, she committed suicide by tying sheets from her bed together and hanging herself from a ceiling light fixture."

Chioma touched a key on her laptop and put a new photograph on the wall monitor.

"Gentlemen, meet the real Pathologist Amelia Martin," Chioma announced.

Amelia Martin looked to be in her early sixties. She had a round, plump face with a double chin, green eyes, curly gray hair and stylish glasses with thin, dark frames and arms.

"So, our new pathologist is actually Jessica Tyson and likely the revengeful, vicious killer we've been looking for," Shane stated with no emotion as he fought to deal with the shock he felt.

"I'm sorry, Shane," Chioma said. "I know you were starting to like her."

Starting to like her! That's an understatement, Shane berated himself. He knew that Amelia was openly trying to push their relationship to something physical and he was dangerously close to considering it. Why was she doing that? Was it part of her plan for revenge?

As these thoughts raced through Shane's head, he heard Franks admonishing Chioma.

"For shit's sake!" Franks said angrily."You should've contacted me the second you had this information!".

"All of this only came together first thing this morning," Chioma protested. "I had to make sure my suspicions were correct. As soon as I was sure, I did, in fact, call you, Inspector Stabler and Shane to get here as soon as possible."

Franks, his face twisted in anger, crossed his arms, nodded his head at Shane and said, "I think, Chioma, that you're like your colleague Mr. Daniels here. You wanted to play detective when you had no business doing it and now it's more than possible you've jeopardized the investigation!"

"I was just reviewing Shane's case files, looking for suspects, when this came up, that's all!" Chioma shot back.

"Okay, that's enough, Sergeant, let Chioma finish," Stabler said in a firm voice.

"I contacted the CEO of Halifax Regional Hospital, Brent McPhail, and after I explained what was going on, he was very cooperative," Chioma said, some tension evident in her voice after the verbal confrontation with Franks. "He told me that Amelia Martin was a highly respected Pathologist, but over the past year she had to take a lot of time off because she suffered chronic pain in her joints. She was diagnosed with fibromyalgia and decided to go on long-term disability."

"McPhail also confirmed that Jessica Tyson was a Physician's Assistant at the hospital, but her employment was terminated three months ago. He wouldn't say why, citing confidentiality," Chioma said.

"He was forthcoming in discussing the real Amelia Martin's situation, so why was he so tight-lipped about Jessica Tyson?" Franks asked.

"I'm not sure," Chioma answered. "I'm assuming it was because it dealt with a termination and there might be some legal implications, but I didn't push the issue. Obviously, Jessica was not showing up for work because she was busy switching identities with Amelia."

"The question is, how did Jessica manage to steal Amelia Martin's identity and get a job as a Pathologist working at Brantford General Hospital?" Shane asked, attempting to sound calm as he desperately tried to process what he was hearing. How did I not sense that Amelia wasn't who she said she was, he asked himself in disbelief.

"As soon as I hung up from talking to Mr. McPhail, I called Doctor Jeffrey Patterson, the retired Pathologist," Chioma said.

"Your next call should have been to me!" Franks interrupted angrily and that drew a stern look from Inspector Stabler. Franks held up one hand to signal he was done.

"I asked Doctor Patterson who hired Amelia Martin," Chioma then continued, "And he told me the Regional Director saddled him with the job of finding his own replacement. He said he put the available position on the usual networks where these things are normally posted and he received about a dozen resumes. He told me Doctor Martin's resume stood out because of her academic credentials and the many research papers she had published, so he contacted her about the position."

"And, what? He didn't bother doing any research, even online, into Doctor Martin, where he might have seen her photograph? Or even make some calls about her?" Franks asked.

"Patterson admitted he was in a bit of a rush to find his replacement so he could get on with his retirement," Chioma said. "He said he and his wife had already booked a cruise."

"Unbelievably lazy and sloppy," Franks commented.

"I agree, but out of some fairness to Doctor Patterson, Amelia Martin has no social media presence," Chioma said. "Her academic papers are only available as PDFs online. She's not on Facebook or Instagram, a very private person by all accounts. I did a search on

Google and I had to scroll through several screens before I found an image of Martin in a group photo taken at a medical researchers conference over ten years ago. Obviously, Paterson didn't take the time to go looking."

"However," Chioma continued, "Doctor Patterson said he did call McPhail about Amelia and received a glowing report about her. McPhail confirmed to me that he did talk to Patterson and praised Amelia's credentials. However, McPhail didn't mention that Amelia was currently on medical leave."

"I assume Patterson didn't bother to arrange a personal interview," Stabler said.

"No, actually, he did," Chioma responded. "He called the number on the resume and asked the person he thought was Amelia Martin if she would be willing to come to Ontario for an interview or, if absolutely necessary, he could fly to Halifax. But the Doctor Martin he talked to said she had an incredibly busy schedule and wondered if they could do a Zoom call. Patterson, anxious to get on with his cruise, readily agreed."

"And, what? He was like Daniels, mesmerized by the good looking woman who appeared on the Zoom call?" Franks asked sarcastically. Shane didn't react to the insult. He already had too much buzzing around his head, trying to come to grips with what he had just found out, to bother getting into it with Franks.

Chioma then said, "Her Grandmother told me that while Jessica did inherit her mother's fine features, she had always been a 'plain Jane', and never cared much about things like clothes, hair and makeup. Obviously, by the time Doctor Patterson interviewed her by Zoom, Jessica had abandoned her plain looks and transformed herself into a younger looking version of her beautiful mother. Patterson hired her on the spot."

"Okay, we've got to locate Jessica Tyson immediately and get her into custody before she kills someone else," Stabler said. "Franks, put a team together and find this woman. And check on the welfare of the real Amelia Martin. Tyson would've had to do something to get her hands on Martin's personal papers, and at least her driver's license, which she would have somehow managed to replicate with her photo on it."

"I'll get a search underway for Tyson, starting at the hospital, and I'll call Halifax police about Amelia Martin," Franks said as he stood up, preparing to leave the conference room.

"Amelia…Jessica told me she bought a condo here in Brantford," Shane said.

"I've already looked and I wasn't able to find an Amelia Martin or a Jessica Tyson as a registered property owner or a tenant anywhere in the city," Chioma said.

"Of course you looked, Chioma, when you should've been calling me!" Franks snapped at her.

This time, Chioma got a hurt look on her face and said, "I was just trying to help Shane."

"Well, don't help anymore," Franks responded. "With all of your amateur poking around, Tyson is probably aware someone is on to her, and she may have fled."

Shane was angry about Franks' verbal berating of his colleague and friend, Chioma, and was about to say something, which he would likely regret later, but Stabler gave him a stern look that said, 'not now'. Out of respect for the Inspector, Shane remained silent, but his anger at Franks didn't dissipate.

Stabler then said, "We appreciate your efforts, Chioma, but Tyson's got to be living somewhere; we'll have to double check rentals."

"If it's a Townhouse or an apartment, it will have a large freezer," Shane muttered, more to himself than anyone else, as he continued to try to get his head around the situation. "Unless she was lying, Amelia…Jessica…told us the body parts which were sent to us had been frozen at one time."

"She likely dissected the bodies in the autopsy suite at the hospital, after hours," Franks said.

"But she would've had to get the bodies of the two people she killed into the hospital and past security with no paperwork," Shane said. "There's always security personnel posted at the back entrance to the morgue. They're strict about proper documentation, especially if the body is connected to a criminal case. And they would be highly suspicious if a pathologist was trying to bring in two bodies and not ambulance personnel."

Shane thought for a moment and then said, "You know, it's possible she rented either a storage shed with electricity or maybe an empty warehouse somewhere."

"I can look into that," Chioma offered.

"No, we'll do that. You don't do anything else," Franks ordered.

"Fine, fine," Chioma said, holding her hands up in surrender.

Franks left the conference room, his head down, already punching in numbers on his phone.

Chioma closed up her laptop, looked at Shane, and asked, "Are you okay, Shane?"

"Thank you so much for what you've done, Chioma," Shane said.

"You can thank my husband for putting up with me working in my office all night," Chioma said.

"I can't believe I missed this!" Shane admonished himself, out loud this time. "I was around Amelia…Jessica…several times. We even had coffee together. She flirted with me…a lot. If she hated me, if she was getting revenge because of what happened to her mother after I had her stepfather arrested, she showed absolutely no signs of it on her face or in her eyes. I've been through this countless times with other suspects I've encountered. If they're lying or trying to hide their real intentions, I find it easy to spot. There was absolutely no malevolence in Amelia's eyes. She's obviously the definition of a stone-cold killer."

"It's actually real simple, Daniels," Stabler said as he stood up. "In this case, you were thinking with your crotch and not your head."

"You're analysis is not welcome, Inspector," Shane responded with annoyance in his voice.

Stabler started to leave but stopped and said to Chioma, "Franks may be right about when you should've pulled the plug on what you were doing and called us, but just ignore his rude comments. You did great work here, Chioma, even outdoing Daniels on this one. Thanks for finding the person who likely killed my wife."

Stabler then walked out of the room, and like Franks before him, the Inspector already had his phone out and was making a call.

"Okay, Shane, what did the Inspector mean when he said you were 'thinking with your crotch'? And what were you talking about when you said that this Amelia was doing a lot of flirting? Did something go on between you two?" Chioma asked.

"Never mind about that, Chioma," Shane said. "I need some time alone to think, and then I've got to call Emma and tell her what's going on."

Chioma picked up her laptop and headed for the door, but before she got there, Shane said, "Chioma, thanks again."

"You're welcome," Chioma said with a smile that lit up her face.

"You know, I really want you to pass the bar exam and become a lawyer because it's your goal and because you'll be a great solicitor," Shane said. "But either way, as far as I'm concerned, you're the best researcher in this country."

"And you're a great investigator, Shane," Chioma responded, "But for some reason, you missed a monster who was standing right in front of you."

And with that said, Chioma left the conference room, heading for her office.

She's right, Shane thought, and so is Stabler. I let my attraction to Amelia blind me to what was probably there the entire time for me to see.

But then Shane thought of something he hadn't considered before. If Jessica Tyson had deluded herself into believing that she really was Amelia Martin, then she wouldn't give off any physical signs of deception to Shane when they were together. In her sick mind, Jessica was Amelia, and it was as the beautiful Amelia that she tried to draw Shane into something more than a friendship.

That's got to be it, Shane tried to convince himself. That's why I didn't pick up any hint of malevolence on Jessica's face.

And, Shane decided, that means I was right when I thought Amelia was a beautiful siren calling me to crash into the rocks and ruin my relationship with Emma.

Chapter Thirty One

Shane called Emma from his office to give her a full explanation of what was going on.

When Emma answered, she asked Shane to hold on, saying she was still at the BGH, in Ben's room with Lan and Michelle, and wanted to go somewhere quiet to talk.

After Shane waited a few moments, Emma asked, "What's happened? Is there some news?" in quick succession.

It wasn't lost on Shane that there were no preliminary niceties from Emma.

There was no, 'How are you? 'How're you feeling?, 'Where are you?', 'Isn't it great news about Ben?' There was none of that.

To Shane, it said a lot about the current state of their relationship. It was all business. It wasn't as if Shane didn't understand why. Emma blamed his intentionally deep involvement in his previous cases for their current situation. And she was afraid, not for herself, but for Lan.

Shane also believed it was another sign of Emma's transformation from being a free-spirited, excitement-loving, independent woman who didn't want children, to an overprotective mother. Sometimes it felt like Lan was all that Emma cared about. And now she upset that her daughter had seen a human heart, which someone had removed from a body and delivered to their home as a warning to Shane.

"There is news," Shane said in reply to Emma's question.

He told her the murders of Mark Stabler's wife and her personal aide, and the attack on Ben, were likely committed by a woman named Jessica Tyson, who was posing as Doctor Amelia Martin, the new pathologist at the BGH. And Shane explained that they also suspect Tyson murdered two people to get the body parts that were sent to them, Stabler and Ben.

"Why? Who is this person?" Emma asked.

"She's the daughter of a woman who committed suicide in a psychiatric facility in Nova Scotia. We believe she's seeking revenge on the people she thinks were responsible for causing her mother's mental breakdown," Shane answered.

"And you were at the top of her list," Emma said and her bitterness came through loud and clear to Shane.

Shane then told Emma the rest of the story about why and how Jessica Tyson ended up in Brantford impersonating Amelia Martin. Emma listened without interrupting and when Shane was finished, she asked, "And where is this Tyson now?"

"We don't know. The cops are looking for her," Shane replied. "If she knows Ben survived her attack on him, and could identify her, she'll be on the run. She won't get far, Emma, trust me. She killed a cop's wife, so they'll be relentless in hunting her down."

Emma didn't say anything and there was a moment of silence on phone before she asked, "And once they catch this psycho Tyson, then Lan and I can go home? She acted alone?".

"There's absolutely no indication that anyone else was involved. It was all her," Shane replied firmly. "Once she's in custody, you and Lan can go home."

"Until next time, right Shane?" Emma said bitterly. "Try and get to the hospital and see Ben now that he's awake," she said and then ended the call.

Shane dropped his phone on his desk and took a couple of deep breaths. He didn't blame Emma for being upset. When this was over, it was going to take a lot of work to get their relationship back to the way it was, if that was even possible.

Shane picked up his phone and sent a text to Inspector Stabler asking if they'd found Jessica. He got an immediate reply: *'Search of the hospital done and no sign of her. Still looking for where she was living. Looking for any registered vehicles. Halifax Police found Amelia Martin's decomposing body in her home. Throat slit'.*

Shane's phone pinged as he got another text, this time from Jason, who said he was in his office and wanted to see him.

Jason was behind the big desk in his spacious corner office, working on his laptop, when Shane knocked lightly on the open door, walked in, and sat in one of the guest chairs.

"Court done for the day? How's the trial going?" he asked.

"I decided to put Noah on the stand today," Jason answered, "He did alright, even up against Evan Gregory. I then rested my case. Closing arguments are tomorrow."

"How do you feel about how the trial has gone? Does Noah have any chance with his claim of self-defence?" Shane asked.

"To be honest, I'm not sure," Jason answered. "I've picked up a lot of sympathy for him on the faces of most of the jurors. And I've undermined the prosecution's case enough that I've seen some questioning looks, which means I've instilled some reasonable doubt. That's what I've been aiming for."

"It's too bad Gregory wouldn't agree to the plea deal," Shane said.

"He's being stubborn. He wants a win," Jason said. "Even the new Judge was trying to push a deal."

Jason leaned forward in his chair, laid his arms on the desk and said, "Enough about the trial. How's Ben? Tell me everything that's going on."

So Shane laid everything out for Jason, start to finish. It took most of twenty minutes and when he finished, Jason said, "And all of this started because of the Gavin Benson trial. It set off a chain of events that's resulted in an obviously mentally disturbed woman seeking retribution."

"I'm angry at myself, Jason," Shane said. "I was in close personal contact with this Jessica Tyson in her guise as Doctor Amelia Martin on several different occasions and not once did I get a bad vibe off her."

"You're not infallible, Shane," Jason responded. "You've become far superior to me in reading faces and body language, but it has never been an exact science."

"Everything that's happened has seriously affected my relationship with Emma," Shane said. "I don't know if I can fix it, but I'll try because we now have Lan in our lives."

"If you need anything, anything at all, please don't hesitate to ask," Jason said sincerely.

"I may need you to start putting the brakes on me when I decide to go outside the parameters of my job and play detective," Shane said.

"I can try, but I think both of us know how that's going to go," Jason said.

Chapter Thirty Two

By the time Shane drove from his office to the Brantford General Hospital and found a spot for the Charger in the visitor parking lot, it was getting dark.

From what he could see looking above the glow of the street lights, which had just come on, there were heavy, dark clouds. It's going to start raining at any time, Shane thought, and when I leave, I'll likely get soaked getting from the hospital to the Charger, which was sitting in the farthest corner of the parking lot.

Shane went through the automatic doors at the main entrance and headed for the elevators. As he pushed the button for the surgical floor, he noticed how quiet it was this evening in the usually busy reception area. There was normally a security guard at the desk, but no one was currently there to watch who was coming and going.

When he exited the elevator and started walking down the hallway, Shane found it was also quiet in the Surgical Department, but was not surprised because elective surgeries were normally performed during the day, and that's when more staff, like Emma, would be around. There will be, of course, emergency surgeries underway, Shane thought, and in the waiting rooms, anxious family members waiting for news.

Shane passed the nurses' station where a man and a woman, both in scrubs, were busy at computer workstations. The woman looked up and smiled at Shane as he passed. Through Emma, he knew a lot of the doctors and nurses who worked on the floor, but he didn't recognize this lady.

Shane next passed the room where he, Emma, Lan and Michelle had spent so much time waiting for word on whether Ben would survive surgery. It was empty now.

On his way to the hospital, Shane had received a text from Emma telling him the three girls were going to get some takeout and then go to their hotel.

As he approached Ben's room, Shane recognized the constable from the Brantford Police who was sitting on a chair outside the door. He had the improbable name Bricker Bingham, but had always been known simply as Brick. He was actually a bit of a brick physically; shoulders in a straight line, a big, square chest and wide arms. Brick would have been physically intimidating when he was younger, but he had added a few pounds over the years and now had a prominent gut hanging over the top of his belt. He had a puffy, red-cheeked face and a thick, gray moustache with upturned waxed tips.

Shane knew Brick had been the training officer for dozens of rookies during his career and was considered an old-school cop who wasn't a fan of many of the community policing methods now used by many Police Services. He also knew Brick was very close to retirement and would be more than happy doing night shift guard duty at the hospital, sitting on a chair with a paperback novel and a thermos of coffee on the floor beside him.

"Hi Brick," Shane said when he reached the officer's chair. He noticed the curtains were closed on both the window and the sliding glass door to Ben's room.

"Hey, Shane," Brick responded and then said, "You're here to see your friend, but you'll probably have to wait. The doctor is in there with him. In fact, she's been in there quite a while, so I hope there's not a problem."

"She? It's not Doctor Khan?" Shane asked.

"No, it's…," Brick started and then reached down beside him and picked up a clipboard that was leaning against the chair. "It's a Doctor Martin. I checked the picture on her security badge."

Shane's panic was immediate and intense.

"Shit, Brick! Didn't you see that her badge said she was with the Pathology Department!" Shane exclaimed. "Get your gun out and come with me!"

Shane was worried that Jessica had locked the door, but it slid open, and he rushed inside and quickly looked over the situation. Jessica, in blue scrubs and wearing a white lab coat with her hands in its pockets, was standing on the right side of the bed near Ben's head. Ben was not conscious.

As soon as she saw Shane, Jessica pulled a surgical scalpel out of her right pocket and held it against the side of Ben's neck.

"Jessica, you need to step away from the bed or this police officer is going to shoot you!" Shane said forcefully.

Brick, who was standing just back from the foot of the bed, was holding his Glock pistol in the two-handed position, aimed at Jessica's head.

"Hello, Shane Daniels. So you know my real name," Jessica said in a calm voice. "I don't think the cop is going to shoot me, Shane, for a couple of reasons. His hands are shaking, which means he's never fired his weapon at anything but a target, so he'll likely miss even at this distance. And, he hasn't moved his finger from the side of the gun to the trigger. So he knows the second he starts to do that, I'll slit Ben's carotid artery."

"I'm not afraid to shoot you, lady," Brick said with intensity.

"You can leave now, officer, and call in the Emergency Response Team, like you're supposed to," Jessica said. "Shane can stay and talk to me until they get here."

"It's okay, Brick, go ahead, do as she asks," Shane said, trying to stay calm, but his heart was beating rapidly and his stomach was doing flips.

Brick walked backward slowly toward the door, keeping his gun pointed at Jessica, who then said, "And close the door behind you."

Once Brick had backed out and the glass door was closed, Shane said, "This is going to end badly for you, Jessica, you know that, so why don't you put the scalpel down and walk out with me."

Jessica ignored Shane's comment and instead said, "You can still call me Amelia if you want, Shane Daniels, because I know you're really attracted to her."

"I was surprised at how slow you were driving here in that muscle car of yours," she said. "I was getting worried that if I was in here too long, that lazy old cop outside would get suspicious. I assumed you'd be coming here to the hospital after work to visit your buddy, so I parked on the street along the side of your office building and watched. As soon as I saw you coming out the back door heading for your car, I drove to the hospital, used an entrance reserved for physicians, and got here in lots of time to wait for you."

"What did you do to Ben?" Shane asked. He knew Ben was still alive because there was activity on the heart monitor he could see over Jessica's left shoulder.

"He was asleep when I came in, but I gave him a little dose of Ketamine in his IV to keep him that way," Jessica said.

"What do you want, Jessica? How can we end this?" Shane asked firmly.

"Where's your cane, Shane Daniels?" Jessica asked, ignoring Shane's question. "I read a feature story on you that said you actually don't need to use a cane for walking anymore because you have a special brace for your bad knee. However, the article said you still carried the cane around because you were very good at using it as a weapon for self-defence. I think that's kinda cool, so I'm disappointed you don't have it with you."

"How can we end this, Jessica?" Shane asked again. He needed to keep the conversation focused and not allow Jessica to discuss other topics.

"If you know my real name, then you know all about me," Jessica said. "Do you remember my mother? She was a beautiful woman."

"You underwent a makeover to look like her," Shane said.

"And I worked hard on Amelia's body, which I know you like, Shane Daniels," Jessica said with a smile on her face.

Shane concentrated on looking at Jessica's eyes, but he did take a quick glance at her hand holding the scalpel against Ben's neck. She must have flinched because the scalpel's razor-sharp blade had cut a thin line on the skin of Ben's neck, and there was some blood slowly trickling out of it. I've got to end this before that scalpel goes any deeper and Ben bleeds to death, Shane thought.

"Do you remember when you went to my mother's house to accuse my step-father of murdering the young woman from his office that he was fucking?" Jessica asked, and Shane could see growing intensity in her eyes.

"I never understood what she saw in that asshole," Jessica said. "I wanted to stay living with my Mom, but my stepfather and I hated each other, and I had to get out of there. Anyway, when you were sitting in the house talking to my stepfather, I bet Mom went into the kitchen to get coffee and cookies. She did that whenever anyone came to the house. She was so gentle and kind."

"I'm sorry about your mother, Jessica, I really am," Shane said sincerely.

"No, you're not! Don't lie!" Jessica screamed at Shane and then quickly returned to a calm but intense voice. "My mother was devastated and went into shock when she found out her husband was a murderer. I got her from the hospital here and took her back with me to Nova Scotia. But she never recovered and I eventually had to put her in a place I knew."

"The same psychiatric facility you had spent time in," Shane said.

"We're not talking about me!" Jessica yelled at Shane, but again quickly returned to a calm voice. "All she did all day was sit and stare at the television. Then one day she decided she didn't want to live anymore, not even to be with me, and she hung herself. I was heartbroken, then I was very angry, and then I wanted revenge."

Shane could hear sounds of activity outside the door and knew members of the ERT had arrived. They would be in full tactical gear and heavily armed.

"Jessica, I don't understand. You've killed five people that I know of, and almost a sixth, my friend, Ben, in the bed beside you, because you want revenge for what happened to your mother. But the fact is, the man who was ultimately responsible, your step-father, is already in prison for the rest of his life," Shane said.

"Look at the two of us standing here, Shane Daniels, just like in the movies," Jessica said, ignoring Shane's comment. "There's always a final showdown, no matter how improbable, between the hero and the villain. Except in this case, we're both villains."

"It's time for this movie to end, Jessica, with everyone coming out alive," Shane responded.

"Yes, the first thing I wanted to do was kill my step-father," Jessica said, returning to Shane's previous comment. "But, of course, I couldn't get to him because he's in a maximum security prison. I thought about finding someone with connections inside the prison who I could pay to have Ethan killed, but I had no idea of how to do that. And, more importantly, I wouldn't be there to look at his face when he died, so he'd know it was me. Then I decided it wasn't about killing the people responsible; it was about seeing them suffer the same pain and anguish I did when someone they love dies. The only reason I tried to kill your buddy Ben here was because you hid Emma and your little girl from me. But I did my homework. Your close relationship with Ben, and his involvement in some of your successful cases, came up a lot in the online stories about you, so I knew if I sent him a body part message, he'd come running to you. And if Ben had died like he was supposed to, I knew Emma would come out of hiding to be with you, and then I would have killed her."

Jessica was completely emotionless and matter-of-fact while she made her speech, and her face was frozen with intensity. Her hand holding the scalpel never wavered from Ben's neck, and Shane realized there was nothing he could say which would convince her to give herself up. He figured that by now, the ERT would have snaked a camera into the room to assess the situation. He expected that Jessica's phone, if she had one with her, or maybe his phone, would ring at any time with a trained negotiator on the other end.

"Can't we end this now, Jessica?" Shane pleaded. "Haven't you got what you wanted? When you look at my face, can't you see how frightened I am for my best friend? I was really hurt when he nearly died. My partner and our daughter were shocked when you sent a human heart to our home, and now they're terrified, which also hurts me. You murdered Inspector Stabler's wife, the love of his life, so he will never be the same. Isn't all of that enough revenge for your mother's suicide?"

Jessica didn't respond. She just stared at Shane while a smile slowly spread across her face.

"Jessica, Please," Shane continued to plead. "You know that if a negotiator can't talk you into surrendering, members of the ERT are coming in here and there's a good chance they'll shoot you. I want you in prison for what you've done, Jessica, but I don't want you to die."

"Is that because, since the first time we met, you've wanted to have sex with me, as Amelia, Shane Daniels?" Jessica asked.

Just as Jessica finished saying that, Ben suddenly opened his eyes and said in a hoarse but loud voice, "What the fuck's going on!!"

That drew Jessica's attention away from Shane, probably because she was surprised the Ketamine had worn off so fast. She turned her head and looked down at Ben.

Shane saw the scalpel move very slightly away from Ben's neck, so he charged.

He rammed into Jessica, who went backwards and slammed hard into the metal cart holding the heavy monitoring equipment. The scalpel flew out of Jessica's hand, and she and Shane crashed to the floor with Shane on top.

The anger he had been suppressing since the heart showed up at his door finally boiled to the surface. This crazy woman had killed five people, nearly killed Ben, and had put this relationship with Emma in jeopardy. Shane felt nothing but rage. He put his hands around Jessica's neck.

"I should kill you right now for everything you've done!" Shane exclaimed as he applied some pressure to Jessica's neck.

"I finally see genuine hurt and pain on your face, and the confusion over your feelings for me," Jessica managed to rasp. "You won't kill me, Shane Daniels, because I made you fall in love with Amelia. But go ahead if you can, then I'll be with my Mom."

Shane's face was burning as his anger started to go over the tipping point.

"Murderers like you and my father should never be allowed to stay alive!" Shane screamed.

He started squeezing Jessica's neck harder.

"No, Shane, stop!" Ben called out hoarsely as he tried, despite the intense pain that ripped through his body, to roll off the side of the bed and get to his friend before it was too late.

The members of the ERT, after hearing the crash of the equipment when Shane shoved Jessica to the floor, rushed into the room. One officer grabbed Shane from behind while another tried to peel Shane's hands off the neck of the now unconscious Jessica Tyson.

Chapter Thirty Three

The last thing a lawyer needs just before giving their final argument at a murder trial is to be mentally distracted.

Jason knew that better than anyone, but he was having great difficulty focusing in the aftermath of what had occurred during the past twelve hours. Not to mention the fact that he was also mentally and physically exhausted.

A brief recess in the Noah Tremblay trial was nearing an end and Jason was sitting at the defence table trying to concentrate on his notes.

Prosecutor Evan Gregory had completed his closing address to the jury prior to the break. Jason had to admit that Gregory was very good; articulate, mentally organized as he spoke without notes, and just the right amount of emotion so he didn't sound over the top to the jury. Jason didn't have a ton of respect for Gregory and some of his prosecutorial methods, but he recognized that Gregory had done some of his best work during this trial.

Jason had only managed to grab a few hours of sleep before he had to be up early this morning to prepare for court. Last evening, he had received a call from Shane, who said he had been involved in a violent situation at the Brantford General Hospital and would, no doubt, require some legal advice.

Jason then kissed his wife, Gillian, told her not to wait up for him, and drove immediately to the BGH.

When the elevator doors opened on the hospital's surgical floor, Jason looked down the hallway and saw that a section had been blocked off by two uniformed police officers. When he approached, one of the officers told him the area was closed and that he would have to return later. Jason explained that he was a lawyer, his client was in the blocked off section, and he wished to speak with him.

"You'll just have to wait here for now," the officer told him.

"Not good enough, go get whoever's in charge," Jason demanded.

Jason and the officer had a bit of a staring contest until the officer reluctantly turned and walked to an area where Jason could see four other cops, two in uniform and two in suits, standing in front of one of the ICU rooms. He watched as a forensics officer, wearing a full, white Tyvek suit, emerged from the room, followed by Inspector Mark Stabler and Sergeant Greg Franks.

Stabler turned, saw Jason, and then said to the approaching officer, "It's okay, let him through."

After Jason walked up to Stabler, he asked, "What's going on, Mark? Where's Shane?"

"He's in a room just up the hall," Stabler replied. "He's pretty shaken up. I'm going to have a doctor look him over."

"What the hell happened here?" Jason asked.

"A woman who had been posing as a pathologist here at the hospital managed to get by the officer guarding Ben Chen's room, drugged Ben, and held a scalpel against his neck while she waited for Shane to come to visit his friend," Stabler explained. "She wanted Shane to be there and watch while she slit Ben's throat."

"Oh no!" Jason reacted. "Was this the woman you were looking for? Shane had filled me in. Ethan Holdaway's stepdaughter?"

"Yes, Jessica Tyson," Stabler said. "They were supposed to revoke her hospital security swipe card, but they didn't, at least not in time."

"Is Ben alright?" Jason asked.

"I understand from Shane that after he jumped Tyson to try and disarm her, Ben tried to get out of his bed to help him," Stabler answered. "He ripped out some of the sutures from his previous operation and his blood pressure spiked. They took him into the OR to replace the sutures and to get him stabilized. I've been told that he's going to be okay."

"I need to talk to Shane," Jason stated.

"That's fine, go ahead," Stabler said and then added, "Sergeant Franks and I have already talked to him about what happened, but we haven't taken a formal statement yet."

"Just so we're clear, Mark, nothing he's said so far is on the record," Jason said in a firm voice.

"I know how it works, Burke," Stabler groused.

Jason left Stabler and walked a short distance down the hall and into the waiting room. He found Shane was sitting on a chair staring at the wall across from him. There was a uniformed officer standing just inside the door.

"I need to speak to my client…alone," Jason said to the officer, who nodded at him and left the room.

Jason sat in the chair next to Shane and asked, with concern in his voice, "How're you doing, Shane?"

Shane turned and looked at him and said, "I'm still tense, Jason, but my hands have finally stopped shaking."

"Understandable, given what happened," Jason said.

"I was going to kill her, Jason!" Shane whispered loudly and Jason could see the fear in his friend's eyes. "I got so angry! I had my hands around her throat and I wanted to choke the life out of her because of what she'd done!"

"Shane, I want you to listen to me very carefully. This is important," Jason said in an intense voice. "You can say you were going to, or you wanted to, kill her to me, or you can say it to yourself, but under no circumstances do you say that to Inspector Stabler or Sergeant Franks, or any police officer for that matter. Do you understand?"

"I understand," Shane said softly and Jason could see that Shane was taking long, slow breaths to try and calm himself down.

"As far as you're concerned, Ben's life was being threatened by a woman you knew had no intention of giving herself up," Jason told

Shane. "You acted to save Ben's life, and in a violent confrontation, you made the split-second decision to hold the woman by the neck in order to subdue her. That's your statement, Shane; that's all you need to say. Okay?"

"Okay. Thanks for being here, Jason," Shane said sincerely and for the first time since he sat down beside him, Jason saw the calmness and resolve he normally saw return to Shane's face.

Jason's thoughts about what happened last night at the hospital were suddenly interrupted when Judge Crowder said, "Mr. Burke, we're ready for your closing statement."

Jason cleared his mind of all the distractions he was dealing with, took one quick final look at the notes in front of him on the table, and walked to the area facing the jury.

"Ladies and gentlemen, I'm going to be fairly brief with my final argument," Jason began, "because I know that you already have a very clear understanding of the decision you must make. You will decide between two conflicting theories about what happened the night Olivia Tremblay died. My colleague, Mr. Gregory, claims that on that night, after consuming a lot of alcohol, Noah and Olivia got into a heated argument over her becoming pregnant and wanting to keep the child. Noah, in a fit of rage, got a knife from the kitchen and stabbed Olivia, killing her instantly. That's the Prosecutor's theory; that Noah Tremblay killed his wife in cold blood."

"But that's all it is. It's just a theory," Jason continued, "No one witnessed what occurred that night. Despite the Prosecutor's best efforts to make it look that way, there's no specific forensic evidence to prove that's what happened. What's that leave? Just two police officers who don't agree on what they heard Noah say that night. Two officers, by the way, with no credibility because they changed their statements, perhaps because they thought it would bolster the prosecution's theory."

"Meantime, you heard Noah Tremblay, still distraught a year later, tell you in his own words what happened that night. Olivia was bipolar, but was often in denial about her mood disorder and wouldn't take her medications on a consistent basis. Noah told you that night started out fine, Olivia was happy, but then she suddenly fell into one of her dark moods and, in an out of control rage, tried to stab Noah. There was a physical confrontation during which Noah managed to disarm Olivia, but she wouldn't stop her physical assault on him, and he admits he jabbed at her with the knife. But he didn't mean for the knife to go deep into Olivia's body and pierce her heart."

"You all saw my client on the stand," Jason told the jury, "He's a broken man because of what happened the night Olivia died. He's under a suicide watch because he's struggling with living with what he did."

Jason took two steps closer to the wooden rail in front of the jury and said, "You have to decide if the Prosecutor proved that Noah had the necessary intent, beyond a reasonable doubt, for murdering his wife. I think there's a lot of reasonable doubt."

"Ladies and Gentlemen, Noah Tremblay admits he stabbed his wife," Jason said. "And under the law, based on the circumstances of what happened that night, he may be guilty of manslaughter, but he's not guilty of second-degree murder."

Jason walked back to his table and sat down. His Associate, Susan Cartright, kept a stoic look on her face but nodded at Jason to signal 'good job'.

During Jason's closing, Noah had sat with his head partially bowed, staring at the table in front of him. Jason reached over, put his left hand on Noah's knee, and said softly, "It's almost over. Stay strong."

Judge Crowder began his charge to the jury. Jason looked closely at the faces of the men and women on the panel. He got the sense that many of them were anxious to get into the jury room and make their decision.

He wasn't sure if that was a good sign or not.

Chapter Thirty Four

Hours after his confrontation with Jessica in Ben's hospital room, when Shane had finally gotten home from the police station and crawled into bed, he was pleasantly surprised to see that Emma had decided to come home from the hotel.

She appeared to be asleep, but as soon as he was under the covers, Emma had turned over and whispered, "You're finally home. Are you okay? What happened?"

"I'm fine. Go back to sleep. I'll tell you everything in the morning. I'm glad you're home," Shane had replied.

After a few hours of tossing and turning, Shane gave up the idea of sleeping, so he got up and had breakfast with Emma and Lan. Lan was chatty as she ate her cereal, happy to be home and going back to art camp.

After Lan was picked up by the mother of one of the other young girls attending the camp, Shane and Emma had a coffee, and he told her, in detail, everything that occurred at the hospital.

Emma listened without interruption or any visible emotion on her face. When Shane finished, she said, "I'm glad Ben's going to be okay after trying to help you. His fierce loyalty to you is remarkable. I will check in on him this morning. I'm sure Michelle is already there."

Shane expected Emma to have more to say and a lot of questions about his violent confrontation with Jessica. But after a moment of hesitation, she had put a hand on top of Shane's and said, "I'm glad you weren't hurt. I need to get to work. I…I'm sorry, Shane, I can't talk about this anymore right now. I need time to process everything that's happened."

Emma had then left without another word.

Last night, Shane had spent two hours sitting in a nearby waiting room while a team of police, led by Sergeant Franks, completed the investigation of the scene. Franks had told Stabler that he shouldn't be there because his wife was a victim, but the Inspector refused to leave. However, Stabler did agree to stay well away from Ben's room and the officers working the scene.

After he arrived at the hospital and spoke to Shane about what his statement to the police should contain, Jason said he was going to stay around, but Shane told him to go home, knowing Jason had closing arguments in the Tremblay trial the next day. But Jason insisted he needed to be nearby when Shane was interrogated, which would likely take place at the Brantford Police Station.

As soon as he felt calm enough, Shane had called Emma at her hotel room. At that point, Shane wanted to keep the conversation brief, so when she answered, he said simply, "It's over, Emma. Jessica Tyson has been arrested. You and Lan can go home now or in the morning, if you like."

"Oh, Shane, that's great news!" Emma said and then asked, "She was behind everything?"

"Yes, it was all her," Shane answered, but didn't add any more.

"Where was she arrested?" Emma asked.

"Listen, Emma, I'm tied up making a statement to the police right now," Shane responded, "But I promise I'll explain everything in the morning."

"Why do you have to make a statement now? Were you involved in the arrest, Shane?" Emma asked, and Shane could hear the suspicion growing in her voice.

"I really can't get into the details right now, Emma, sorry, but I will tomorrow," Shane said.

"Okay, tomorrow," Emma conceded, but Shane could tell from her tone that she was not happy. "But you're okay?" she asked.

"I'm fine, just tired. It's been a long day and it's not over yet," Shane said.

"And Lan and I can go home?" Emma asked.

"Yes, you can go home. It's safe," Shane said.

At one point while he was sitting in the waiting room waiting to be interviewed, Constable Bricker Bingham came to the door and said, "I'm sorry, Shane, I never should have let that woman into the room."

"It's okay, Brick. As far as you knew, you were allowing a doctor with the correct security badge in the room to tend to Ben," Shane said.

"No, it's not okay, Shane," an obviously upset Brick responded. "I should've seen she was from Pathology and questioned why she was there. It was a rookie mistake."

"Brick, you're one of the best cops I know," Shane said. "You had my back in that room and that's all that mattered."

"I was more than ready to shoot that bitch between the eyes, and what she said was wrong. I wouldn't have missed," Brick said angrily as he purposely pulled up his gun belt higher on his hips and left the room.

By the time he sat down in a room at the Elgin Street Police Station to give his formal statement, Shane had calmed himself down substantially; the adrenaline that had coursed through his body the second he saw Jessica in Ben's room had long since dissipated and had been replaced with mental and physical exhaustion.

As instructed by Jason, Shane made no mention of his anger-fueled attempt to kill Jessica. When Franks, in an accusatory tone, asked about the visible bruising on Tyson's neck when they took her into custody, Shane said he was simply trying to subdue her as quickly as possible and may have applied too much pressure.

Franks stared at Shane for a long time, with skepticism written all over his face.

Chapter Thirty Five

After Emma had left abruptly for work the next morning, Shane poured himself another coffee and tried to decide what he was going to do with himself for the rest of the day.

Jason had told him, actually, more like ordered him, to take several days off and decompress from everything that had happened, to spend some time with Emma and Lan, and maybe talk to someone, perhaps Charlene Anderson.

Shane wasn't sure what he wanted to do, and all he could think about was his conversation, or rather non-conversation, with Emma earlier that morning. He knew he had put Emma through a lot over the past few days, and now their personal relationship was in trouble because Emma was worried about how Lan would be affected if he continued to go deeper into cases involving potentially dangerous people.

Shane wandered around the house for a bit, thought maybe he would get the vacuum and do some cleaning, and even considered going through his DVD collection and picking a couple of classic westerns to watch.

But, in the end, nothing was appealing; there was too much rattling around his head, so he showered, put on some dress pants and a button-down, short sleeve shirt, and drove to the office.

As he walked through the common area at Burke and Associates, Shane noticed that Tin Tran was sitting in a cubicle. He walked over and said, "Hi, Tin. I'm really sorry for what I suspected about you, and for putting you through a police interrogation. I was wrong and I apologize."

Tran looked up at Shane from the laptop on his desk that he was working on. He had no expression on his face, so Shane wasn't sure what kind of reaction to expect from the young man.

"I understand why it happened, Mr. Daniels, I really do," Tran said. "There's nothing I can do about the family I'm from and I did try to hide my connection, which was wrong."

"Well, it appears Jason understood your situation," Shane said with a smile. "I'm glad you'll be staying with us, and like I said when we first met, I hope I can connect you with my daughter, Lan, so she can keep up on her Vietnamese language skills."

"I'll be more than happy to do that, Mr. Daniels," Tran said, his face now showing emotion.

"And, please, it will always be Shane, never Mr. Daniels," Shane said lightheartedly as he walked away, heading for his office.

Shane spent the majority of his time during the rest of the morning and early afternoon working on the backlog of unfinished reports he owed various lawyers with the firm, but often found himself staring at his laptop, going over the events of the past week. Specifically, his total blindness to Jessica Tyson's intentions when she was posing as Amelia Martin.

Office Manager Jill Langley appeared at his door at two in the afternoon and said, "I thought you might want to know that the jury has reached a decision in the Tremblay trial. The Judge has reconvened the court for four. Jason is already on his way to the courthouse to talk to Noah."

"That didn't take the jury very long, Shane said. "Thanks, Jill. I'm going to go and hear the verdict."

When Shane arrived at the courtroom twenty minutes before the jury was expected back, the visitors' gallery was already full, not surprising given the amount of media attention the trial had generated. Social media had been buzzing with activity during the trial as well, and Shane was aware that a lot of the posts contained comments that were not very favourable for Noah.

Her mother, Charlotte Crombie, had set up a Facebook memorial page for Olivia, but Charlotte had not been using the page for fond memories of her daughter. Instead, it was filled with vitriolic rants against Noah.

Shane managed to find a space to sit on the bench along the rail directly behind Jason's table, where the lawyer was sitting with an open chair between him and his Associate, Susan Cartright. After Shane touched Jason lightly on his shoulder to get his attention, Jason turned around, the two men shook hands, and spoke briefly.

Shane then took a quick look around the gallery and saw two of the police officers involved in the case, Sergeant Duncan Campbell and Constable Monica Mosher. Shane knew they would be interested in the verdict because Jason had seriously undermined their credibility when he accused Campbell of using his position as her superior officer to make Mosher change her statement about what she heard Noah say the night of Olivia's death.

Shane also saw Olivia's parents, Jim and Charlotte Crombie, sitting at the end of the bench behind Prosecutor Evan Gregory's table. The Crombies sat close together, holding hands. They had grim expressions and it appeared Charlotte had already been crying.

At exactly four o'clock, everyone in the courtroom stood as Judge Crowder entered through a door to the left of the bench. After he signalled everyone to sit, Crowder nodded to a court security officer who opened a door on the left wall and Noah Tremblay, handcuffed in front, was escorted in by another officer.

Noah was pale and even thinner than the last time Shane had seen him, and his dark suit looked like it was one size too big. Knowing the different kinds of trial strategies his friend employed, Shane wasn't surprised Jason hadn't made an attempt to improve Noah's ill-looking appearance, hoping it invoke some sympathy from the jury.

Judge Crowder asked a court officer to bring in the jury, and as they entered the room and took their seats, Shane studied their faces. He didn't see any visible emotions, but there was a determined look on each face, which told him they were satisfied with their decision.

As soon as the jury was seated, Judge Crowder then asked, "Madam Foreperson, has the jury reached a unanimous verdict?"

A well-dressed, statuesque, middle-aged woman, who was sitting in the middle of the first row of seats in the jury box, stood and said, "Yes, we have your honour."

"You may proceed," Judge Crowder said.

The woman looked down at a sheet of paper she was holding and said, "In the matter of the Crown V. Noah Tremblay, we, the jury, find the defendant not guilty of second-degree murder but guilty of manslaughter."

"No!" Shane heard someone yell and turned to see Olivia's mother, Charlotte Crombie, on her feet, her face twisted with rage.

"What's the hell is the matter with you people!" Charlotte screamed. "That man killed my daughter in cold blood! He's guilty of murder! He needs to rot in prison!"

The courtroom erupted in a cacophony of voices. Judge Crowder hammered his gavel repeatedly on its wood block while shouting, "Order, Order!

When the noise in the room finally faded, Olivia's parents were still standing, and Jim Crombie, with a look of disgust on his face, was holding his wife, who had her hands over her face, sobbing loudly.

"Mrs. Crombie, if you don't sit down and be quiet, I will have you removed from this courtroom," Judge Crowder said in a loud and firm voice.

Jim Crombie held up his hand to the Judge as a signal to wait and then led his still sobbing wife into the aisle. Shane assumed they were going to leave the courtroom, but he was wrong.

Jim left his wife's side, rushed toward the end of the bench where Shane was sitting and propelled himself over the railing and onto Noah Tremblay's back. Jason got knocked out of his chair and onto the floor by Crombie's lower body, and the defence table slid away.

Crombie, now on top of Noah, started repeatedly hammering his right fist into the side of Tremblay's head, which was pinned sideways on the floor.

"You killed my daughter and destroyed my wife, you piece of shit!" Crombie screamed as he continued to punch Noah.

Shane, who was knocked sideways when Crombie leaped over the railing and on top of Noah, quickly recovered, jumped over the rail and grabbed Olivia's father from behind.

"Stop, Jim, that's enough!" Shane shouted as he yanked Crombie off Noah's back and pinned him to the floor.

By this time, three security officers had run over to the scene from their positions elsewhere in the courtroom. One of them took over from Shane and put Crombie in handcuffs, and one tended to Noah, who had blood trickling from his right ear, a dark bruise forming on his cheek, and his right eye was swelling closed. The third officer took a position to ensure no one else got involved.

When Shane got up from holding Crombie down, he immediately went and checked on Jason, who had gotten to his feet, shaken but not injured.

"I'm okay, no harm done," Jason said as he used his hands to brush the sides of his expensive suit coat.

Shane then went to Susan Cartright, who had been sitting to Noah's left and was pushed off her chair when Crombie landed on Noah.

"I'm okay too, I'm not hurt," Susan assured Shane and then said, "But we'll need an ambulance for Noah."

As expected, everyone in the courtroom had stood up to see what was happening and the sound of their voices filled the room. Judge Crowder banged his gavel several times and shouted, "Everyone sit down and be quiet!"

After the two officers pulled the handcuffed Crombie to his feet, he shouted at Crowder, "The justice system in this country is a joke!"

"Be quiet, Mr. Crombie!" Crowder loudly responded and then said to the officers, "Remove this man from my courtroom and put him in police custody."

One of the officers escorted Crombie out a side door. By this time, Shane and Susan had helped a battered Noah up off the floor and onto a chair.

"You Honour, my client needs immediate medical attention," Jason said to Crowder.

The Judge nodded at Jason, then turned his attention to Noah and said, "Mr. Tremblay, I'm terribly sorry this has happened to you. No one deserves to be assaulted and I'm very upset it has occurred in my courtroom. You will be now be taken into custody, but then immediately to a hospital for treatment. You have been found guilty of manslaughter. Your lawyer, Mr. Burke, will be notified when a date has been set for sentencing."

Noah didn't react to what the Judge told him. He just stared at his hands.

Judge Crowder turned his attention to the members of the jury, who had by this time returned to their seats.

"I apologize for what has happened," Crowder told them. "I thank you for your service."

He then tapped his gavel and said, "Court adjourned."

Shane, Jason and Susan stood close by as two officers helped Noah to his feet and then handcuffed him in front.

"I need you to stay strong, Noah, please," Shane heard Jason say to Noah before the officers led Tremblay away.

When Shane turned to leave, he noticed the courtroom was empty except for one person. Charlotte Crombie was sitting on a bench, her face a pale mask of shock and her eyes locked in a vacant stare.

Chapter Thirty Six

Mark Stabler was sitting on a chair beside the bed in the master bedroom of his house, the same chair he had occupied for many hours since his wife was murdered.

Stabler's grief was like a cloud hanging over his head, but he was refusing to let it show physically. His late father, a stern, humourless, religious man, always insisted that getting emotional about anything was a waste of energy. When he was a young man, his father had also told Stabler, on countless occasions, that men do not cry. The last time it happened was when Stabler's mother died and as he stood beside her coffin at the funeral home with a few tears running down his face, his father whispered to him, "You know, son, a man who cries looks like a spineless fool."

Stabler was always looking for his father's approval and feared his wrath.

Stabler was well aware that the people he worked with thought he was a stoic, grouchy man, and he really didn't have a problem with that. His father was right in many ways; emotion was a waste of time, particularly if you were a cop. You have to be cold, calculating and smart to be a good detective, and Stabler prided himself on being all three.

Stabler put his hand on the bed beside him, which had been freshly made up. He couldn't bring himself to remove the bloody sheets, but it was done by a female constable on his squad, Ariel Rodriguez. She had told him that if there was anything she could do to help, anything at all, don't be afraid to ask. When others had asked the same thing, he had waved them away, but there was a real sincerity in the constable's voice, and he knew he wouldn't be able to deal with the bedroom on his own. So he swallowed his pride and asked for her help, and she readily agreed.

Ariel removed the bloody sheets from the bed, replacing them with new ones, and did the same thing with the blood stained pillows. She collected the various bottles of medications from the nightstand and told Stabler that she would donate them, on his behalf, for distribution to people who couldn't afford them.

Stabler sat downstairs in the kitchen while she did all of this.

But even now, with everything replaced on the bed, when Stabler looked at it, he still saw bloody sheets.

I'm selling the house, Mary, Stabler said in his mind to his wife. I can't live here anymore, not without you, and I can't sleep on the couch for the rest of my life because I will never use this bed again. Besides, Mary, you know how much I hate yard work, and you did most of the cooking and cleaning. I think our heartbroken son will understand that I can no longer live in his childhood home.

Stabler thought about one of the last conversations he had with Mary. She was amused when he suggested he would retire or take a leave of absence so that he could spend more time with her during her recovery. You'd go stir crazy hanging around the house all day, and that would drive me crazy, she had told him. You're a cop, she had said, just keep doing that, because it makes you happy.

But now, Stabler was angry with himself because he should have ignored what Mary thought and taken at least a leave from work. If he were at home, that mentally deranged woman would never have gotten in the house, and both Mary and Jalissa would still be alive.

Stabler knew that Shane Daniels was not being truthful when he told him and Sergeant Franks that he wasn't trying to kill Jessica Tyson after he overpowered her in Chen's hospital room. He claimed he was holding Tyson by the neck only to subdue her. But Stabler knew that if Daniels hadn't been stopped, he had every intention of strangling Tyson for threatening his family and trying to kill his best friend.

Mary, Stabler said silently to his wife, I promise you that if Jessica Tyson ends up in a comfortable psychiatric facility and not a federal prison for slitting your throat and taking you away from me, I will find a way to finish what Shane Daniels started.

Chapter Thirty Seven

That evening, as they worked together preparing dinner, and Lan was in her room playing Minecraft on her tablet, Emma gave Shane an update on how Ben was doing. She had been able to drop in and see him twice during her shift at the hospital.

"He's decided to try and keep his use of the words, 'fuck', 'shit' and 'asshole' to a minimum while the medical staff are around because he claims they're giving him dirty looks and he's worried they'll give him a placebo instead of his pain meds or maybe spit in his food," Emma said.

"Sounds like the Ben we know and love is back," an amused Shane remarked.

"Personally, I was hoping what happened to him might result in a new Ben, but no such luck," Emma said. "Either way, he's got a long road to full recovery ahead of him."

"I'll go and see him in the morning before I go to work," Shane said.

"I told Michelle to come and stay with us instead of continuing to pay for a hotel room," Emma said. "I'm sure Lan won't mind having a roomie for a while."

"She likes Michelle, so I'm sure she'll be thrilled," Shane said, and then he told Emma about what happened in the courtroom after the jury delivered its verdict in the Tremblay trial.

Emma was carefully slicing celery while Shane talked, but by the time he had finished, she had substantially picked up the pace of her cutting, and Shane knew she was getting upset.

"Why is it that trouble always seems to find you?" Emma asked with frustration in her voice.

"What happened had nothing to do with me, Emma," Shane said defensively. "The Crombies hate Noah, they always have. Jason told me they had sat in the courtroom every day of the trial with anger on their faces. Their hostility toward Noah boiled over when he was found guilty of manslaughter and not second-degree murder."

"But you managed to end up in the middle of it anyway," Emma retorted, "You're like a magnet for this kind of stuff."

Shane didn't respond and that was the end of any conversation between him and Emma. It remained that way even after Lan had joined them at the table and they started eating.

"Something's wrong around our house," Lan said as she moved the stir-fry around her plate with her fork, her standard signal that it wasn't her favourite meal.

"What do you mean there's something's wrong, Lan?" Emma asked. She had forgotten just how perceptive Lan was for her age.

"You and Dad are obviously not talking to each other," Lan said and then, in rapid succession, asked, "Are you mad at each other? Are you mad at me? Did I do something wrong? Are you guys splitting up?"

"No, no, sweetheart, you haven't done anything wrong," Emma answered firmly. "Your Dad and I are not fighting, and we're not splitting up. There's been a lot going on lately, and I'm sorry we're not talking like we normally do during supper, but your Dad and I are only being quiet because we're thinking about everything that's happened."

"Like because someone sent a real heart in a box to our house and we had to stay in a hotel because we were in danger?" Lan asked as she continued to play with the food on her plate.

"Yes, that's part of it," Shane said, speaking for the first time. "But, Lan, there's no longer any danger and no more body parts will be coming to the house."

"That's good because it was pretty gross!" Lan exclaimed.

"Yes, definitely gross," Shane agreed and then added, "But what your Mom says is true. We're not fighting, just quiet because it's been a very busy week. Okay?"

"Okay," Lan said and then asked, "How much of this stuff do I have to eat?"

Later in the evening, Shane sat in the living room mindlessly flipping through the channels on the TV, trying to decide on something to watch while Emma listened to Lan read, which was part of Lan's bedtime routine. When Emma was finished getting Lan settled for the night, she came to the living room, sat down on the sofa beside Shane, and said, "We need to talk."

"You're right, we do," Shane responded. He pointed the remote at the TV and turned it off.

"Have you heard yet when the funeral for Mary Stabler will be ?" Emma asked.

"Next Monday," Shane answered. "She has already been cremated. It will be a small, very private service, but we've been invited."

"It's going to be very sad," Emma said. "Mary had just completed another round of chemotherapy and the prognosis was good. Then this happens. Have you had an opportunity to talk to the Inspector specifically about his wife's death?"

"I've tried a couple of times, but you know Stabler, he has little to say even on a good day."

"So, Shane, was there something going on between you and this woman, Jessica Tyson, when she was posing as pathologist Amelia Martin?" Emma asked, as she suddenly changed the subject.

"I thought we were becoming friends," Shane replied. "That's all."

"Come on, Shane, you know what I mean. She's a beautiful woman and a few of the more nasty gossipers at work have been going out of their way to mention to me that they heard you were spending extra time in the Pathology Department with her and you were even seen having coffee with her."

"I did have coffee with her and I admit that I enjoyed her company because she came across as a highly intelligent and genuine person. And, yes, as you said, she was also a very beautiful woman," Shane said, and then quickly added, "But Emma, absolutely nothing went on between us."

"I believe you, Shane, I really do," Emma responded. "But here's the thing that I'm worried about. I've seen you around beautiful women countless times and I've never known you to even take a second look. Did you getting friendly with Jessica have anything to do with the fact that things haven't been that great between us lately? I know I've been making demands about how you work your future cases and we've not been exactly burning up the bed with passionate sex."

"No! It had nothing to do with any of that!" Shane replied firmly. "Do you remember Homer's Odyssey? There's a story in it about these beautiful women called Sirens who sing to the passing sailors, to lure them to crash their ships against the rocks. In the myth, these Sirens represent temptation. Jessica, posing as Amelia Martin, was my Siren. She aggressively flirted with me, which, I admit, I didn't mind. But she was doing it on purpose to blind me from seeing her hate, her desire for revenge and her murderous intentions."

"Jessica was a Siren? You're going with that? Really?" Emma said and Shane heard her skepticism loud and clear. "It had nothing to do with the fact that she was hot and you wanted to screw her?"

"Emma, you're smart, beautiful and sexy," Shane said defensively. "I love you and you're the only woman I want to be with! It's just that, in my mind, I needed an analogy to explain why I didn't see even a hint of malevolence in Jessica's eyes."

"It's fine, Shane," Emma responded in an even voice. "I appreciate your honesty; it's one of the things I've always admired about you, even if it includes, I suppose, you telling me about lusting after another woman. It just shows you're not perfect, you're human, and because you're a male, it's part of your DNA. I mean, it's not as if I don't lust after other men all the time."

Shane's eyes went wide and his mouth dropped open.

"You do!?" he asked, shocked by an admission he never would have expected from Emma.

"Of course not!" Emma said as a smile spread across her face. "I'm just yanking your chain."

"Oh," was all Shane said.

"Shane, you're a very intelligent man with a brilliant analytical mind, but I think sometimes, when it comes to women, you're as dumb as a brick."

Shane, take aback, and a little hurt by Emma's comment, was about to say something, but Emma didn't let him.

"But Shane," Emma continued, in a return to a serious tone, "Only you know, in your heart, what your true intentions were when you were with that woman. If you say she purposely acted as a temptress to mess with you, I accept that, but you have to accept how it appears to me. That you were looking around because the current woman in your life wants to put conditions on your perceived calling as a crime solving detective."

Shane felt ashamed because he had, in fact, previously considered what Emma was saying may have been his unintentional motivation.

"Shane, I want you to know that I'm not angry with you about what we've just been through," Emma said. "You had no way of knowing that an obviously disturbed woman would murder people, and even dismember some of them, to get revenge for her mother's mental breakdown and eventual suicide."

"But what is concerning to me," Emma continued, "is the fact that this woman's actions were a direct result of you doing your Shane Daniels super sleuth thing and insisting on personally confronting a killer. Because it was you who was sitting in Ethan Holdaway's house, accusing him of murder in front of his wife, not a police officer. That's why you became Jessica Tyson's target."

Emma moved closer to Shane on the couch and said, "We really do need to finish discussing what I've already asked you to do regarding how you handle your cases with the firm from now on. I know I've been guilty of going way beyond my mandate as a councillor for recent amputees because I sense there's been an injustice, or maybe there's a mystery to be solved. I find myself wanting, no, needing, to get involved. It's like I need the adrenaline rush. Well, I've put the brakes on that, and now I'm asking you to guarantee to me that you are going to do the same thing. No more super sleuth stuff, Shane. When you get a solid lead in a case, if you discover some proof or, most importantly, if you identify a suspect, then you hand it over to the real cops."

"I understand what you want, Emma, but as I've said before, you're asking me to change my nature, to change who I am," Shane said with some intensity.

"I know that, but when you bring danger to our door, you bring it to our daughter," Emma said. "I can't live with that possibility anymore, and neither should you."

"I will try to change, Emma, I promise. But, I'm sorry, I don't know if I can guarantee it will work," Shane said sincerely.

"I love you, Shane," Emma said. "But I will do anything to protect Lan from being put in harm's way ever again, even if it means the end of us."

Emma then kissed Shane on the cheek and left the room. Shane sat in silence.

Chapter Thirty Eight

"Will the defendant please stand?" Judge Crowder said, and Jason joined Noah Tremblay as they stood up behind the courtroom's defence table.

It had been a week since the trial ended in an uproar when a distraught and angry Jim Crombie, Olivia's father, assaulted Noah after the jury delivered its verdict. Crombie was charged with assault and was later released on bail.

Noah still showed some of the results of the punches he took from Crombie. The area around his right eye was a yellowish green and a spot of blood was visible in his eyeball near the iris.

But Jason noticed that, in general, Noah appeared a lot healthier than he did before and during the trial. Aside from the bruising, there was some colour in his face and it looked like he had put on a bit of weight. Still, Jason sensed an aura of sadness around Noah and he continued to worry about the state of the young man's mind.

There were only a few people in the courtroom to hear Noah's sentencing, other than a couple of members of the media that Jason recognized. He knew they'd be looking for a statement from him after the session ended.

"Noah Tremblay," Judge Crowder began, "You have been found guilty of manslaughter by a jury of your peers. I have reviewed your pre-sentence report."

Crowder looked down at a document sitting in front of him and said, "It notes your deep remorse over the death of your wife and recommends that you receive counselling during any period of incarceration that you receive. Prior to your arrest, you had steady employment but minimal family support. You were estranged from your wife's parents well before you were arrested. You have no siblings and seldom have contact with your parents, who live in Alberta. They apparently were unable to visit you while you were remanded in custody or to attend your trial. You have a previous criminal conviction for assault. However, the report says your risk of re-offending is considered low."

Crowder looked up from the document and directly at Noah. "Mr. Tremblay," he continued, "Only you know exactly what happened the night your wife died of a stab wound you admit you inflicted. Whether or not it happened the way you claim it did, you do have to pay the consequences for what was a tragic event. I have taken into account the almost eighteen months that you have already spent in custody. I hereby sentence you to a further two years less a day in jail."

"Good luck to you, Mr. Tremblay," Crowder said. "You will be taken back into custody and transported to a provincial institution to serve your sentence. Court adjourned."

After Judge Crowder left the courtroom, an officer who had been standing nearby walked toward Noah to put him in handcuffs.

"Give me a minute," Jason said to the officer, who nodded in agreement and stopped his approach.

"Listen to me, Noah, please," Jason said to his client. "I know you still grieve over Olivia's death and you believe, in your heart, that you deserve to be punished. Well, you're now being punished. Go and serve your time in a provincial jail, where you'll have a better chance of getting help than you would in a federal prison; a place, trust me, where no one wants to be. Serve your time and then get on with your life."

"Thanks for everything you've done for me, Jason," Noah said in a soft voice and then he nodded at the officer, who then handcuffed Tremblay and took him out a side door.

Jason noticed that Evan Gregory hadn't left the courtroom yet and was in conversation with one of the clerks. Prosecutors and defence lawyers often shook hands at the end of a trial as a show of mutual respect for the work they did either on behalf of a client or the Crown. It appeared that Gregory wasn't interested in shaking hands, which didn't bother Jason because he honestly felt the same way.

But Gregory surprised Jason when he walked over and said, "You did a good job for your client, Burke, because he should be on his way to a federal prison for twenty five years."

"You know, Evan," Jason said. "If you had just taken the plea deal, this trial could have been avoided and Olivia's parents wouldn't have suffered through so much pain and anguish."

"If he hadn't died, Judge Wendal would never have even considered the plea deal that you were proposing," Gregory said with an edge in his voice.

"Well, he did die, and based on his review of the case that you were presenting, Judge Crowder strongly suggested you take the deal," Jason shot back. "But you, Evan, were determined to have a trial because you needed one, you needed a win because your reputation with the Crown Prosecution Service was shot."

"The size of your ego continues to amaze me, Burke," Gregory said angrily. "You think everything and everyone works only the way you see it. Noah Tremblay stabbed his wife, and in your world, two years less a day in jail was enough punishment for a cold-blooded killer. Goodbye, Burke."

Gregory turned his back on Jason and walked briskly out of the courtroom.

"Have a good day, Evan," Jason said with a smile on his face.

Chapter Thirty Nine

I thought that I was going to be with you by now, Mom, but it didn't work out that way.

I was convinced Shane Daniels was going to send me to see you. He had his hands on my neck, and he had the look in his eyes, but in the end, he couldn't do it.

Of course, I completely understand why.

I made him fall in love with the smart and beautiful Doctor Amelia Martin. What a clash of emotions, love and hate, Shane Daniels would have felt as he started chocking the life out of me. I don't know why, but he included his father when he screamed killers like me shouldn't be allowed to live.

A painful memory? If so, how wonderful!

When they took me to the police station from the hospital, they put me in a tiny, smelly room with two police officers who told me that Jessica Tyson was facing multiple murder charges.

I told them my name was Amelia Martin, I didn't know a Jessica Tyson, and that the Jessica they were talking about must have stolen my identity and killed all those people.

The two officers told me that trying to act like I didn't know who I was wasn't going to work because I knew exactly what I was doing when I dissected the bodies of two homeless people, murdered Mary Stabler and Jalissa Dale, and tried to kill Ben Chen.

They grilled me for hours, but I just kept telling them I didn't know any Jessica and I didn't know what they were talking about.

One of the officers, an ugly brute of a man named Sergeant Greg Franks was particularly nasty to me. If I ever manage to get out of custody, I think I'll go visit this Franks, or maybe better yet, his wife, if he has one.

Anyway, Mom, the two officers eventually gave up and brought me a young, goofy looking Legal Aid lawyer named Mason Bennett, who tried to explain the situation to me.

I told him I would be pleading not guilty because I, Amelia Martin, didn't kill anyone.

When they finally put me in front of a Judge, they read off all the charges I was facing and the Judge asked if I understood what was going on. I just shrugged my shoulders and stared at the floor.

Then, there was a bunch of talking between my lawyer, the Prosecutor and the Judge. Blah, Blah, Blah. The Judge eventually ordered that I must undergo a psychiatric evaluation.

So, Mom, you're now up to date on my situation.

My lawyer, Bennett, says I might be transferred to St. Joseph's Hospital in Hamilton, where they do psych evaluations, but more likely it will be done right at the Brantford courthouse.

That means I'll be put in a locked room, alone with a forensic psychiatrist, while either a cop or a Corrections Officer watches through a window, if there is one.

I wonder if they'll leave me in handcuffs? If so, will they be attached to a ring on the table?

If not, what would happen if I suddenly went across the table and started to throttle the psychiatrist?

Does the officer come in through the locked door to rescue the doctor? If he or she does, then I can take them down and walk out of the courthouse.

That's my plan, Mom.

I don't know if it'll work. If it doesn't and they eventually put me away somewhere, I'll just find a way to join you.

If it does work, then I think I'll go to my love Shane Daniels' house and see if Emma and Lan are home.

www.ingramcontent.com/pod-product-compliance
Lightning Source LLC
Chambersburg PA
CBHW072013110726
47910CB00005B/1745